# Month of Sundays, Book One: Time of Tragedy

The smile slid slowly from Vaughn's face and was replaced by a look of inquisition. "Were things really that bad?"

"Well, they definitely weren't typical. Every couple of years a teenager went missing or was found dead. Really shook up the town. Everybody thinks this is such a tight-knit community. They tried like hell to explain away the problems. Then, as suddenly as it began, it just stopped." Mike spoke about the incidents as if they hadn't involved human life. Indifferent.

Vaughn was sorry he'd stopped to talk. "Well, I'd better get going then."

The rain started again as he jogged across the parking lot, attempting to avoid the puddles. As he settled into his pickup truck, he thought maybe he *should* attend one of Perry's poker games. Maybe he could talk to the former chief and get some sort of background on this town. It seemed every time he asked questions, he received more and more information suggesting Rochester's perfect façade was covering some kind of dark, decaying secret.

# MONTH OF SUNDAYS, BOOK ONE:
## *TIME OF TRAGEDY*

by

Courtney E. Michel

*BEACON BOOKS PUBLISING*
www.beaconbookspublishing.com

Published by
BEACON BOOKS PUBLISHING

PO Box 152
Tovey, IL 62570
www.beaconbookspublishing.com

ISBN: 978-0-6151-3535-9

Credits
Cover Artist: Nathan Tumulty
Managing Editor: Dave Field
Associate Editor/Mentor: JoEllen Conger
Copy Editor: Steve Johnson
Proofreader: Jamie Wingo

# REVIEWS FOR
## MONTH OF SUNDAYS, BOOK ONE:
### *TIME OF TRAGEDY*

**4 ½ Lips from Two Lips Reviews**
"… **Courtney Michel** superbly weaves a tale of quiet small-town life with subtle touches of humor, interlaced with suspense. From the opening moments when a bridge over a new bike trail seemingly vanishes, to the unfolding of the mysteries and secrets in Rochester … the reader will be kept turning the pages as fast as possible to discover what the next denouement will be. I highly recommend this one to fans of mystery, suspense, and great characterization and plotting. **Month of Sundays** promises to be a trilogy, and be assured this reviewer will be waiting on tenterhooks for the next installment."
**www.twolipsreviews.com**

"… This book made me laugh, gasp, and want to cry all in one. From the first line… I was not disappointed at all. I am looking forward to the second installment of the *Month of Sundays* series, *Book 2: Grace of God.*"
**Kathryn Niles, author of**
**He Knew The Time Had Come**

"… This is an unusual book with a startling ending. Underneath the small town facade, there is an ugly, grim side that, though downplayed, is terrible. Don't read with a faint heart."
**Huntress Reviews**

# REVIEWS FOR
## MONTH OF SUNDAYS, BOOK ONE:
### *TIME OF TRAGEDY*
### (continued)

**4 Cups from Coffee Time Romance**
"… Ms. Michel has a deft hand with suspense; she often had me on the edge of my seat. All of her characters are well written, with their own special roles to play in this mysterious plot… Time of Tragedy is a fascinating story, although one which I had to read in the daylight. However, I am eager for the next installment."
**Marcy, Reviewer for Coffee Time Romance**
**www.coffeetimeromance.com**

# DEDICATION

To my husband, Scott… because true love is more than just saying 'I love you.'

# ACKNOWLEDGEMENTS

Special thanks to my mentor, JoEllen Conger, my copy editor, Steve Johnson and proofreader, Jamie Wingo. Just when I can't read one more word you seem to re-spark the fire of excitement I have for these stories.

I would also like to extend a personal thank you to Chief Bill Marass of the Rochester Police Department. Your willingness to meet with me and answer questions relating to this book was invaluable. Thank you for the tour of the station and providing me with the necessary information it took to make this series a reality.

To Sangamon County Coroner, Susan Boone... it isn't every day that someone in your capacity would take time out of their busy schedule to provide knowledge of crime scenes and dead bodies. It was fascinating and I thank you!

A special thank you to Mandy Getz, my friend and the winner of my "Name A Character After You" contest. I couldn't think of a better person to have in my book. Although the character might not be a true reflection of your person, your spirit is definitely in the pages... all the way to Book Three.

# AUTHOR'S NOTE

The town of Rochester, Illinois that is portrayed in this book is an existing town located only a couple of miles south of Springfield, the capital city. I have referenced many true to life landmarks that will be recognized by those familiar with the area, but the characters are completely fictional.

When construction began in 1990 and the mystery of the "lost bridge" presented itself, I knew immediately that one of my suspense novels would be home to this setting.

Finished in the summer of 1995, the asphalt pathway, rich with densely covered peaks and valleys, is built atop the old Baltimore and Ohio Railroad line. It runs parallel to the busy stretch of Route 29 and meanders over Sugar Creek. Nearly five miles in length from Rochester to Springfield, it is enjoyed by those both local and from afar, young and old.

May this novel do it justice…

## Prologue

"Would someone please explain to me how in God's name we lost a goddamn bridge?"

Ed Vey bellowed at his reflection in the office window. He could see his hands planted firmly on his hips, his chest heaving rapidly. Fortunately he couldn't see his face turning a bright crimson, but knew that his wife Betty would be saying he looked like a tomato, ripe for the picking.

Ed had worked for the Illinois Department of Transportation for twenty-six years and had never had to explain why he and his crew couldn't find a one hundred and sixty-five-foot bridge. He stood rooted in front of his reflection and watched himself unbutton the sleeves on his dress shirt and roll them up to the elbow. When he thought himself to be sufficiently calmed down, he turned back into the room and faced the three uncomfortable men making up his immediate staff.

"Well, do any of you have an explanation for this cluster fuck we've gotten ourselves into?" Ed moved to the plush leather chair behind his desk and plopped heavily into it. It knocked the wind out of his lungs and deflated the last of his anger. He looked around the room and silently analyzed the men.

Ed had worked with Tom Darcy for nearly fourteen years and considered him as a good a friend as any. They golfed on Saturdays and often shared a beer in Tom's backyard when the wives went to Bingo together on Thursday evenings. Les Shepard was a hot head but a damn good engineer. He stood all of five foot nine, but made up for the height in attitude. They'd gone head to head once or twice, but Ed couldn't think of anyone else he would rather have on his team.

Then there was Will Curtis. Will had only been working with the department for five months. At first he had shown great potential, but lately Ed had doubted his abilities to be a real professional. Ed could see Will squirming in his chair like a grade-schooler needing to use the bathroom. "Will? Do you have something to say?"

The young man looked positively ill at the thought of having to speak. He cleared his throat twice and croaked, "Well, Ed, it's not so much we *lost* the bridge. More like it was stolen."

Ed leaned forward onto the desk and placed his head in his hands. He could feel his blood pressure rising and thought it best to just leave the room before he fired everyone.

"What he means, Ed," Tom broke in, "is that the salvage company that was hired to recover any valuables has seemingly dismantled it right out from under our noses."

"The steel alone would have fetched a hefty price on the market," Les volunteered.

"Okay," Ed conceded to the entire conversation, "someone needs to get a hold of that new police chief in Rochester. What's his name Victor...?"

"Vaughn Dexter," Tom volunteered.

"Right. Tom, you call Chief Dexter and tell him we lost his bridge, err sorry," he corrected, "someone *stole* his bridge. And we'd better let the wives know too, gentleman. We might be pulling an all-nighter trying to rework this budget if we are going to open that bike trail on time. It's beginning to sound like we are going to have to factor in the cost of building a new bridge."

## Chapter 1

### *Saturday, May 14th*

"Hey, Chief, Ms. Weirdly, I mean, Yardley's here to, umm, see you again."

The new Chief of the Rochester police department finished the sentence he was writing before looking up from his paper work. His pen caught a glimmer of the sunlight breaking through the rain clouds, streaming in from the small window behind him. It reflected onto the officer's face. Vaughn Dexter blew a deep breath out from underneath his neatly trimmed mustache and sat back in the creaky office chair.

Most of the women in town would agree that their chief was quite a hot commodity. A bachelor for all of his thirty-seven years, Vaughn was as fit and firm as most of the high school football team. He stood six foot three in his policeman's shoes and always kept his uniform pressed and polished. His blond hair was worn longer than Pastor Sampson approved of, but was, for the most part, accepted into his newly acquired hometown.

Vaughn had been more than happy to uproot from his life in Northern Illinois and relocate to Rochester after the Mayor had selected him as Chief of Police.

Now after six months on the job, Vaughn was still getting acclimated to the local flavor.

"What is it this time, Mike?" Vaughn addressed the police officer, who was by comparison just a weasel of a man.

Mike Simms wore his black hair slicked off his large forehead from root to tip and chewed his nails incessantly. He worked the night shift at the station and Vaughn could tell he was anxious to get this over with so he could get home.

"I'm not sure, Chief, something about a dead bird and a wicked chair..."

"A *wicker* chair, Officer Simms, a wicker chair," a voice sounded from over the young deputy's shoulder.

Mike shrunk down from the harshness of the voice and stammered, "Ms. Yardley, you aren't supposed to be back here."

"Its okay, Mike. Come in Ms. Yardley. What can I do for you today?" Vaughn sat forward again and placed his laced hands over the paperwork in front of him.

Margaret Yardley shouldered past the policeman in a whirl of flowing cotton. The dozen or so beaded necklaces she wore around her neck clacked together in upset as she made her way into the center of the room.

"Someone placed two dead crows on my wicker porch chair, Chief Dexter, two! I could chock one up to coincidence, but two dead crows is not a coincidence, sir, it is a sign. Oh and I think you should arrest Larry Fairfax."

Margaret's last statement caught Vaughn off guard and he even allowed a small chuckle to escape before pulling himself into check. "Why ever would I arrest Mr. Fairfax? Did you see him putting the crows on your porch?" Vaughn rattled off some questions to cover his astonishment.

"No, I did not see him on my porch. But I saw him at the store this morning and..." Margaret hesitated, fingering the shortest strand of beads around her throat. The chief raised his eyebrows and cocked his head to prompt the rest of her story.

"I saw him through the store window getting into his car and he had, well he had a dirty halo." Margaret rushed the last of the story out of her mouth and snapped it shut. She smoothed her wiry, gray hair with bony hands and then crossed her arms defiantly over her ample bosom.

Vaughn Dexter prided himself on keeping the emotion out of his voice when he asked, "Would you care to elaborate on this 'dirty halo' Mr. Fairfax was wearing?"

"I see things, Chief Dexter. Things that other people don't see and I see a black ring encircling Larry Fairfax's head. A black ring, or a dirty halo as I call it, Chief Dexter, means something bad is about to befall Mr. Fairfax. Something deadly," Margaret explained dramatically.

"And tell me why is it again that I should arrest him?" Vaughn was beginning to lose patience with the whole situation.

"Chief," Margaret huffed, "are you even *listening* to me?"

Vaughn stood from the chair and stretched to his full height, which caused even the self-proclaimed town witch, to retreat a step. "Ms. Yardley put yourself into my position. If I went around arresting every innocent person who was wearing one of these dirty halos, then I imagine I would have half the town in lock up."

As he talked, Vaughn moved slowly towards the door, ushering the old woman with him. With every word he spoke, Margaret Yardley nodded her head in agreement. When she reached the door of the Chief's office, she suddenly jerked her head out of the trance the handsome chief had put her in and scowled at him.

"Chief Dexter, I don't have to remind you that you have not lived in Rochester for very long. I have been a citizen of this town for nearly sixty-four years and I can tell you that there is evil everywhere. It is around the houses, down the streets and in the people. It may lay dormant for eleven years, but it is still here and it will run full circle. I can assure you that…"

Without warning the doors to the police station banged open and two officers struggled in with an uncooperative Larry Fairfax. The chief shepherded Margaret the rest of the way out of his office and stepped into the hallway.

"What seems to be the trouble here, Perry?" Vaughn asked the sergeant. Larry who had been swaying back and forth between the officers began singing loudly, "Swing low, sweet chariot, comin' for to carry me home."

"Hush it up, Fairfax," Perry Newlon grabbed the man's cuffed arm and gave it a shake before turning to Vaughn. "Just a drunk and disorderly, Chief."

The chief turned back to Margaret and threw his hands up, "well, there you go. He'll spend the night drying out in a cell. Nothing bad can befall him there. Problem solved."

"It isn't quite that easy, Chief. He will wear the dirty halo until the deed is completed," Margaret said in a quiet voice, eyeing the drunk man as he rocked, half asleep into the wall, "I will come back tomorrow to check on him."

The chief dropped his shoulders and shook his head. Vaughn already knew that Margaret Yardley would have to be his cross to bear in this otherwise content town. He started back into his office to finish his paperwork. The elderly woman sauntered to the door as swiftly and assuredly as a super model on the runway. She put her hand on the doorknob and turned back to face Vaughn.

"Oh, Chief Dexter?"

The chief stopped in mid-step to face the woman again.

"In case you were wondering, he is *still* wearing the dirty halo." With that she was gone, in her flurry of skirts and beads.

Perry Newlon handed the drunk Larry Fairfax off to the other officer and followed Vaughn into his office.

"Tell me, Perry, what's the use of having a dry town if your biggest problem is still going to be a fifty-nine year old alcoholic?"

"Oh it ain't old Larry's fault. His daughter was killed some years ago. Don't think he ever got over it. It literally took his wife to the grave."

"Hey, Perry," a voice called out from the hallway.

"Yeah, yeah, I'm coming." Perry turned back to Vaughn, "You know a bunch of us are getting together tonight for a game of poker. You're, uh, welcome to come."

Vaughn smiled at the gesture, "Yeah, Perry, thanks. I might just make it tonight." Vaughn knew he would never go to the card games Perry organized with a couple of his high school buddies, but he appreciated being invited. Eventually, Perry would stop asking and Vaughn would question whether he had done the right thing by keeping his distance from the men of the town. Right now he was out to prove his leadership and authority. He wanted to be respected as an officer of the law. Besides, he still hadn't had a chance to scope out all of the stand-out characters in Rochester. People like the town drunk that was now spending the night courtesy of the city, and the teenager down at Bear's Auto Body who always seem to find trouble. Those situations he could handle. But all be damned if he'd signed on for this dirty halo business.

~~*~~

Margaret Yardley left the complex housing the police station and public library in a huff. Her mood matched the dirty gray thunderclouds looming overhead. She muttered viciously under her breath and stared intently at her skirts swishing about her legs as she walked. The motion of the color soothed her inner self. She was so involved in the swirling shades of pink, purple and blue that she ran straight into the head librarian carrying an armload of books.

"Oh Ms. Yardley, I'm so sorry," Cameron Cody bent to retrieve the books that had slipped from the pile in the collision.

"Mr. Cody, my apologies," Margaret replied curtly and moved to walk around the man. Cameron stood without finishing his task and stepped in front of her attempt to escape. Margaret stopped short and looked up to meet the man's curious brown eyes.

He casually ran a hand through his thick brown hair and smiled. "Is everything all right, Ms. Yardley? I saw you coming out of the police station there."

Margaret reached up to finger her beads again and sighed. "I'm fine. Just a little upsetting business on my front porch this morning."

Cameron nodded his head slowly and moved his frame out of the old woman's way. He had expected her to push past him and was intrigued when she stood rooted to the sidewalk.

"You know, Mr. Cody," Margaret breathed, "you should just let it go."

Cameron squinted his eyes in question and dropped his arms to his sides, "let go of what, Ms. Yardley?"

"The anger."

"I'm sure I wouldn't know what you're talking about. I'm not angry," Cameron stammered.

"Not on the surface," Margaret interrupted his shaky speech, "but deep down you hold an anger that will destroy you."

Fury flared in Cameron's eyes and he bent to retrieve the fallen books.

"You don't know what you're talking about and even if you do, you'd better keep your mouth shut." He slammed the last of the books onto the stack and marched towards the entrance to the library.

Margaret watched him go.

The dazzling red halo encircling his head left a smudge of color in the air in front of her. She resisted the urge to reach out and touch it for fear that the Chief was watching her through the police station window.

~~*~~

Cameron unlocked the doors of the library with a shaky hand and launched himself and the stack of books through the opening. He quickly shut the heavy oak door behind him and re-locked it. He could feel his lungs seizing up so he reached for the inhaler in his pocket. A few quick puffs and his breathing calmed.

*She couldn't possibly know. She's just an old woman for Christ's sake.*

Since he was little, Margaret Yardley had always been referred to as a witch. He remembered staying the night in a tent at Peter McNamara's house in the fourth grade. All the other boys dared him to sneak through the yard and ring Margaret's doorbell. He'd been so scared creeping through the damp grass, his mouth dry and his palms wet. He'd only made it halfway up the front steps when a creaky board had sent him scurrying back into the bushes. The other boys had made fun of him, laughing and calling him a sissy.

Cameron slammed his hand down on the counter and cursed. He would make sure she didn't talk.

## Chapter 2

Elizabeth Lawrence slammed the kitchen window shut and shook her head disapprovingly. Even at her advanced age, her hair remained a wicked shade of red and she wore it long like her late husband liked. Even though her mother always told her that after forty, hair should be worn above the shoulder.

Just beyond the wooded edge of her property, the state workers were putting in overtime to secure the finishing touches on the newly built bike trail. Liz could sense the urgency in the whines and hums of the machinery as the workers pushed on, motivated by the impending storm. The springs in Central Illinois were as predictable as the sun and moon. This year was no different. It had been raining for almost a week straight and the river was ever rising toward the newly built, aptly named Lost Bridge Bike Trail.

"Jesse, finish your breakfast," Liz prompted her ten-year-old grandson. Even though Liz had never enjoyed the demands of motherhood there was something about being a grandmother that had changed her.

Jesse Lawrence couldn't bring himself to eat. He picked the spoon up out of his cereal again and watched the milk slowly trickle back into the bowl. When Liz wasn't looking, Jesse slipped the piece of toast off of his plate and under the table for Sunshine, his Golden Retriever. "Grandma, can I stay here with you tonight?"

"Sorry, Jesse, but it's Sunday. You know you have to go back to your mom's on Sundays." Liz was heart-broken by the disappointed look on her only grandchild's face and disturbed by the dark circles under his eyes and amount of weight he had lost.

When her son, Walter, had separated from Jesse's mom, Nina, almost six months ago, he had moved back in with Liz to save money. The couple had no formal custody arrangements, but it seemed to Liz that Jesse didn't get to spend enough time with his father or with her for that matter. The effects of the impending divorce were showing in Jesse's grades and now in his appearance. She poured herself a cup of coffee and leaned against the counter top.

Walter Lawrence's robust frame appeared in the doorway a moment before he spoke. "Good morning, Sport. Mama," Walter entered the kitchen with mighty gusto. Jesse's down turned mouth instantly leapt upward into a huge smile, which made Liz smile as well. Sunshine stood from his vigil at Jesse's feet and wagged his hairy, yellow tail until the elder Lawrence reached down and scratched her behind the ears.

"Morning, Bear," Jesse giggled.

"Jesse. Don't call your father that," Liz admonished half-heartedly.

"Why not? Everyone else does," Jesse said as his father's callused hand ruffled his rust-colored hair.

"Yeah, everyone else does," Bear mocked.

"You two," Liz trailed off as she finished her coffee and placed the mug into the sink. Another quick glance out the window showed that a small drizzle of rain had started. A knock at the door made all the Lawrence's look toward the foyer.

"It's Ryan," Jesse explained excitedly, wiggling off of his chair and heading to the front door, his furry friend at his heels. "We're gonna check out the finished part of the trail today."

"But Jesse, its already starting to rain," Liz frowned and rubbed at the pain in her arthritic fingers. She glanced at her son for some back up, but he just shrugged. They heard the door open and excited voices came back towards the kitchen.

"How about if you guys ride down to the shop with me? If the rain lets up, you can head out to the trail." Bear watched the boys silently wrestle with a decision and then nod in unison.

"Go get your packs then... and don't forget Sunshine's leash," Liz ushered their animated chatter back out of the kitchen and waited until she heard their footsteps on the wooden staircase.

"He asked if he could spend the night again, Walter," Liz said, turning back to her son. Bear, as he was called by everyone but his mother, shook his head as he slid a coffee mug off the hook under the cabinet.

"It seems like more and more often, he doesn't want to go back to his mom's house at the end of the weekend. And have you noticed how thin he is? Do you think I'm spending too much time at the shop?"

Liz crossed her arms and shrugged, "I don't know, Walter, he's a ten-year-old boy. This is a crucial time for him and he needs his father full time. Not just on the weekends. He is taking this separation very hard." Liz dropped her arms and walked over to her son. "I know you're doing the best you can." Bear shook his head, but before he could reply, the boys bounced back into the room and surrounded him.

"Let's go, Dad."

"You got it, Sport." Bear ushered the boys out through the garage and held open the passenger door of the tow truck as they scrambled in, then waited while Sunshine found a comfortable spot in the floorboard under the boys' dangling legs. Bear often watched Jesse and wondered if he and Nina had done the right thing by not having any other children. He knew the separation was taking its toll on Jesse. His grades had been steadily dropping since the return to school after Christmas break, but for the life of him, Bear couldn't figure out how to make it right. Jesse's dog and best friend seemed to be his only solace.

Nina and Bear had lost their love for each other shortly after Bear bought the auto body shop almost five years ago. After his dream to play football had fallen though, Bear wanted nothing more than to own it. Being a mechanic was the only thing he was really good at.

After working for John Tavish most of his adult life, it seemed only natural that Bear take over when the old man retired. Nina hadn't seen the purchase of the shop as an asset to their family. It had consumed most of Bear's time and the more time he spent away, the angrier she became.

Bear shut the truck door firmly and ran his hand over the metallic lettering that spelled 'Bear's Auto Body'. "Buckle up, boys."

"Hey, Dad, is Shannon working today?" Jesse asked as his dad climbed into the driver's seat and started the mighty engine.

"Yeah, Jess. I think Shannon might be there this morning, but if we don't get going we're going to miss him." Bear raised a hand and waved to his mother, who had followed them outside. She returned the wave then dropped her arms to her sides.

As if she knew of the conversation inside the truck, Liz frowned at the thought of Jesse spending time with the juvenile delinquent employed by her son. Bear always defended Shannon Marshall and made excuses for his past troubles, but Liz didn't trust him.

*Maybe it would be wise if Jesse and Ryan just played at my house this afternoon.*

Liz opened her mouth to holler after the truck, but at the same moment the roar of the heavy machinery sounded behind the house. It was back to work on the bike trail.

Liz watched the truck pull into the street and out of sight. It was times like these when Liz wished her daughter still lived in Illinois. She may not have always seen eye to eye with Katrina, but she knew her children had a special relationship. Liz sighed and crossed her bony arms across her chest suddenly feeling very cold and very old.

She knew it was time to give Katrina a call.

~~*~~

Shannon Marshall stood in front of Bear's desk in the grimy office of the auto shop and stared intently at the wall. It wasn't the wall, but what was *on* the wall that had his attention captivated. He absently pulled a greasy rag from the back pocket of his equally greasy jeans and wiped his hands. In fact everything about Shannon Marshall was greasy. His dirty dishwater blond hair had grown way too long in the back but he couldn't afford to get it cut. He was of average height and weight for a nineteen-year-old, although his arms were a tad too long making his gait look awkward.

His body was toned and muscular from lifting the tools in the auto shop all day and walking to and from his job. Small, dark eyes were set close together on his thin face and flitted about, making him appear untrustworthy. He ran his skinny, nimble fingers one by one through the oily fabric of the rag and then tucked it away.

Shannon reached his right hand out to touch the picture of the woman's face. To him, she was exquisitely beautiful. A perfect, porcelain-white face framed with a mane of ruby red hair.

In the photo, Katrina Lawrence was laughing at a two-year old Jesse smeared in peanut butter and looking as innocent as freshly fallen snow. Katrina's own hands were sticky with the brownish substance and she held them out towards the young child as if to pick him up.

Every time Shannon looked at the picture he was seized by emotion. Even though he knew that Katrina was Jesse's aunt and not Jesse's mother, the sight made Shannon wonder about his *own* mother and whether or not they had ever shared a moment slathered in peanut butter. He very much doubted it.

His mother had been a very angry woman, drunk more days than not. The only kind of affection she showed Shannon was usually in the form of a slap to the back of his head. His father had not been much different, but at least he functioned enough to get Shannon fed and dressed most days. Neither cared whether their young son made it to school or took a bath and Shannon quickly learned that the only way to get their attention was to cause trouble. He'd been expelled more times than he could count and finally quit six months before his scheduled graduation.

Shannon was thankful that Bear had hired him on. The salary would never make him rich but Bear appreciated the quickness of his work and the pay was steady. Something he'd needed for a very long time.

Around his seventh birthday both mother and father had decided that a life on the road would be more exciting than this narrow-minded town. Of course that life didn't include Shannon. He was dumped with his father's mother, a giant of a woman who barely moved between the rooms in her house, let alone outside. It was a dismal existence for a small boy but Shannon had always been grateful that the old woman took him in. He didn't think she understood him and she certainly wasn't aware of his nocturnal activities. She was now nearing eighty-years old and Shannon knew it was only a matter of time before she died.

His narrow fingers darted out again towards the picture when he heard the distinct sound of the engine in Bear's truck. There was a steady pinging and Shannon made a mental note to have Bear pull it up on the lift for a tune-up. Seconds before he actually made contact with the one-dimensional redhead, Jesse, Ryan and Sunshine bounded into Bear's office and pulled up short. They had no idea that Shannon shouldn't be in the office and their excited voices filled the small space before he had a chance to usher them out.

"Shannon, hey Shannon, guess what we are going to do today?" Jesse asked, breathlessly trying in vain to keep his book bag on his shoulder while the dog wagged excitedly around his ankles.

"We're going to check out the bike trail when it stops raining," Ryan interjected before Shannon had the opportunity to answer.

"Do you want to go with us, Shannon?" Jesse gave up on his backpack and set it down in his father's guest chair.

"I've got to work guys, or else you know I'd go." Shannon took both boys by a shoulder and led them back into the main area of the garage just as Bear came around the corner.

"You boys leave Shannon alone so he can work, all right?" Bear's tone was half-serious. He knew Shannon would get his work done and still be able to give some attention to the boys. Most of the people in town didn't trust Shannon but Bear had found no reason not to give the boy a chance. His parents had been no good and the town was quick to assume that Shannon would be no good either, especially since he'd dropped out of high school at seventeen, just months before graduation. Now bordering on his nineteenth year, Shannon seemed to fit in at the shop more than anywhere else on Earth.

Outside the drizzle of rain had turned into a steady pour and Bear settled in behind his desk to finish paperwork on Kelvin Maylor's prize Chevy Impala.

Kelvin's son had recently turned fourteen and on a dare backed his father's magenta wonder out of the garage and took it for an hour long joy ride that resulted in a broken headlight and bent front bumper. Bad for Kelvin but good for Bear. The ringing phone stopped his pen from finalizing the bill and he snatched it up.

"Bear's Auto Body."

"Bear, its Nina." Bear's entire body tensed at the sound of his wife's voice and his grip tightened on the phone.

"Yeah, Nina what is it?" He tried to sound nonchalant as if he were busy, but to his own ears his voice was strained and he waited for the verbal attack that was sure to ensue when talking to Nina.

"I need you to bring Jesse back a little early tonight," Nina said, tightly.

"I can't do that, Nina. I don't get to see him enough as it is and I'm not going to cut short my weekend with him."

"Come on, Bear. You don't see him any less than when you lived in this house with us. You're at that shop all the time. To you there's no other *home*." Nina's voice became shrill. A sound he'd become accustomed to over the last few years of their marriage.

"Dammit, Nina," Bear tried to keep his voice restrained so it wouldn't carry out to where Jesse was pushing Ryan in a wheeled office chair. "How am I supposed to provide for my family if I don't work? You sure as hell never made the effort to contribute."

"That is *it*, Bear. I'm not having this conversation again. Just bring Jesse back at six o'clock."

Bear watched the boys race back and forth along the slick floor of the garage, sliding and spinning in the chair. Sunshine barked her encouragement. Bear closed his eyes and took a deep breath. "You're right, Nina that *is* it."

After a long pause, he heard her speak, "You still have things here at the house that you should probably pick up someday. I've tried to clean everything out as best I could."

"Yeah, I'll do that. I've got to go, Nina." Bear placed the phone back onto its cradle and pushed the papers away from him. He was no longer interested in the large sum of money Kelvin Maylor owed him. It seemed nothing would please Nina. He'd tried so hard to make their young family work but it had been apparent very early on that Nina had wanted more than Bear could offer.

He was sad for Jesse.

Again, Bear watched as the two friends tired of the chair race and moved onto a new point of interest. They each pulled a wrench from the giant toolbox in the corner and began a mock sword fight. The metal clinked together and rang out into the garage. Shannon moved deftly between the same toolbox and a workbench, arranging and rearranging the contents. He wiped down each tool before putting it in its own special place and then moved onto the next piece. The shop wasn't nearly busy enough for Bear to pay Shannon full time but he felt he owed it to the kid. Even so, Bear was sure Shannon would still be around, wiping down the already clean tools, even if Bear wasn't paying him. After a few minutes, he went back to the paperwork on Kelvin Maylor's Impala.

~~*~~

"Hey Shannon?"

Shannon Marshall turned at the sound of Jesse's voice and found himself staring at both boys, just feet from where he was working. They wore matching looks of both anticipation and dread, which made Shannon uncomfortable. He wanted to look away, cough, do anything that would cause a distraction, but found himself the target of the young boy's stares. In Shannon's mind, they were accusatory, bearing down on him, daring him to tell the truth. Under his t-shirt, Shannon felt the cold trickle of sweat start from his shoulder blades, making a path down his back to the waist of his dirty jeans. "What's up, guys?"

The wrench in Shannon's hand became heavy and he took consolation in its weight. "I was telling Ryan about your animals."

"You were?" Shannon's entire body tensed.

"Yep," Jesse replied and glanced sideways at his best friend. "He wants to know if we can come over to your house and see the graveyard."

"Well there isn't really much to see." Shannon's grip on the wrench tightened until his knuckles showed no visible signs of the blood pumping under the surface.

Silent until now, Ryan took a step forward. "I thought Shannon was a girl's name."

The statement was simple but somewhere in Shannon's mind, a breaking point was reached. He was thrown backward in time. Shannon never had any friends growing up. The other children taunted him mercilessly.

*"Shannon's a girl's name."*

*"Are you a girl, Shannon?"*

*"Shannon Marshall is a little sissy girl."*

Always the same, always cruel. Shannon took two quick deep breaths and replied, "just forget what Jesse

- 34 -

told you. There is no graveyard. It was just a story. Kids will believe anything. Now get out of here and let me work."

He turned his back to the boys.

Jesse had never seen Shannon so angry. He knew he shouldn't have told Ryan about Shannon's animals but he couldn't help it. The story was so cool and Ryan was his best friend. Now Shannon was mad at him. Jesse turned and followed Ryan out of the open garage door. They were outside before Jesse even realized it was still raining.

## Chapter 3

Katrina Lawrence slammed the phone down and took several deep breaths before she was able to remove her hand from the receiver. She moved through her tiny apartment gathering her thick red hair into a sloppy ponytail. She drew back the curtain of her bedroom window and leaned against the sill to catch the small sliver of the city barely visible around the brick building next door.

No matter how small the view, Katrina was comforted by the quick movements of New York and was soon able to rationalize the conversation with her mother. Regardless of the distance Katrina had put between herself and her hometown of Rochester, Illinois, it didn't sever the family ties. One quick call was all it took to reduce Katrina back to the intimidated little girl she'd left behind.

"Damn you, Alexander Graham Bell, for inventing the phone," Katrina mumbled to the window, her breath causing a small opaque circle on the glass. She rubbed at it absently and then retreated to the kitchen for some Windex and a rag. One thing her mother instilled in Katrina was a neurotic tendency to clean. When she was upset or depressed, happy or nervous, Katrina cleaned.

Katrina misted the window covering the remainder of her view and thought seriously about changing her phone number. Of course, she'd never do that. There was Bear and Jesse to think about. If there was one thing Katrina missed it was her little brother, Walter Jr., whom she'd affectionately nicknamed 'Bear' when she was just a little girl. She was five years his senior.

Growing up, Bear had been her baby doll and tea party guest of honor. Then later a student in her make-believe classroom and groom at her mock wedding, when Katrina was twelve. Bear never seemed to mind. He was happy to have the attention of his big sister. The summer when Katrina became a twelve-year-old bride was also the same summer Marie Fairfax went missing. She was a sixteen-year-old local beauty with sunshine in her hair and smile.

At first, everyone thought Marie had run away. It was the most logical explanation and one that kept the reputation of the town squeaky clean. It wasn't until a badly decomposed body showed up five months later in a cornfield off New City road that the suspicions started flying. Of course Margaret Yardley had voiced her declaration of the town's evil until Chief of Police, Gordon Newlon, said the words that every resident had been waiting to hear.

A vagrant just passing through must have killed poor Marie Fairfax. Just in the wrong place at the wrong time, Chief Newlon explained. These were simply the dangers of living so close to the capital city, right off the well traveled Route 29.

The theory was swallowed whole, followed by a collective sigh of relief. No longer was the town evil.

No matter what Margaret Yardley said.

Even Betty and Larry Fairfax, parents of the deceased, accepted the explanation of their only child's demise and the case was closed. Of course no one blamed them when at dinner they had more to drink than eat until Betty was hospitalized with a nervous breakdown. Not three years later Betty took a few too many sleeping pills and died on her bathroom floor.

As it does, time passed and Katrina and Bear grew up. Bear became a tall, broad man who pleased the family and the local football coach. His hair and coloring had escaped the shocking red genes of Liz Lawrence and took on the deeper more auburn tone of their father, Walter Sr. While Katrina finished up her degree in journalism from Southern Illinois University, Bear led the Rocket football team to state and dedicated his terrific year to the undying devotion of his family. Katrina herself had never intended to settle for the small town life of Rochester and figured Bear would also travel beyond the city limits.

After graduation, Katrina took a job for a small Chicago paper writing cooking tips and horoscopes. She didn't care if it was small-time work. It paid her bills while putting her nearly four hours from the critical eye of her oppressive mother.

During Bear's senior year of high school as the star quarterback searched the field for an open man, Walter Sr. clutched his chest in pain inside the small Rochester clinic where he served as the local doctor. Bear, seeing no receiver, barely avoiding a sack, ran forty-two yards for a touchdown securing his full ride scholarship to the University of Illinois while his father took one last breath and died.

The blow of the good doctor's death resonated through the town and settled into a small dark place in Katrina's heart. She stood stoically between her mother and Bear in front of her father's casket, while her mother accepted the sympathy of the townspeople. The funeral had been moved from the small downtown funeral home to the high school gym to accommodate all of the people who came to pay their respects.

Inside the gymnasium, the temperature reached a critical point until Katrina was forced into the late fall afternoon of the parking lot where the air was cooler.

On her way out, Katrina passed Mandy Getz's parents as they moved in to exchange tearful words of praise for all of Walter Sr.'s amazing contributions to the town. Mandy had been in Katrina's class at school until they were fifteen. A cheerleader and an honor student, Mandy was headed for Stanford until one day after cheer practice she flounced through the door her parents had just entered and was never seen again.

Katrina rounded the back of a station wagon and, being careful not to dirty her dress, sat on the bumper. When she looked up, Margaret Yardley stood silently before her. "My God," Katrina exclaimed as she grabbed the bumper to steady herself, "you scared the shit out of me."

The old woman didn't apologize but narrowed her eyes as if to look deep into Katrina's soul. "Your sadness is infinite."

"Yeah, well, my dad just died. Of course I'm sad."

The old woman shook her head of wiry brown hair and touched a small stone she wore on a chain around her neck. "No, it's much deeper than that. Your sadness has lasted a long time. I see you wear a deep blue halo with just a faint ring of yellow." The woman reached a hand out as if she could touch the mythical halo of which she spoke. Reflexively, Katrina pulled away.

"What could the yellow be?" Margaret asked rhetorically. "Relief, perhaps. One less reason to remain."

Anger flashed through Katrina's veins and heat flooded her face, leaving the creamy white skin blotchy and red. "I am not *relieved* that my father's dead. You don't know anything about me."

The woman didn't seem offended by Katrina's outburst, nor was she sorry that she'd offended Katrina. "I know you want to escape—and escape you should."

Katrina had opened her mouth to lash out when Bear's voice traveled across the tops of the parked cars. "Kat? Mom needs you." She lowered her finger from in front of Margaret Yardley's face and smoothed her dress around her waist. Glancing back momentarily at her brother, Katrina lost sight of the woman but wasn't surprised that upon turning back, she was gone.

Three days later, as Katrina retreated to the safety of her Chicago apartment, she couldn't help but replay the conversation with Margaret Yardley. She'd been furious with the witch's accusations but in truth was furious because of the accuracy of her statement.

Cruising down Lake Shore Drive, Katrina tightened her hands on the wheel and came to the hard realization that she'd wanted out. Out of the small town eye with its intrusive residents and missing teenagers. And now with her beloved father dead, and no real love linking her with her mother, there was only one reason why she would ever return to Rochester.

Bear.

When their father had died, Bear's seemingly perfect existence had shattered like the Petri dish his father dropped as the pains shot up his arm and sunk deep in his chest during the heart attack. The younger Walter finished out the football season with less than spectacular stats. He managed to rack up more sacks in a month's time than he had his entire high school career. Coaches were sympathetic even as the steady decline in his grades threatened the hard-earned scholarship.

The clincher, however, came several months later in the sterilely clean room their mother referred to as the salon, which was actually nothing more than a dining room with no table. It would seem that young Bear, who was always popular with the opposite sex, had gotten classmate, Nina Jansen, pregnant. Liz Lawrence was calmer than Bear ever thought possible. With a curt nod of her head, Bear's football scholarship was dismissed and a wedding was planned.

Katrina received the call with mixed emotions. Of course, her mother was harsher with Katrina as if it were her fault instead of Bear's that Nina Jansen was pregnant. Katrina had met the girl only once before in passing and was instantly jealous. Anyone close to Bear wanted to be the focus of his attention. For so long that had been Katrina.

On the other hand, Katrina felt free. Bear would now have to take care of his own family. He would have to be the man of the house and would no longer need her to look after him. So the summer of his nineteenth year, Bear became a husband and the father of six pound, two ounce Jesse Ray. There was never mention of the lost opportunity of Bear's football career. Instead, he took one dead end job after another until John Tavish finally hired him on at the auto shop.

Katrina knew Bear had taken an instant liking to the world of car mechanics and Nina took a part-time job at the grocery store to make ends meet. She knew it wasn't the glamorous life Nina had seen for herself. By hitching her star to Bear, Nina had seen a way out of this small, backwards town. A baby had not factored into those plans.

Two years after Jesse's birth, Katrina got a syndicated column in a more widely-known New York magazine called 'The Day Timer', and moved to the Big Apple. Now, eight years later at thirty-three years old, she was no more adjusted to her new life than when she'd left Rochester.

She meandered through the apartment and put the Windex back under the kitchen sink. She tossed the damp rag in her bathroom hamper before settling onto the couch. Putting a hand on her belly, Katrina felt like she could throw up, but willed the vile creature crawling up her throat back into the dark depths of her stomach.

*How will I tell him?*

By 'him', Katrina meant Jackson Graham, the prominent attorney she had been seeing for over two years. That was, of course, when he wasn't busy with his wife and two young daughters. Katrina hated herself for dating a married man. The possibility of wrecking a home  hadn't exactly appealed to her, but even so, she found herself falling in love with his debonair demeanor and charismatic ways.

Katrina had no delusions about their relationship. She didn't expect Jackson to one day walk out on his wife and children to make an honest woman of her. She did however intend to keep seeing him. Now, she'd jeopardized that by going and getting herself pregnant. It was purely by accident and except for the hourly purging of everything she'd eaten, Katrina could almost believe it was untrue. The double, dark pink lines of the pregnancy test had dispelled that argument.

Jackson was due at Katrina's within the hour and she would have to tell him. Not because she thought it would change things, but because she thought Jackson deserved to know. She felt no motherly, or maternal, instincts toward the baby within her, even though it had been conceived in love. Katrina supposed it was due to Jackson's impending reaction and not just because she had inherited her own mother's indifference towards children.

In one heated argument with the stubborn Liz Lawrence, Katrina had been told that Walter Sr. was the one who'd wanted children, not her mother. She hadn't been surprised by the revelation but had been repulsed nonetheless.

A sharp rap on the door brought Katrina off the couch fast and she fought wave after wave of nausea. The last thing she wanted to do was meet Jackson with vomit on her shirt and breath.

"Just a minute," Katrina called out. She heard a key rattle in the door and it swung inward. Sudden fear and nervousness rooted her to the floor. Jackson Graham floated in looking as if he'd spent the day on a yacht, or perhaps vacationing in the Hamptons. He wore a white button-down shirt that peeked out from the collar of his navy blue sweater. His khaki pants were creased sharply down the middle and looked fresh.

"Katrina?" He moved into the apartment, tossing his keys back and forth from hand to hand. Katrina thought it amusing that he kept her apartment key on the same ring as his home, office and car keys and wondered if his wife ever questioned what lock it belonged to.

He stopped and eyed her. "What's going on? Why are you sitting in the dark?"

At once, Katrina didn't want to tell him. She didn't want things to change between them. Maybe it would be best if she just got rid of the baby and never told him. Would life be simpler? She swirled numerous scenarios around in her head. What if she aborted the baby and Jackson found out? He might be furious. He might actually want the baby and was just looking for the right push to leave his wife and settle down with her.

*Oh who am I trying to kid?*

"My mother called. You know how that is." Katrina waved a hand and willed her feet to move. She walked through the kitchen and put the counter top between them to hide any indication of a belly, although at six weeks there was no physical evidence of her condition. "Are you hungry? I can fix you something."

Katrina pushed her canisters into a neat, even row and wiped at non-existent spots on the fridge door.

"No." Jackson was already shaking his head before Katrina stopped speaking. "Annie's ballet recital is tonight and I promised Felicia I'd go."

Katrina cringed involuntarily. You'd think after two years she'd be used to Jackson speaking his wife's name so casually in their conversation. As if the two women were friends. The sound of the woman's name made the bile swell again in her throat. She moved through the kitchen and retrieved a glass from the cabinet next to the sink. She deposited a small amount of water from the tap into the bottom of the glass and drained it, wishing for something stronger than the tepid contents.

"Hey, what's wrong?" Jackson circled the counter and placed his hands on Katrina's hips, dangerously close to her abdomen. Katrina sighed and leaving her water tumbler on the counter, encircled Jackson's neck with her slender arms.

"Oh, Jack, I don't know what to do."

"What is it? You can tell me. Maybe I can help." Jackson attempted to pull away from the hold Katrina had on him, but she kept him firmly in her grasp. She couldn't look at him right now.

"I'm pregnant, Jackson," Katrina muttered into his neck. She pulled in a deep breath of his scent the moment before he pulled away. This time wild horses couldn't have kept him in Katrina's arms. She could suddenly feel an icy barrier descend between them and the look in his eyes broke her heart in two.

"You're *what*?" Jackson questioned, even though she was sure he'd heard her plainly. His voice cracked and he cleared his throat. Now they both looked as if they would vomit.

"I'm pregnant, Jack. I didn't plan it but it happened." Katrina reached out to him, but he moved back through the apartment as if trying to reverse time by retracing his steps.

"How did it happen?"

"Come on, Jack, you know how it happened." Katrina's terror of telling him was slowly turning into white-hot anger at his reaction. It had been expected, but now the truth of how he felt was written in plain English all over his face.

Jackson stopped behind the couch and placed both arms out to steady himself. He had his back to Katrina but she could tell that he was taking in deep breaths, probably with eyes closed and saliva pumping an ocean into his closed mouth. "It's mine?"

"What do you mean 'It's mine?'? How dare you? You know perfectly well it's yours, Jackson Graham," Katrina shrieked the words across the apartment. She watched as he slowly turned to meet her gaze, his shoulders slumping with acceptance.

"I can't do this, Katrina. I can't have a baby. What would Felicia say?"

*That name again.*

Katrina lunged at the opportunity.

"What would Felicia say if she knew you were having an affair?! She doesn't have to say *anything*. I don't want anything from you, Jack. I just thought that you should know."

"You mean you're *keeping* it?" The tone of Jack's voice was so incredulous that Katrina almost laughed out loud. She hadn't seriously considered whether or not to keep the baby. Getting through this conversation was the furthest ahead she was looking.

"I think you should go," Katrina said and pointed towards the door.

"Katrina, be reasonable," Jackson said, taking a step towards her. When she raised a hand to stop him, he appeared taken aback.

"I love you, Jackson, but I'm not going to put my life on hold for you. I've wasted two years of my life on a relationship that I knew was never going anywhere. You might spend the night once a month but at the end of the day, you go home to your wife and daughters. I'm here alone. Now I didn't plan this pregnancy, but this might be my only opportunity to have a child. And how wonderful for me that I get to have it with you." Katrina's voice broke with emotion and she silently chastised herself for losing it. She blamed the raging pregnancy hormones coursing through her body. She hoped she wouldn't be one of those women who cried over Hallmark commercials and puppy calendars.

Jackson fished his keys out of his pants pocket and busied himself removing Katrina's apartment key from the ring. When that was accomplished, he produced his wallet out of his back pocket and counted out five one hundred-dollar bills. He placed both in a Carnival glass dish on the end table and turned back to Katrina. "Get rid of it, then call me."

"You can't be serious." Katrina was not so much taken back by what Jackson said as by what he did. Giving back her apartment key and then leaving her with five hundred dollars like she was some cheap whore. She flew across the room to the table and picked up the wad of money in her fist. The touch of it sickened her and she almost dropped it out of disgust. Throwing it back at Jackson, she screamed, "I don't want your damn money, Jack. I don't want anything from you. Would you have ever told Felicia to get rid of Annie or Sydney? How *could* you?"

Jackson never broke his stride as he floated through the darkened apartment looking as calm and fresh as when he'd first entered. He had moved beyond the topic as if in the courtroom. Having argued his point and unwilling to listen to the opposing views, he'd shut down. Although Katrina was shocked to see him hesitate at the door and turn back for one last statement.

"I love you, Katrina. I want to be with you. You know that. We met under circumstances that make it impossible for us to be together all of the time. If you have this baby, I never want to see you again. Please, for *us*, have an abortion."

And with that he was gone.

Katrina stood long after he'd left, rooted to the spot on the carpet. The vulgar money was strewn in a crude semi-circle on the carpet in front of her.

*How dare Jackson demand that I get an abortion?*

Never mind the fact that she'd run that very scenario through her head only moments before he arrived.

*It's my body, my baby. I'll decide.*

Without really being aware of her own motion, Katrina moved through the darkened apartment and found herself again at the bedroom window. She gazed out over the busy city street and a sense of calm settled over her. She'd figure this out on her own. Whether or not Katrina thought she could raise a baby by herself, she knew that things between her and Jackson would never be the same. Her life had changed in just a few seconds.

Telling her mother would be much worse than her confrontation with Jackson. Now she knew how Bear and Nina felt. The only exception was that Katrina was an adult—not the young teenager her brother had been. Of course, with Liz Lawrence that wasn't the issue. Liz had never had much faith in Katrina or her abilities. You'd never catch Katrina saying she had a loving relationship with her mother. Even after Bear had squandered his opportunity for a career in football with his untimely child, Liz was still able to find the good of the situation. Katrina doubted her mother would be so supportive with her.

Their child had devastated her relationship with Jackson and now it would upset her family as well. She sank onto the bed and pulled a pillow over her eyes. Maybe tomorrow things would look better; then again she'd *still* be throwing up.

## Chapter 4

It was quarter 'til six when Bear pulled the truck in front of his former house and turned off the noisy engine. During the short trip from the shop to the house, Jesse had become sullen and silent. One hand gently stroked the nape of his dog's neck as he stared out the window at nothing. Finally the rain had eased and Jesse seemed shocked when the sudden silence of the engine permeated the cab.

Bear slung his forearms onto the steering wheel and sat hunched towards the windshield as he scrutinized the place he once called home. The yard was just starting to sprout the full green grass of spring but Bear knew that Nina would never keep up the mowing and trimming needed around their landscaping. She wanted to sell the place and move. Her folks had moved back up to Peoria when Jesse was five and Nina had mentioned on more than one occasion how nice it would be to live closer to her family. But every conversation had turned into an argument and Bear had thrown a fit. He could barely stand Jesse living a couple blocks away, let alone hundreds of miles. Bear moved his gaze to his son who was giving him an intense stare.

"Dad?"

"Yeah, bud."

"Can you tell Shannon that I'm sorry?"

"For what?" Bear angled his body to get a better look at his son.

"I told Ryan a secret that Shannon told me and I shouldn't have. Just tell him I'm sorry, okay?" Jesse hung his head and fidgeted with his fingers.

Bear's eyes narrowed.

*A secret? Exactly what kind of secret should a nineteen-year-old boy be sharing with my ten-year-old son?*

"What was the secret, kiddo?" Bear tried to keep his tone light. Jesse looked over at his father as if to gauge whether he should break confidence again. After a moment of silence, Jesse said, "I told Ryan about Shannon's animals."

"Animals? Shannon never told me he had pets."

"They aren't pets, Dad, they're just...Could you just tell him I'm sorry?"

Bear knew it wouldn't be wise to push Jesse so he let the subject die. He made a mental note to bring it up next weekend when Jesse came back to stay with him. On second thought, maybe he should just confront Shannon at the shop.

"Dad?" Jesse's voice was tiny inside the cab. "Can I tell you something?"

"You bet, Jesse. You can tell me anything." Bear reached out a hand to pat the boy's bony shoulder.

"I want to live with you, Dad. You and grandma," Jesse's voice was suddenly filled with tears and it ripped Bear's heart clean in two. He would give anything if Jesse could come and stay with him full time but Nina wouldn't let go that easily.

"I want you to live with me and grandma too, but it's just not that easy. You know that. I explained how the court has to decide the custody arrangements."

Jesse shook his head in defeat and reached for the door handle before pulling his hand back. "Dad, there's something else."

"What is it, Jess?" Bear asked but his attention was already focused on the front door of the house opening slowly. Nina appeared out of nowhere, her arms crossed over her chest, hands clutching elbows. She was dressed in a white t-shirt and jeans, her feet bare. She had slung a white sweater over her shoulders to step out into the May evening despite the heat.

Nina was a raven-haired beauty. As gorgeous as when Bear had first seen her. Her parents had moved to Rochester their junior year of high school and it wasn't long before the two were an item and Jesse was on the way. Bear had always lost himself in Nina's piercing aqua-colored eyes.

Now from the truck, Nina's eyes appeared hard and cold. Jesse had followed his father's intense look out across the yard and noticed his mother. As suddenly as the conversation had begun, Jesse clammed up and clamored out of the truck as if it had just burst into flames.

"Wait, Jesse—I thought you wanted to tell me something," Bear called after the boy, but he was already halfway across the lawn. He watched the boy slink past his mother and disappear into the house while Sunshine sniffed at a spot in the yard. At that moment, Bear was filled with self-loathing at what the separation was doing to Jesse. He continued to stare at Nina until it became obvious that she would win the contest. He pushed open the door of the truck and lumbered across the yard like a convict on death row.

"He asked if he could live with me again."

"Well, I'm not shocked. Your mother promises him the world, Bear," Nina replied spitefully and clenched her hands tighter on her elbows. Bear sighed. The argument was the same, just happening on a different day.

"I gotta go. Does Jesse need anything? Summer clothes or money for camp?" Bear attempted to peer around his estranged wife into the house to assess its condition. Nina shifted her weight and blocked the opening.

"No and Jesse isn't going to camp this year."

From somewhere behind Nina, Jesse's voice pierced the rapidly approaching night air. "What? I don't get to go to camp?"

Jesse shouldered past his mother to stand beside her on the porch. His own dark eyes were blazing with anger and hurt. "But you promised. Dad, tell her I can go."

Bear watched a sheen of tears wash over his son's eyes and he wished like hell he could tell Nina what to do. He knew she was punishing Jesse because of him. It wasn't fair and Nina knew it. "Jesse, we'll talk about this later…"

"No, I want to talk about it *now*. I want to live with you, Dad. Please take me home with you."

"Jesse, you can't stay with your father tonight," Nina's eyes hardened until Bear thought her very stare would turn him to stone, "It's Sunday. There's school tomorrow."

Again, Jesse shoved past his mother, sobs racking his small frame. Somewhere deep inside the house a door slammed and Bear flinched. "You don't have to do this to him, Nina."

For a moment, Nina faltered and her brow furrowed before she regained composure. "I don't know what you're talking about. You did this to us, Bear. *You* left." She turned on her bare-footed heel and started through the front door. Over her shoulder she called out, "come on, Sunshine."

"You pushed me to it, Nina and you know it. I couldn't live like this anymore. I worked so hard to make that business work and you resented it. Resented it even as you happily spent the money I made from it."

"What money, Bear?" Nina stopped just inside the threshold, "That business is nothing but a cut-rate mechanic's shop. I thought you were really going to be somebody, Bear. Somebody special. Your football career would have taken you a long way from here and... I would have followed you anywhere." Her last statement took on a note of whimsy and longing. Without another word, she slammed the door in his face. He was left on the lawn with the rapidly approaching darkness and the gentle chirping of crickets.

Maybe he could have been a big football star at one time, but those days were over. He'd let them go so easily. The death of his dad and then Jesse's birth had all but ended his ability to even play the game. In all of Jesse's ten years, Bear hadn't so much as tossed the ball around with him. The memories of what could have been were too painful. Bear pushed both heels of his hands to his eyes and then slowly lumbered back to the truck, feeling more alone than ever before.

## Chapter 5

*Monday, May 16<sup>th</sup>*

"**A**ll right, Mr. Fairfax, let's go," Perry Newlon unlocked the holding cell door and slid the bars to one side. The old man was snoring softly on the cot, still wrapped in his overcoat even though the temperature outside was turning warmer by the minute. His face was a series of deep lines and creases, weathered by his days in the cornfields. In another life, one that included a loyal wife and a beautiful teenage daughter, Larry had been a successful farmer and businessman. Now he looked no different than the homeless who littered the streets of the capital city.

The old man appeared to be in deep thought, contemplating the most complex intricacies of the world, even though Perry knew this wasn't possible. Larry Fairfax's brain was probably still swimming in a sea of alcohol even though he'd been sequestered in the Rochester police station all night.

From where he stood, Perry thought he could see his own future in the old man's face. Larry Fairfax had been a good friend of Perry's father. Gordon Newlon, the former Chief of Police, was well-liked and respected by the community, just as much now as when he was on the force. Back then it had been Gordon who held the weekly poker games at their house. In attendance had always been Larry, Doc Lawrence, Roger Thompson from the grocery store and Perry's Uncle Fred on his mother's side. Gordon and Fred didn't get along that well but Esther Newlon insisted he be included or Gordon and his buddies could go without the fancy snacks that she prepared for their game night. Thus Fred's place at the table was secured.

Young Perry had never been allowed into the basement when the game was being played and he certainly wasn't allowed to help his mother prepare the snacks in the kitchen. So as an only child, Perry had no other entertainment than to retreat to his room. It was decorated in cowboys with muted greens, blues and browns that Perry was quickly outgrowing. When he was a small child, Perry had fiddled with model cars and blocks to pass the evening. But in time, Perry grew up and it wasn't long until he realized that in his parent's modest ranch-style home, more than just the heat was transferred up through the vents into his bedroom.

On those nights after the men retreated to the basement, Perry would escape to his room and huddle close to the heating vents to take in all the conversations wafting up along with the choking scent of cigar smoke.

Most of the time, Perry had no idea what the men were talking about. Other times, their dialogue was unmistakable. In the year of 1971, hot topics consisted of the Beatles breakup, new Monday Night Football commentator Frank Gifford and the lovely Jane Fonda in her role as a New York call girl in the movie 'Klute'. It would win her the Academy Award.

The men always seemed so proud of themselves, masters of the universe in this small Illinois town. Perry knew early on that he never wanted to be like his father or the other fat cats sitting around the table stuffing in his mother's cooking and laughing at their own jokes.

Through it all, even at Perry's young age, he could feel their discontent in life. It came shadowed in comments about their wives and jobs, their lost dreams and fading youth.

And yet here he was, following right in the shadow of Gordon Newlon. Perry had become a cop when nothing else seemed to fit, even holding the same poker games in the same basement of the same house. Those thoughts made him bitter, but he was unwilling to do anything about it.

*If only...*

"Morning, Perry," Vaughn said, entering the station. He removed his hat and ran a hand over his blond hair. At the sound of the chief's voice, Perry was startled back to the present. "Is our guest awake yet?"

"Hey there, Chief," Perry replaced his dazed countenance with a smile, "missed you at the game last night."

"Yeah, sorry about that. Had some business to take care of," Vaughn continued into his office while Perry called out after him.

"I was just gonna wake up old Larry here and take him home unless there's something else you needed."

"No, that's fine. Turn him loose," Vaughn said, appearing again in his office doorway, "and warn me if you see Ms. Yardley coming this way."

"Sure thing."

Vaughn watched Perry rouse the still drunken man out of his peaceful slumber and usher him toward the door of the station. They stepped out into the sunshine of the morning, and through the window, Vaughn could see Perry's lips moving in soundless conversation. Soon the sergeant was behind the wheel of the police car and gone.

Even after six months, Vaughn was unsure of Perry's attitude towards him as Chief. At first Vaughn had anticipated problems because he knew Perry had been acting Chief when Perry's father, Gordon Newlon retired from the position. Everyone in town just assumed Perry would follow in his old man's footsteps, and move up the ladder from officer to Sergeant to Chief. Nevertheless, the city went outside their limits and pulled in an outsider to fill the position. Perry had never seemed to harbor any animosity in his lack of promotion and treated Vaughn with respect. But Vaughn always had a doubt in the back of his mind that on some level Perry had wanted the job. Having never met the elder Newlon, Vaughn often wondered how Perry's father had reacted to the news.

Alone in the station with his thoughts, Vaughn walked over to the holding cell and stared down at the cot that was so recently vacated. He searched over the pillow and blanket with quick eyes for any sign of Margaret Yardley's dirty halo nonsense. Chuckling under his breath, Vaughn ducked back into his office to start the day.

~~\*~~

"Just a couple more weeks of school. Man I can't wait to go to camp this summer."

Ryan Bentley ran a hand along the white picket fence bordering the sidewalk, his hand thumping from post to post. The last bell of the school day had just rung and like all the days before, Ryan and Jesse had met up by the swing set to begin their walk home. Jesse hadn't said a word since leaving the school grounds and became even more sullen when Ryan mentioned camp. He didn't want to admit that his mom wasn't going to let him go this year. He didn't know what he would do if he had to be cooped up in the house with his mom all summer. Maybe he could convince his dad to let him stay the summer at his grandmother's. Jesse knew his mother would never allow it but he was going to ask anyway. Beg if he had to. Maybe even ask his dad to go back to court to get full custody.

"Hey are you even listening to me?" Ryan had stopped several steps back on the sidewalk and was squinting at Jesse through the late afternoon sun.

"What? Yeah, totally. Camp, I know. It's going to be so cool." Jesse reached up and pulled a leaf off the tree above his head so he could avoid looking in Ryan's eyes.

"What's up with you, man?" Ryan asked, beginning to walk again, "you've been a first class space cadet for like weeks."

Jesse reached out a hand and grabbed Ryan's arm. "I don't want to go home yet."

Ryan stopped again and looked at his friend. He wondered how tough it would be if his parents split up. Ryan thought he'd go crazy. Especially if he had to live with just his mom and two little sisters. He shook his head in what he thought was understanding and then a sudden light brightened his eyes. "Let's go check out the trail. Come on. We didn't get to go yesterday cause of the rain. Now there'll probably be all kinds of worms and bugs crawling in the dirt piles."

For the first time that day, Jesse's face broke into a smile and he exclaimed, "Race ya."

With that, both boys tore off like rockets, their back packs slapping heavy books roughly against their backs. They raced in the opposite direction of their neighborhood.

Jesse wished he could just keep running away forever. Soon they pulled up short next to the sign at the beginning of the trail, doubling over and gasping for breath. Jesse felt alive at the possibility of their impending exploration and he was anxious to begin.

"Wait," Ryan said, holding back his friend, "wait till the cars are gone." Ryan motioned toward Route 29 as the stoplight changed from red to green and the cars started slowly creeping forward, drivers eager to continue their journeys. Jesse nodded and kept a watchful eye until the last of the cars had slid through the intersection and disappeared. When it seemed that the roadway was as clear as it was going to get, the two boys ducked around the sign and entered the wooded trail.

The canopy of trees was tightly holding in the smell of fresh asphalt . The strong scent was thick in the humid air. Jesse knew that not much of the trail had been paved and further down, somewhere behind his grandma's house, machines were still clearing the foliage and packing down the earth in preparation for the trail.

For a while the two walked in silence, absorbing the new surroundings and familiarizing themselves with the terrain. The black road pack beneath their feet was hot and sticky and Jesse knew his mom was going to be mad when he came home with tar on his shoes. The thought made him want to tramp harder on the tarmac, shoving the vile substance farther into the tread on his sneakers. So involved was Jesse with hateful thoughts towards his mother, he didn't even realize they'd walked the length of the finished trail and were now venturing onto the uneven dirt path where the train tracks used to lie.

"Whoa, check it out," Ryan motioned ahead of where they stood to the half-finished bridge and the giant machinery there to assemble it piece by piece. The massive equipment now lay as still as a bone yard and left long looming shadows.

Jesse was unnerved by the still behemoths but Ryan appeared undaunted. He sprinted ahead to examine every nook and cranny. A tiny sliver of sunlight had penetrated through the canopy of trees and was bouncing brightly off his white-blond hair. The boys were so completely opposite in appearance. For all of Jesse's dark hair and eyes, Ryan was fair in his coloring. The vision reminded him of a couple of months ago when the pair had been at the library.

They loved going to the annual paperback sale. The boys had scrambled to retrieve all of the western novels they hadn't read and took them to a nearby table to pour over their finds. Jesse had glanced up to see Margaret Yardley approaching their table, a wry smile playing on her lips. She moved a gnarled hand in a sweeping motion over the top of Ryan's pale hair and then did the same to him.

Of course, there was nothing magic about the action, but Jesse swore he felt an electric buzz come off the woman's hand and trickle down the nape of his neck. Margaret leaned in closely and whispered, "You boys are the perfect balance between light and dark, peace and war, good and evil. Never lose sight of each other and you won't get lost."

Ryan stared up at the old woman, his blue eyes round and unblinking, shocked at what the woman had said. Jesse on the other hand became instantly agitated. Was he the dark one? The evil one?

Before Jesse could reply the woman was gone. Swallowed up in the stacks of books and racks of magazines.

But that was then—now Ryan had scrambled to the top of the mighty machine and was peering in the window of the cab.

"Jess, come here! They left the keys in this one!"

Jesse dropped his backpack onto the ground and raced after his friend. Maybe he was the evil one. Maybe that's why his dad had split up with his mom. Maybe that was the reason why he hated his mother so much. Right now he just wanted to be a kid again.

A kid that didn't know so much. That hadn't seen too much.

~~*~~

Shannon Marshall watched as the bird's chest took one last final heave in attempt to breathe, and then it was still. Even though the death of the creature was always a relief to Shannon, a single tear slid down his grimy cheek and fell onto the bird's feathers. This one had been long and hard. The death agonizingly slow.

He rubbed at the wet feathers and smoothed them back into place along the breast of the bird before placing it in the tiny box he'd fashioned from scrap wood. The lid fit perfectly atop the small coffin, just as the others he'd made had.

Shannon glanced out of the small window in his room. His view was of the yard behind the house. It was a postage stamp of crab grass surrounded by a wooden fence in dire need of painting. The slats between the fence posts were so choked with weeds that you couldn't even see through them, whether you were trying to look in or out. The entire property backed up to a cornfield and beyond that was country as far as the eye could see.

It was one of the advantages of living at the edge of town. People could speculate about Shannon Marshall, but no one really knew him. Or knew what he did.

The daylight was fading into the West and Shannon knew he would need to scout for a plot soon while he could still see. He moved through the house as quietly as possible, but the old structure's creaking floorboards gave away his presence.

"Shannon, honey, is that you?" His grandmother's feeble voice reached out from the living room. Shannon could hear her favorite game show coming from the television set.

"Yes, Grandma. Just going outside for a bit." Shannon bypassed the entrance to the kitchen and stood before his grandmother. She'd grown so large that he had no idea how she got in and out of the chair most days. Shannon had seen her lumbering to the bathroom in the early evenings but for the most part she remained seated. He knew one day that he'd find her in that chair, unmoving.

"Well, don't be too late dear. You know I don't like being in the house at night alone."

"I know," Shannon said and bent to kiss the old woman's forehead. Her smile was caught flickering in the glow of the television and reminded Shannon of a fun house clown. He quickly retreated through the kitchen and stole into the back yard.

The far edge of the fence was dotted with tiny mounds of muddy earth. They resembled molehills but Shannon knew better. Miniature graves holding the remains of dead animals. Some long since passed. On those burial places the earth was tightly compacted and only a few sprouts of grass were showing.

Shannon settled down on his haunches and began clearing leaves and debris. When he had decided there was sufficient room, Shannon fetched a small trowel out from behind a discarded flowerpot and began digging. In no time, the hole was big enough to accommodate the makeshift coffin he had built and, like always, Shannon didn't realize until he was finished that the earth was also wet with his tears.

He lumbered slowly through the house again and retrieved the animal from his room. This time his grandmother didn't call out.

Once again before the grave, Shannon couldn't bring himself to put the bird in the ground.

"Why does it always have to end this way?" he whispered to no one in particular. The daylight had turned into dusk and the brilliant sun sitting on the horizon seemed almost eye level with Shannon.

Clutching the box to his chest, Shannon let himself out of the rickety-gated yard and began walking quickly down the street.

In record time, he'd passed the Catholic Church, the post office and the bank on the corner. He glanced quickly left and right before darting across the busy intersection of the highway. If Shannon turned right, he'd be walking back towards Bear's Auto Body but instead he turned, crossed the street and made a path along the sidewalk till he reached his destination.

The great house loomed before him. It was painted olive green with eggplant colored trim. Neat white wicker furniture was assembled in one corner of the massive porch. All of the windows were covered with dense, heavy curtains, but even so, the door opened before Shannon completed his climb up the porch steps. Margaret Yardley eyed the boy with sympathy and reached out both of her hands.

At first Shannon thought she intended to hug him and at that moment he wanted desperately to be hugged. Then he realized she was holding her hands out to take the box from his tight grasp. "This one was just too beautiful to bury, Ms. Yardley."

"I understand, dear. Now run along. I'll make her beautiful again," the old woman's mouth twitched at the corners and then she disappeared back inside her house with Shannon's dead bird.

As depressing as it sounded inside his head, Shannon had no choice but to return home.

## Chapter 6

"Hey, Dad," Perry shut the door quietly behind him and ventured into the living room of his parent's house. Gordon Newlon shuffled through the empty space in his robe and house slippers, wheezing and gasping for air. If Perry hadn't been used to the scene, he'd have been alarmed at the sound of his father's labored breathing.

Behind him, the elder Newlon pulled an oxygen tank. The slender green bottle of life-sustaining gas rattled back and forth in the wheeled cart's steel cage with each step he took. His greeting to Perry came on the heels of a wretched hacking cough that made Perry wince. It seemed the only thing connecting Gordon Newlon to life was the long, clear tube running from his nose to the tank.

Thirty-two years of smoking had given the man a raspy voice and lung cancer. Diagnosed nearly a year ago, his once strong, intimidating appearance was now reduced to a shrunken version of himself. Perry was sure his father hadn't been out of that same bathrobe in nearly a week. His still-brown hair, only gray at the temples, was slick to his head with grease. Indentations had formed on his cheeks where the oxygen tube was trying to permanently burrow into his face.

"You shouldn't be up walking so much, Dad."

Perry went to his father's side and attempted to help him across the room. Gordon shrugged off his assistance and continued to gasp and pant long after he'd settled into the worn living-room recliner.

"I'm not a baby, Perry. Don't treat me like one."

Gordon's words were broken up by long draws of air, which lessened the intensity of his reply. "Oh, and I fired Jackie today."

"Dammit, Dad."

Perry moved through the house, taking off his weapon holster, and began unbuttoning his shirt, "You can't keep doing that. One of these days Jackie's going to get fed up with your shit and not come back. Then what would we do, huh?"

Gordon shrugged as if he couldn't care less what happened if Jackie really quit. Perry continued to shed his blue policeman's uniform down to his t-shirt, and then retrieved a bottle of beer from the fridge.

Jackie Agans was a petite blond who worked as Gordon's home health aide. Even though she appeared to be an innocent pixie of a woman, she was tough as nails and the only person Perry could find to put up with his father's crotchety attitude.

Besides, Perry knew deep down the old man adored Jackie and her fifteen-year-old daughter, Amy. Amy was a beautiful teenager with a lust for mystery novels. She planned on going away to Northern University in a couple of years to major in Criminal Justice. Even though she wasn't quite sure what she wanted to do with the degree quite yet, she loved to tag along to the Newlon house and question Gordon endlessly about his days on the force.

Perry knew he'd have to call Jackie in the morning and apologize again for his father's behavior and beg her to come back. The thought made him sigh heavily and take a long swallow from his bottle. Starting down the hall towards the bathroom, Perry shouted out, "I'm going to take a shower then make us some dinner."

After several moments of working up enough breath to speak, Gordon shouted back, "I'm not hungry."

"You've got to eat, Dad. That's final."

*Jesus Christ,* Perry thought as he stepped under the hot spray of the shower. *How much more of this can I take? If only Mother was here, things wouldn't be such a constant battle with Dad.*

But three years ago, a deadly case of breast cancer hadn't even given his mother a chance to have a mastectomy before taking her life. Perry often wondered if his mother knew long before her death that something was wrong but just didn't want to face it.

Until the day she died, Esther Newlon had taken care of her husband, cooking and cleaning with a ferocity that Perry had never seen before, or since. Maybe she'd been doing all of that for herself in attempt to scrub away the disease ravaging her body. Perry would never know. Esther had been a private person, keeping all of her feelings and frustrations locked inside. Perry knew that his father hadn't been an easy person to be married to but Esther's Catholic background didn't even allow one to think the word 'divorce'. She had made it work for herself and for Perry.

He always wondered if that was the reason why his marriage to Joyce didn't work out. It was just too difficult—and, of course, Perry had spent a lot of time trying not to replay history by becoming his father to a woman who deserved so much more. Because of that, the distance he kept between himself and Joyce finally forced her to leave.

Thankfully there had been no children, but not because they hadn't wanted them. Perry had been determined to be a better father than what he'd had but after years of trying, Joyce's doctor had given them the devastating news. Endometriosis had all but taken over Joyce's uterus and there was no chance for a baby. It put tremendous pressure on the already-strained relationship and gave Joyce the final reason she needed to leave. The last Perry had heard, she lived back in Salisbury with her parents. One of these days he would try to make things right.

For now he was here, taking care of the old man. Perry shut off the water and grabbed his towel. He felt himself at the breaking point and questioned how long he would be able to keep his sanity.

~~*~~

Katrina shut the lid on her laptop computer and moaned. The latest topic for her column in 'The Day Timer' wasn't flowing well and Katrina knew it was best just to put the story to bed for the night. Several days ago, she'd spoken to her editor and asked for some time off to collect herself. From experience, Katrina knew Molly wouldn't be happy with her request but in the end she agreed to run a previous piece of Katrina's writing.

Through it all, Katrina kept up the research on her latest project, but couldn't find the concentration to do the column justice. She found herself pacing through the apartment feeling more alone than ever before, which she thought to be ironic since she was now not alone.

Katrina touched her abdomen just below her belly button and sighed.

*I don't know what kind of mother I'd be. I can't even take care of myself.*

It had been over a week since her confrontation with Jackson. Although she hadn't expected to hear from him, she couldn't help but be disappointed in his actions. How could he just turn his back on her? On his child?

As a kid, Katrina remembered being her daddy's little girl-- sitting on his lap and hugging his neck, her arms barely reaching around him. Then later when she graduated with honors from college, even now she could still picture the pride in his eyes. Even though he'd wanted her to attend medical school, he had supported her decision to be a journalist. Would she ever be able to make her child understand that his or her father was too busy with his *other* family to be a part of their world?

These thoughts bounced back and forth in her mind until she thought she might go crazy. In the end, she still wasn't sure if she was going to have the baby or not. For all the pros, Katrina's mind found a con and *vice versa*. Above all, she wished she didn't have to make the decision alone.

But who could she tell? Certainly not her mother and Bear had his own problems, what with the separation and all. Except for a few acquaintances at the magazine and, until recently, Jackson, she had no real friends in the city. It wasn't as if this fact depressed her, she really liked leading a solitary life. She attributed it to growing up in a small town where everyone knew everything about you. Escaping to the anonymity of New York City had been like a stay of execution for her. She loved it and never saw herself going back to Illinois.

Katrina found herself at the refrigerator, staring at the meager contents. She selected a peach from the crisper and went back to the couch. Before she could sit, the phone rang. The sudden noise reverberating off the walls in the otherwise quiet apartment.

"Hello."

"Katrina, it's your mother." Katrina heard the voice and cringed. It was as if thinking of the woman only moments ago had somehow summoned her. Continually, Liz Lawrence would call her daughter for no other reason than to relive all of her daily aches and pains, all the while trying to make Katrina feel guilty for not being in Rochester to see her through them.

"Mother," Katrina said after several seconds of silence.

"Is this a bad time?" Liz's tone was curt as usual.

"Well actually, I was working—"

"I just called to say you should talk to your brother," Liz interrupted before Katrina could complete her sentence.

"Why? Is something wrong?" Katrina was notably concerned and it sounded in her voice.

"Jesse doesn't seem to be handling the separation very well at all and because of that neither is Walter. I just don't know what to do any more. I think he might be contemplating a reconciliation with Nina, for Jesse's sake."

Katrina closed her eyes and held the phone away from her ear.

*Why don't I have caller I.D.?*

"Mother, I can't tell Bear what to do with his life. No matter how badly he needs to be away from Nina."

"Honestly, Katrina I don't know why I call."

*This is how it always starts,* Katrina thought. *Why does she think the effect of Bear and Nina's potential divorce on Jesse is my responsibility? And how will my moving back to Rochester make things go back to normal?*

Katrina hung up the phone feeling worse than before. Maybe she *should* take a trip back to her hometown. Visiting with her brother and nephew would be great—but that would mean staying at her mother's house.

On second thought maybe she would send Bear and Jesse a plane ticket to come stay with her. School was almost out and now would be the perfect opportunity for both of them to get away. Katrina couldn't picture her little brother feeling at home in the big city but she hadn't seen them in almost five years. Even then she'd flown in for a weekend visit and stayed in Springfield rather than traveling the fifteen additional minutes to Rochester.

A lot had changed. They would look different and act different.

And then, of course, there was the baby.

## Chapter 7

*Friday, May 20<sup>th</sup>*

"Are you ready, Jess?" Bear asked from the doorway of his former home. It was Friday night and Bear was there to pick up his son for the weekend.

"Yeah, Dad, just a second while I grab something," Jesse replied and ran towards his bedroom.

His wife, Nina, sat cross-legged on the couch flipping through the television channels with the remote while Sunshine snoozed on the floor beneath the window. Bear knew she wasn't interested in anything else than what was going on between him and Jesse. She didn't even bother to turn and face him when she said, "Don't forget there are still some of your things in the closet."

"Yes, Nina, I know. I wanted to talk to you about some things before I completely move out," Bear tried to keep his voice low so Jesse couldn't hear. This time Nina did turn and regard him.

"What kind of 'things', Bear? You aren't thinking about moving back in here are you?" Nina's tone was unreadable and this was certainly not the time to talk about it.

"I just think we should think everything through before we do anything drastic," Bear replied.

"I think we've already talked this subject to death, don't you?"

Bear put a finger to his lips to quiet her raising voice. "I'm just worried about Jesse. Have you looked at him lately? This whole thing is taking its toll on him. I just want to do what's right."

"Jesse is fine," Nina said, perhaps a little too quickly and harshly, "I don't know why you would say such a thing."

With that she turned back to the television and Bear knew the conversation was over. He set his mouth in a line of disgust. How he could ever contemplate moving back into this house, he didn't know. But for his son, he would do anything and everything necessary.

Jesse stood just inside his bedroom door, his hand hovering just above the knob. Was he hearing this right? Was his dad thinking about moving back in? Jesse smiled slowly and felt his chest begin heaving with deep breaths. That would be the answer to everything. If his dad would just come back home, then everything would go back to normal and he wouldn't have to carry around such a burden. There must be something he could do to convince his dad to come home.

~~*~~

Once in the truck, Jesse couldn't keep the happiness off of his face. "I heard you talking to mom."

"Oh yeah?" his dad said as they backed onto Sherry Street and started towards his grandma's place.

"Yeah and I think it's a good idea if you came home. *Please* come home."

Bear sighed and reached a hand over to rustle the boy's thick auburn hair. "Your mom and I need to do some serious talking before we make any decisions, okay? I didn't want you to get your hopes up. That's why I haven't said anything to you yet."

"I understand. It's just..." Jesse's voice trailed off as he glanced out the side window.

"It's just what, bud?" Bear felt Jesse shy away from him again. It seemed like every time he was alone with his son, Jesse would start to say something and then stop. "You know you can tell me anything, right Jess?"

"It's just that I need you, Dad. That's all."

"I need you too, Jesse." Bear felt his heart swell and could barely keep the tears out of his eyes and voice as he said, "Hey, I've got an idea. Why don't we stop by Ryan's and see if he can stay the night?"

Jesse nodded his head vigorously and a smile replaced any upset from the unpleasantness of their conversation.

Maybe he didn't need his dad to move back into his house. Maybe it would be better if he just moved with Bear into his grandma's house.

*Bad things don't happen there.*

~~*~~

Nina watched the truck disappear around the corner. She hadn't wanted to admit to Bear that she'd seen the change in Jesse. It was drastic and severe and she felt she was to blame. She wouldn't take Bear back. She just couldn't. He'd let her down and there was no turning back now.

Nina tightened the cardigan sweater around her middle and crossed her arms over her chest. It was the end of May in central Illinois but Nina couldn't shake this dreadful cold feeling that had settled inside of her.

~~*~~

"I'm outta here, Mike," Vaughn stepped through his office door and shut the lights off behind him. Now the only illumination came from the harsh fluorescent tubes in the squad room. Mike Simms filed some paperwork and slammed the filing cabinet shut. "Have a good night boss. You should have been out of here hours ago."

"Yeah, you know how it is. I thought this town was supposed to run itself." Vaughn chuckled good-naturedly and was confident to leave the police work to his overnight officer.

Mike laughed too and shook his head. "This town's come a long way. When I was a kid, this town went crazy for a while. That's probably why Perry didn't go after your job. He saw what his father had to deal with. I'm surprised he even became a cop at all, really."

The smile slid slowly from Vaughn's face and was replaced by a look of inquisition. "Were things really that bad?"

"Well, they definitely weren't typical. Every couple of years a teenager went missing or was found dead. Really shook up the town. Everybody thinks this is such a tight-knit community. They tried like hell to explain away the problems. Then, as suddenly as it began, it just stopped." Mike spoke about the incidents as if they hadn't involved human life. Indifferent.

Vaughn was sorry he'd stopped to talk. "Well, I'd better get going then."

The rain started again as he jogged across the parking lot, attempting to avoid the puddles. As he settled into his pickup truck, he thought maybe he *should* attend one of Perry's poker games. Maybe he could talk to the former chief and get some sort of background on this town. It seemed every time he asked questions, he received more and more information suggesting Rochester's perfect façade was covering some kind of dark, decaying secret.

~~*~~

Cameron Cody watched the last of the teenagers leave the library around closing time. It was Friday evening and many of the kids had better things to do than hang out reading books. Cameron himself had nothing to do. No one to go home to. He would stay at the library long after the doors had shut and walk among the books. The library was so peaceful, especially at night. He found comfort in the old volumes lining the shelves.

He moved stealthily to the window overlooking the parking lot and cautiously spied on the teenagers as they moved through the dim parking lot to their cars.

*So young and beautiful. An entire life before them.*

They had choices to make and experiences to live through.

Cameron closed his eyes and willed away the images behind his lids. It had been so long since he'd loved someone. But how could he? He was a monster. Who would ever love such an abomination of God?

~~*~~

Margaret Yardley opened the box and exclaimed in delight. This one was more beautiful than the last. Shannon would be so thrilled with her latest creation. Margaret meandered through the house touching this and that. She'd spent most of her days alone, especially after the death of her beloved mother. Most people kept their distance from her although they would never admit to the reasons why. They didn't want to believe she had special powers to see into people's souls. Powers to view their thoughts and feelings. Only one person seemed not to care about Margaret's reputation.

Shannon Marshall.

Margaret considered Shannon to be the most misunderstood person in the town. Even more so than herself. She knew how awful his home life had been and couldn't help but feel for the young man. At first, she'd been unable to see the boy's halo because of his age. The younger they were, the harder it was to determine true feelings, because of a child's ignorance to the world. As the boy grew into a man, Margaret slowly but effectively became able to see the colors that swirled about him. Although most shunned his very presence, she couldn't help but be drawn to the boy because of what she saw.

Perhaps her friendship with Shannon Marshall wasn't the most normal but their commonality transcended age and gave each of them a solace from the harsh judgments of others.

Margaret picked up the phone and dialed quickly. While she listened to the ringing tone, she toyed with the contents of the package.

"Bear's Auto Body."

"Shannon, dear, it's Maggie. Our beauty arrived."

"I'll be over right after work. And Ms. Yardley," the boy talked in a rush, "Bless you."

~~*~~

"Walter, don't you think that Jesse should be spending more time with you?"

Bear watched the two boys scamper up the stairs before regarding his mother. "I know, Mom. I'm going to take Sunday off and spend all day with Jesse. I just thought tonight he could have a little fun and stop thinking about his mom and me. You should have seen the look on his face when he thought I might be coming back home. It nearly broke my heart."

Liz Lawrence sighed and ached for her grandson. How she wished her husband, Walter Sr., could be here to enjoy the boy as well. Jesse could have learned so much from his grandfather. The youngest Lawrence was so bright and quick to become skilled at whatever he put his mind to. She wouldn't be surprised if Jesse was the one to attend medical school and take over where his grandfather had left off. She still owned the small storefront where Walter Sr. had practiced. All of his medical files still were locked in the rusted filing cabinets. He could have been a great surgeon but...

"Mom, what is it? You have this really sad look on your face."

Liz shook off the memories and forced a smile on her lined face, "It's nothing, dear. I think I'll go start dinner.

## Chapter 8

Larry Fairfax rolled unsteadily off the couch and tottered to his feet. He couldn't remember the last time he'd had a sober day or night. Truth be told, he couldn't remember a lot of stuff. More often than not he stumbled in from a hard night of drinking and fell dead to the world on the couch, or floor, or chair in the living room of his quiet house. Larry had long since stopped making the trek up the stairs to the second floor. It housed only three rooms and two of them Larry couldn't bear to enter.

When his daughter had been murdered so long ago, the Fairfax's closed the door to the girl's bedroom and never set foot in there again. Then when Larry's wife had taken her own life, Larry could think of no reason to ever use the bed he'd shared with her for all of those years. Now he was alone. Eventually, he might get around to selling the place and moving somewhere that didn't have so many memories.

Larry moved through the house to the kitchen and mulled over the lack of food in the cabinets. He hadn't eaten a decent meal in years but then again all that food just dulled the affect of the alcohol. Pulling open cabinet door after door, Larry slowly came to the realization that along with no food, he was also out of his favorite beverage, Johnny Walker Black Label.

Without bothering to shower or even change his shirt, Larry retrieved his car keys from the coffee table and set out in search of a drink.

~~*~~

"Ryan, you still awake?" Jesse Lawrence asked into the darkness of the room. The red numbers of his digital clock read nearly eleven thirty.

"Yeah, is it time?" Ryan's whisper came back through the room. Jesse's body twitched involuntarily with excitement. He threw off the covers to reveal himself fully clothed in jeans, a t-shirt and a blue hooded sweatshirt. He heard Ryan do the same from the matching twin bed across the room. Jesse retrieved his backpack from beside his nightstand. Inside were two flashlights, a couple of extra biscuits from dinner and a can of soda.

As the two snuck as quietly as they could across the wooden floor, Jesse whispered, "My Aunt Kat told me about this." He unlocked the window and slowly eased it away from the sill. "This used to be her room and she sneaked out all the time."

Ryan giggled involuntarily and slapped a hand over his mouth to suppress the sound. Jesse threw a leg out the window and grabbed onto the TV antenna standing sentry against the house. A mist of rain had left a slick film on the cool metal and he slowly started moving downward, grabbing tightly to each rung of the antenna's rudimentary ladder. He heard Sunshine whine somewhere above him as she paced in two-step intervals. Her toenails clicked loudly on the wooden planks. About a third of the way to the ground, Jesse looked up and motioned for Ryan to follow him. His friend nodded silently and began the same descent. The dog poked her head out of the open window, shaking nervously. "Stay, Sunshine," Jesse admonished in a harsh whisper.

Once on the ground, Jesse was careful to keep his head under the windows of the house although he was certain both his grandma and dad had gone to bed. Jesse felt himself shiver with excitement as the two boys reached the edge of the lawn and crossed through the tree line onto the new trail. For the last week, the boys had been coming to the work site after school. They would dodge in and out of the trees, climb the massive mounds of dirt and explore the heavy machinery. Tonight they were going farther than they'd ever been— all the way to the "lost bridge." The trail had been named for the bridge because once 'lost' it had to be reconstructed to give access over the South Fork River.

"Hey, slow down," Ryan trailed behind, his tennis shoes making light slaps on the hard-packed earth.

"Come on, before someone sees us," Jesse said, pushing on. Now out of view from the house, Jesse took one of the flashlights from his bag and aimed the beam at the ground. He hated to admit his relief when the light cut through the dark night. He'd never been a fan of the dark and was especially leery of it now that his dad had moved out. Tonight, he would be brave in front of Ryan.

"There it is," Jesse whispered and pointed to the massive iron structure. Its skeleton framework was a mere shadow against the night's backdrop and couldn't be penetrated by the weak illumination of the flashlight. Both boys rushed ahead and climbed up on the lower rung of the bridge's railing. Long ago the trail and bridge had served as a railway, lined with tracks as far as one could see. Jesse fantasized on what it would have been like to live all those years ago with horse and buggy instead of a car—and no television.

"Look," Ryan spoke out and Jesse turned to where he was pointing. "It's a backhoe."

"Let's go sit in the bucket." On fast feet, the best friends raced the length of the bridge and clamored into the bucket of the machine. The space was cramped for two growing boys and they scrambled back out.

"I'm gonna sit on the top of the cab," Jesse decided and started up.

"I don't know, Jesse, its awfully high."

"Come on, little baby. You just climbed down the TV antenna. What's the difference?"

Jesse couldn't see Ryan below him but the blond boy shrugged and started up after his friend.

Once on top, the two stared up at the clear sky, full of stars.

"I wish I could just stay out here forever, you know. Camp out and be an explorer," Jesse said, his face tilted toward the sky.

"I know. It is so awesome but what would you do when it gets cold?" Ryan asked.

"I'd find a cave, like a bear does, and live there." The answer seemed perfectly acceptable to both and they lapsed into a comfortable silence.

Although not talking, Jesse's mind was racing at full speed. He wasn't sure he could keep it to himself any longer. He glanced at Ryan. The boy's face was shiny with the light of the moon. Margaret Yardley said they needed to stick together so they wouldn't get lost and right now Jesse felt as lost as he could get.

"Hey, Ryan, can I tell you something?"

## Chapter 9

*Saturday, May 21st*

"*N*ow you stay in your room until I tell you to come out, okay?"

"But Leigh..."

"Vaughn, listen to me. I need to talk to Shawn alone. I want you to play in your room, then we'll make popcorn and watch a movie. Got it, kiddo?"

"Okay, Leigh. But hurry, the movie starts in half an hour."

Vaughn Dexter woke with a start at the shrill ring of the phone and couldn't help but glance at the clock before answering. It was a quarter after three in the morning and he felt as if he'd just shut his eyes.

*That damn dream again.*

If only there was something he could do to keep those images out of his head.

The Chief of Police took a deep breath to clear his mind and sat up against the headboard. "Hello."

"Chief, something real bad's happened. We need you up at the intersection of 29 and Walnut, now."

"How bad are we talking, Mike?" Vaughn asked as he swung his legs out over the side of the bed and stood, shaky with sleep.

"It's Larry Fairfax, sir."

"Damn," Vaughn cursed, a horrible feeling settling into the pit of his stomach, "Please tell me he's just been picked up for drunk and disorderly again."

"No, sir, he's, uh, gone and, um, killed the Bentley boy. He was driving drunk and the boy must have been crossing the street. Anyway, the paramedics just notified dispatch to call the coroner."

That wasn't a good sign. The paramedics wouldn't have asked for the coroner if there was something that could be done. That meant there really *was* a dead ten-year-old boy. Vaughn dressed in record time and headed off to the scene of the accident, praying that Mike Simms had been wrong about the situation.

Some time during the night a shower of rain had soaked the pavement and caused the humidity to soar. Vaughn flipped on the air conditioner just as much for the blast of air as to calm his nerves.

As he neared, Vaughn could see the flashing beacons of red and blue lights. They pulsed in time with Vaughn's heartbeat and suddenly everything felt like it had turned to slow motion. He slammed the truck door shut a little harder than necessary and made his way through the gathering crowd. Ducking under the police tape, Vaughn swung his gaze around to take in the scene. To his immediate left, he saw Larry Fairfax's silver Taurus. On first glance, he figured Larry to have been driving north on Route 29. Probably heading out of town. The car was now parked up on the curb about fifty feet past a white sheet-clad lump lying in the middle of the road. Instantly, Vaughn was thrown back in time. They'd covered his sister with an identical white sheet.

*Of all nights to have the dream.*

Larry was handcuffed and currently was being escorted to a police cruiser by one of Vaughn's officers and when the light from the car's cherry strobed on the old man's face, Vaughn could see he was crying.

Two other policemen stood huddled near a gathering crowd of people asking questions and one of them was writing furiously in a small notebook. In the dark, Vaughn was only able to determine that one of the officers was his Corporal, Phillip Rothwell, because of his imposing height. All of the other policemen were faceless and unidentifiable in their matching blue uniforms. Vaughn absently noted that his entire police force was currently accounted for, and somewhere else in the town crime could be running rampant, offenders without the fear of being caught. The paramedics moved slowly between their ambulance and the body. They were in no hurry. There was no life to be saved.

"Tough night, eh boss?" Perry Newlon stepped up beside Vaughn, hands on his hips.

"It's certainly turning out to be," Vaughn commented, "What are you doing here?"

"Heard it on the scanner. Thought I'd see if you needed any help. Besides, this is the most excitement this town's seen since Fairfax's daughter went missing."

Vaughn sized up his Sergeant. Perry was dressed casually in dark jeans and a hooded sweatshirt. His hands were stuffed deep in the front pockets of his jeans and he was bouncing carelessly on the balls of his feet.

"No uniform?"

"What? Oh yeah, hey, I'm not on duty. Just the first thing I grabbed, I guess."

Letting it go, Vaughn pointed ahead of them. "Let's go see what Phil's got for us."

Vaughn and Perry moved across the newly wet pavement to where the two officers were collecting statements from the people who'd filed out of their house to see what all the flashing lights and sirens were about.

Surely someone had seen something. After only six months in this town, Vaughn couldn't believe this was happening. He'd moved here to get away from violence and death, yet it seemed to have followed him. Vaughn was merely a few steps away from his officers when he spotted her through the crowd. Margaret Yardley stood just behind a couple, all three dressed in their bathrobes and slippers. Her eyes were anxious and he could see she was straining above the heads of the other people, trying to get his attention. He tried like hell to ignore her but her persistence was winning out and people were starting to stare.

"I need to see him, Chief," Margaret's voice rang above the crowd and she motioned him over. Vaughn nearly growled out loud as he passed through the wall of people and grabbed the older woman's arm above the elbow.

"Keep your voice down." He pulled her to the side of the road where a small bench sat on the grassy median. "Now what's this all about?"

"Larry. I need to see him up close." Margaret's voice was breathy and her cheeks were flushed bright pink from Vaughn's brisk escort.

"Now why should I let you anywhere near him?" Vaughn tried not to let his impatience show. But, of course, something had happened, leaving a ten-year old dead in the street and if Margaret knew something, Vaughn wanted to know.

"I need to see him," Margaret repeated.

"Margaret, I can't let you waltz up to the squad car and stare at a suspect."

"The dirty halo, Chief." Her voice had become meek and Vaughn could feel her visibly shrinking away from him. Margaret knew what the reaction would be but she was determined.

"Dammit, Margaret, I've heard this story before. I don't have the time for your feelings and psychic vibrations. There's a little boy dead. Now go home and let me investigate." Vaughn was angry—but not at Margaret Yardley. He was mad that after only six months as Chief of Police he was dealing with a reckless homicide in this otherwise quiet community.

He left Margaret standing by the bench, a look of pride still on her face. She solely believed that some mystical cloud of colors above a person's head could tell their future—but right now Vaughn needed cold, hard facts. He pushed back through the crowd of onlookers to a puzzled Perry Newlon. The Chief shook his head as if to say, 'don't ask'.

"He's D.O.A., Chief," Susan Barnes said, suddenly appearing behind the chief. The coroner didn't even bother to exchange pleasantries with him before cutting to the chase.

"Yeah," Vaughn ran a hand over his mustache and down the sides of his mouth, "I was afraid you were going to say that."

Susan, dressed in jeans and a light blue t-shirt, was an attractive brunette with long legs and full lips. She would seem better suited in a major motion picture rather than gurney side at an autopsy. She casually removed the latex gloves from her hands and pulled out a pen and paper. Vaughn had met Susan only months before when he'd requested to be present at an autopsy. He'd never had the experience and thought that before he accepted the position as Chief of Police he should know all parts of the job. Susan had been extremely helpful and took her time explaining all of the cuts and analyses. Vaughn had to admit that he'd been mortified at the sight of the necessary procedure and silently hoped he died of obvious causes so the procedure wouldn't be required on him.

After the corpse had been re-sewn and placed back in the freezer, Susan led him into the hallway and then asked him out. At first, Vaughn didn't know what to say. The question had been so unexpected after what he had just witnessed that he stood rooted to his spot on the squeaky tile floor. He was trying desperately to regain his composure and to his utter dismay, he turned down the beautiful coroner.

Dating was complicated for Vaughn. He knew first hand how fragile a person's life was and couldn't quite bring himself to get involved in a relationship that might end suddenly.

And by 'end', he didn't mean breaking up.

Vaughn had loved his sister. After she was killed, he'd never wanted to love anyone again. Having to live everyday as if the person you love might be inhaling her last breath was a grave strain on any relationship. One that eventually took its toll. It wasn't that he didn't date. In high school, a brunette named Tracey had captured his heart, but when she learned he wanted to be a cop she dumped him. Later in life there'd been Andrea. She was a waitress at the coffee shop he'd frequented when he worked the beat in Rockford.

Andrea wasn't exceptionally beautiful or smart but after the coffee shop closed she'd go home to her one-bedroom apartment and paint the most amazing art that he'd ever seen. After nearly a year of being together, Andrea wanted more. One night after dinner, Andrea presented to him a portrait she'd painted. It was a picture of himself. The likeness taken from a photograph she'd snapped months before. She told him it would look great hanging in *their* apartment.

Long after that night, he'd try to think back if he'd even heard her say those last words. But at the time, as he gazed at the swirling colors resembling his reflection, Vaughn suddenly realized Andrea loved him more than he would ever be able to love her. He couldn't commit. And not because he was one of those carefree, Peter Pan bachelors who wanted his eternal freedom. It was because of his mortality and more importantly, Andrea's.

That night he'd left behind the portrait and a devastated girlfriend.

He wasn't sure he ever recovered fully from his experience with Andrea, but after that dating became easier. He would go out with a woman once, maybe twice. They'd have a good time, but always up front, Vaughn insisted that he wasn't in it for a relationship. He wanted the woman to understand that when he left, or stopped calling, that it wasn't personal. It wasn't because she couldn't cook, or was obsessed with salmon-colored toenail polish. It was Vaughn.

The unfortunate part was that he *wanted* a relationship. He just knew early on that he was no good at it. Why date seriously unless he could feel strongly about someone and would potentially marry her? Now at thirty-seven, he'd settled comfortably into his lonely life. Susan Barnes wasn't part of the plan.

Besides, Vaughn wasn't sure that a union between a cop and a coroner would lead to anything but dismal dinner conversation with the replay of gruesome crime scene details. Susan had been polite as he had stumbled over his explanation. She was still pleasant when they ran into each other, and occasionally asked him if he wanted to reconsider turning her down. He loved that she had a sense of humor about the whole deal.

At the scene, Susan finished jotting a note before meeting Vaughn's gaze. What he saw there wasn't the normal sparkle of her good nature. Tonight she was all business. "Do you know if anyone's moved the body?"

Vaughn and Perry exchanged glances. "We just got here," Perry answered and then addressed his boss. "I can check with Phil if you want."

Before Vaughn had a chance to respond, Perry left in search of answers. Susan hesitated only a moment.

"There's something you need to see."

Moving back towards the body, Vaughn was stopped by a voice coming out of the crowd. "Chief Dexter?"

Vaughn turned just in time to see members of the Springfield Police Department and Illinois State Police Crime Scene Unit filtering through the horde of people like an invading army of soldiers. Most of the law enforcement already knew what their job entailed and he watched as several of the officers passed him by on the way to Ryan Bentley's body. An act that made Susan Barnes very nervous.

She touched his arm. "I have to go, but please, Vaughn, see me before you leave the scene."

Vaughn nodded and turned to the man who'd called his name. What he saw was Detective Donnie Parsons, the cardboard cutout of every television cop. Crew-cut, round glasses, walk of an authority figure. No way could this guy ever work an undercover investigation. He would be made in a matter of seconds. Vaughn referred to him as 'Macho Cop' and the thought was the only thing amusing to Vaughn about this entire evening.

"We've got our best guys on this, Chief. You should have no problem with this cut-'n-dry case," Macho Cop said, confidently.

"Thank you," Vaughn replied automatically.

"Have you viewed the body?" Macho Cop put his hands on his hips and glanced around like a king observing his kingdom.

"No, I was actually just heading over there…" Vaughn began.

"Chief," Perry Newlon jogged up to where the men stood. "Phil said he's got a guy that may have seen something."

Beside the Corporal, Vaughn could see an elderly man flailing his left arm in animated conversation. In the crook of his right arm he held a tiny, white poodle.

The Chief walked over and spoke. "I understand you saw something, sir."

The man was flushed and breathless with the knowledge. His jittery anticipation to tell the story was obvious on his face. His dog was nervous too, wriggling ineffectually inn his arms. "Yes. Yes, I did see something. Betsy here was barking something awful so I finally got up to take her out. She still goes out on a leash even though she's nearly seven years old. Oh, anyway, while I was in the yard I heard this car. I thought it was awfully early in the morning for someone to be out on the road so I looked. That's when I see this silver car. I knew it was Larry. He was swerving all over the place and then suddenly jerked the wheel. The car bounced right up on the curb and he slammed on the brakes."

Vaughn was listening so intently to the ramblings detailing Betsy's bladder habits that he didn't even realize the man had stopped talking. He quickly composed himself with a change of facial expression and inquired, "And then what did you see?"

"That's it. Well I saw Larry stumble out of the car and he was shouting for someone to call for a doctor. I thought he was crazy," the man's voice was exaggerated and high-pitched. He was obviously proud of the information he was supplying.

"Did you see Ryan Bentley at all?" Vaughn's tone was bordering on impatient.

The elderly gentleman's features took on a look of pondering as he recalled exactly what he had seen. "Now that you mention it, no. I didn't see the boy. Just Larry's car bouncing up on the curb."

Vaughn was no longer listening as he focused in on Larry Fairfax's car. "Thank you, sir. Um, Phil, make sure you get the complete statement."

Vaughn motioned for Perry to follow him and the pair walked closer to the vehicle. They made three complete rotations of the vehicle before stopping at the front of the car. Vaughn knelt down beside the bumper. "Look at this, Perry."

Perry squinted at where Vaughn was pointing and shrugged his shoulders. "I don't see anything, Chief."

"That's right. There's nothing. No dent or ding, no blood. You'd think if you hit someone with your car there'd be some evidence."

"Maybe he didn't hit him. Maybe the boy was bent down, tying his shoe or something. Maybe the old guy just plum ran him over," Perry suggested.

"Make arrangements for the car to go to the impound. I think it's time I talk to Susan." Vaughn walked back to where the body lay in the middle of the street. Staring at the white sheet covered lump, he couldn't bring himself to lift the cover. Vaughn had always considered himself a tough cop, committed to facing even the most horrific crimes to find the truth. But when there was a young boy involved, the job became a burden on his back.

Susan wasn't with the body. As Vaughn looked around, the scene gave way to a liquid landscape and for a moment he thought he might get sick. The pulsing of the police car lights was causing a pounding headache right at the point where his head met his neck. And the collar of his uniform felt tight and hot. Something wasn't right but he couldn't quite put a handle on what it was that bothered him.

*Why isn't there any evidence on the car? Maybe Perry's right. Maybe the boy did just get run over. Dammit, where's Susan?*

Two crime scene technicians were finishing with their examination and one of them motioned for the paramedics to bring the stretcher.

"Have you guys seen Susan Barnes?" Vaughn's voice was thick and didn't sound quite right inside his head, but if the technicians noticed they didn't say anything. They continued to pack up their equipment as one of them answered his question.

"I think she went to call the forensic pathologist. She wants the boy in autopsy as soon as possible."

Before he moved away, he watched the paramedics surround the boy and prepare him for transfer. In their haste, the top corner of the white sheet pulled back and exposed what lay underneath. Vaughn was struck by the vision. Again, he had the feeling something wasn't right. One of the crime scene technicians took one last photograph and the flash burned into Vaughn's eyes.

He wished Susan were here. She could explain to him the reason why something began gnawing at the back of his head the moment the body was exposed. Instead, he watched as they loaded the tiny remains of Ryan Bentley onto a stretcher, lifted him into the ambulance and drive off into the night. No lights or sirens required. A quick trip to the morgue and then on to the next call. Very much like the night Vaughn's sister died.

The past had grabbed a hold of him again, pulling him down like quicksand. He struggled to free himself of its hold. A glance at his watch and Vaughn realized he'd been on the scene for more than two hours, although it felt like only minutes. He knew he needed to keep moving, needed to keep his mind focused on the crime. And he knew eventually he'd have to be the bearer of bad news. He would just have to talk to Susan later. Vaughn signaled to Perry Newlon. "Come on, Perry. Let's go tell Ryan's parents."

Perry followed his boss back to the police cruiser and settled into the passenger seat. "What are you thinking, Chief?"

"I don't know yet, but something isn't right." Vaughn put the car in gear and had started away from the scene when he spotted her again through the crowd. Margaret Yardley still stood along the curb. If not for the probing beam of his headlights he might have missed her.

Perry felt the car come to a slow stop and glanced through the passenger window to see what Vaughn was staring at. Throughout the night, people had come and gone. The original crowd of onlookers had been replaced by a second shift as if the town was keeping a constant watch on the happenings at the crime scene. "Just a bunch of rubberneckers. Who wouldn't miss a chance to satisfy their morbid curiosity?"

"Yeah," Vaughn agreed, quietly. Although he was sure Margaret had stuck around for more than just that. He swung his gaze to where Ryan's body had laid on the pavement and tried to recall the old woman's words.

*"He will wear the dirty halo until the deed is completed."*

Was it gone now, this so-called dirty halo?

Right now, Chief Vaughn Dexter didn't even want to think about it.

## Chapter 10

After her confrontation with the Chief, Margaret Yardley had strained her neck over the crowd to catch a glimpse of Larry Fairfax as he was cuffed and placed in the back of the police cruiser. The arresting officer had his hand on the old man's head disrupting the energy that produced the halo image. That, coupled with the swirling lights of the car made it all but impossible for Margaret to see whether or not the dirty halo had dissipated. She wanted so much to know that it was gone. You couldn't get much deadlier than killing a child. But it never hurt to be sure.

She pulled her tattered, red robe tighter together at the throat despite the mild temperature and watched the Chief leave along with Perry Newlon. There was no reason for her to stay now. Larry had been taken to the police station. Margaret turned back towards her house.

*If only the chief had listened to me. But then again how could I expect anyone to take me seriously...*

Her thoughts and feelings, no matter how well in tune with the universe, would never be understood by mere mortals.

She shuffled up the front steps of her house and sat down in the wicker chair where, less than a week ago, the dead birds had laid. Margaret had seen the small body of Ryan Bentley lying motionless on the pavement. Even though she'd watched as Larry Fairfax was arrested for the boy's death she still couldn't shake the feeling that something else was very wrong with the situation.

Something was dead wrong.

~~*~~

Shannon Marshall rolled away from his bedroom window and shut his eyes tight. He'd heard the sirens. Everyone in the whole town had probably heard them. Shannon wished sometimes the sirens would just come and take him away.

That was when he heard the scratching coming from the open shoebox under his bed. He willed his body to be as still as possible and tried to keep his breathing slow and even. After a few minutes the scratching ceased and Shannon knew it was over. He let out a deep breath and turned to stare at his bedroom ceiling. A single tear ran down the side of his face and dripped noiselessly onto his pillow.

There was going to be trouble, he could feel it.

~~*~~

Ellen Bentley opened the door of her house and then shielded her sleepy eyes from the harsh porch light. With her other hand, she clutched her robe tightly around her neck. "Perry? Chief Dexter? Is there a problem?"

Vaughn took his hat off and held it in front of him while Perry hung back on the tiny porch. "Mrs. Bentley, I'm terribly sorry to be disturbing you at this hour but there has been an accident."

"What? What kind of accident?" Ellen shook her head, trying to make sense of the situation.

"Can we come in, Mrs. Bentley?"

"Of course and Chief, please, call me Ellen." She held the screen door open for the two police officers and directed them into the living room of her home. Vaughn had met the Bentley family at his welcome reception at the village hall. They seemed like very nice people. They were a simple all-American family who loved their religion and valued their family ties. So much like his own parents. Just then a light came on down the tiny hallway of the ranch style house and Ellen's husband, Robert, appeared.

"Ellen, what's going on? Chief, is everything all right?"

"No, Bob, I'm afraid there's been an accident." Vaughn hated this part of the job. He hated having to wake these nice people from their sweet dreams to tell them that a drunk driver had been accused of hitting and killing their only son. Besides, just what the hell was Ryan doing out of the house so early in the morning?

The Chief knew how the Bentleys would feel because he knew how his parents had suffered when Vaughn's sister had been taken from them so suddenly. Vaughn remembered the look that haunted his mother's face from that day forward. No one ever got over the loss of a child.

Ever.

Ellen moved across the room to join her husband and he lovingly placed an arm around her shoulders as she worried her hands together, the robe forgotten. The two looked more like a brother and sister pair than husband and wife. Vaughn could see that all of their children got their blond hair and blue eyes honestly from both parents. "Please, what is it?"

"It's Ryan. I'm sorry but we believe Ryan was hit by a car about an hour ago and was killed," Chief Dexter braced for the worse but Ellen only glanced at Robert and shook her head.

"No, Chief there must be some mistake. Ryan spent the night at Jesse Lawrence's house. I'm sure he's safe in bed right now." Her smile was pleasant and she seemed extremely relieved at her own explanation. Somewhere behind Vaughn, Perry cleared his throat and stepped forward.

"No, Ellen. I saw the body. It was Ryan."

The woman took a long deep breath to compose herself and said, "I'm going to call Liz Lawrence and get this straightened out."

While Ellen attempted to dial the phone with shaking fingers, Robert moved toward the policeman. His face was as white as the sheet that had covered his son's body. He ran fingers through his bed-flattened hair and stared wide-eyed at Vaughn. "It's him, isn't it?"

Vaughn could only shake his head and glance down to the hands that held his hat. For once he wished he'd not dressed in his formal police uniform.

"How could this be? What was he doing out of the house at this hour?" Tears formed in the father's eyes as the reality of the situation became evident.

In the background Ellen crossed her right arm over her chest and rested her hand in the crook of her left arm that held the phone. She was hoping against hope that Ryan would come groggily to the phone and ask her in this sleep-thickened voice what she wanted. From the receiver came the endless ringing at the Lawrence's place.

~~*~~

"Jesse, wake up."

The overhead light in Jesse's bedroom came on simultaneously with the sound of his dad's voice. Jesse sat up in the twin bed and rubbed his eyes although he hadn't been sleeping. Sunshine, who had been dozing at Jesse's feet, also raised her head. After returning home from the Lost Bridge Trail, Jesse had changed from his jeans and t-shirt into his pajamas before sliding under the covers, so his dad wouldn't know that he and Ryan had snuck out. Behind Bear, Jesse's grandma stood with a worried look on her aged face.

"Jesse, where's Ryan?" Bear marched into the room and threw the covers of the matching twin clear to the floor.

"What?" Jesse asked, cautiously.

"Ryan's mom is on the phone, Jesse and she wants to talk to Ryan. Where is he?" Jesse had never before heard the desperation in his father's voice and it scared him.

"He went home."

"What do you mean 'he went home'?" Bear grabbed Jesse's shoulders and gave him a shake. "When?"

"Walter, don't," Liz Lawrence stepped to Jesse's side and rescued him from Bear's grasp.

"I don't know what time. We were telling ghost stories and he got scared," Jesse spouted. "He said he wanted to go home."

"Why didn't you wake me up?" Bear stood casting Jesse in his massive shadow.

"I told him to but he said he'd just walk home. It wasn't that far. You believe me don't you, Dad?" Bear pulled Jesse to him and stared over his head at his mother.

How was he going to tell his son that his best friend was dead?

~~*~~

"I didn't kill him. I didn't," Larry Fairfax shouted from inside the holding cell at the Rochester Police Station.

"I said shut up, Fairfax. I ain't gonna tell you again," Mike Simms sat heavily in his chair in the squad room and started filling in the paper work.

"I swear I didn't do it," the old man retreated to the far corner of the cell and slid down the wall, hugging his knees. His chest heaved with great sobs. His head was clear from the usual alcoholic fog but he couldn't make the young policeman listen to him. No one took him seriously until now. And now they were accusing him of killing a little boy. There was no way he could have done it. He would never harm anyone, especially someone's child. Especially not after what happened to his own daughter. Oh how he wished Betty were here. But he had no one.

No one was on his side.

## Chapter 11

Katrina stood in the hallway outside of her apartment, trying to balance the grocery sack and her purse all while trying to get the key properly inserted into the lock of her door. The contents in the bag shifted suddenly and almost sent everything in the sack crashing to the tile floor. Katrina lunged forward with both hands to save the cartons of ice cream before they wound up lid down on the tile floor.

Being only eight weeks pregnant, Katrina wasn't sure whether food cravings were yet an issue, but somehow all six flavors of the Ben & Jerry's Ice Cream sold at the local market had found themselves in her cart. She'd stood for twenty minutes outside of the freezer section in the small establishment, trying to decide between the Chunky Monkey and Cherry Garcia when the sudden urge to grab all six flavors and run was too overwhelming to deny. Now she could barely contain her anticipation of getting into the apartment, snatching up a spoon and sampling each and every flavor with large, delectable bites.

Making the decision to keep her baby was a constant struggle in her mind. Katrina knew she wouldn't be able to concentrate on anything else until she had come to a firm decision. The right decision. Of course, she wouldn't have it just to spite Jackson, but she did need to know she'd be able to care for a child. New York City wasn't exactly the place to raise a baby. Besides, she would want her child to know its family, but even the thought of moving back to Rochester made Katrina want to throw up again.

The shrill ringing of the phone made Katrina hasten her attempt to open the door. Finally successful, Katrina left the sacred sack of ice cream on the tile foyer and ran to answer the call.

"Yes," she said out of breath.

"Kat, its Bear." Even with those few words, Katrina knew something was not right with her brother's voice. The very sound made the hair on the back of her neck stand on end.

"Bear, what is it? What's wrong?"

"You remember Jesse's friend, Ryan?" Bear's voice was barely audible now.

"Yes, I think so. Jesse can't ever stop talking about him when we're on the phone. Why?" Katrina slowly moved to the arm of the nearest chair and sat down. "Is Jesse all right?"

"Jesse's friend was killed this morning. Hit by a car. Larry Fairfax did it." Bear's sentences became short and choked with emotion.

"Oh God, Bear, how awful. How's Jesse taking it?" Katrina felt her heart sink lower in her chest and she instinctively covered her belly with her hand.

"He's not good, Kat. He's been in his room all day. I don't know what to do. Mom took him some lunch but he won't eat."

"Bear, this isn't something that he's going to get over so quickly. Ryan was his best friend and has been there for him throughout your separation from Nina. Really, the only constant thing in his life was just ripped away from him."

She paused a moment, but Bear said nothing.

"Oh this is just terrible. Poor Jesse. And what that child's parents must be going through." Katrina stopped talking and listened to the utter silence on Bear's end of the line. After nearly a minute, she wasn't sure if he was even still there.

"Bear?"

"I'm here, I just...I called to ask if you would come home. Jesse needs you right now. He has such hostility towards Nina for some reason and although mom means well she just isn't consoling."

Katrina placed a hand over her mouth. In any other circumstances, she'd be on the first plane back to Illinois if Jesse needed her but this pregnancy was complicating things. She wasn't ready to tell her family and she knew it wouldn't take long for her mother to see right through her. It was selfish, but she just couldn't bring herself to do it. Then Katrina recalled her plan to have Bear and Jesse come visit her.

"I have a better idea," Katrina said, skirting the issue of her return to Rochester. "I'm going to send you and Jesse plane tickets. I think you should bring him out here for a while. Get him away from that town and Ryan's death."

"You really think that's a good idea?" Bear's tone was tentative.

"Absolutely. School's out next week but I'm sure they'll understand if Jesse doesn't go back. You could wait till after the funeral and then fly out. I could show him all around the city. I think that would be good for him. And it would be good for you too, Bear. I can tell this separation's getting to you. Maybe you need some time away from Rochester too."

"But the shop?"

"Forget the shop. Close it down for a couple of weeks. That's the beauty of having your own business,"

Katrina tried to keep her voice light despite the seriousness of Bear's call.

"I suppose I could have Shannon look after things," Bear said, warming to the idea.

"See there. It's settled."

In New York City, Katrina frowned. She had listened to stories of Shannon Marshall from her nephew and always the mention of the boy's name made her uncomfortable. Many times, she'd tried to ask to her brother about the strange boy, but Bear always shut her down saying what an asset Shannon was to the shop. Regardless of his contributions to Bear's Auto Body, Katrina didn't care for Jesse hanging around Shannon. Hearing his name was enough to incite a cold chill up her spine. Katrina's dislike of Shannon Marshall was one of the few things she knew she had in common with her mother.

It was then that she realized Jesse needed to get away from that town for a lot more reasons than just the death of his friend.

~~*~~

"Well?"

Perry dragged himself into the house, practically dead on his feet and shook his head at his father. "Killed him."

"Damned old drunk," Gordon Newlon gasped. He'd been sitting vigil next to the police scanner since they'd first heard the call. Although no longer a member of the police force, Gordon just couldn't give up the life. Now he lived it through Perry.

Jackie Agans came from the kitchen holding a plate of toast and a cup of coffee. "He's been glued to that thing all morning. Maybe you can talk some sense into him, Perry and get him to eat."

"I'm not hungry," the old man grumbled and shooed her away.

"Dad, you need to eat," Perry grumbled back without much conviction. All he wanted to do was to fall into bed and not think about that dead little boy and his distraught parents.

"I swear, Gordon one of these days you're going to be sorry for the way you treat me."

Jackie talked with a smile on her face and when she turned toward Perry, he caught a wink of her eye. Jackie was a godsend when it came to dealing with his father. Perry knew he'd be lost without her.

"I need to stay focused on this case, Jackie," Gordon Newlon shouted as she disappeared back into the kitchen. "You said Amy's coming over this afternoon and she's going to want to know details. Specifics about how to handle this type of situation."

Perry smiled to himself as he retreated to his boyhood room and lay down. Maybe he should have given his crotchety old father a grandchild. He seemed to be getting soft in his old age.

Gordon hunched closer to the scanner and tried to catch some words through a crackle of static. His oxygen tube was hissing and the wheeze of his breathing made it just that much more difficult for him to determine the conversation. He hadn't asked Perry how Vaughn was dealing with the little boy's accident because he didn't want to know.

Gordon had never spoken to the new Chief of Police but wondered if the man knew how damn lucky he was. This situation was cut and dried. Everyone knew Larry Fairfax had hit that boy. It wasn't like that mess he had to clean up when he was chief. All those missing and dead girls and their terrified parents. Such a nightmare.

*But that was a long time ago. And we're talking about a little boy hit by a car—not teenage girls disappearing in broad daylight only to be found dead days, weeks or months later. Or sometimes never found.*

It was something he vowed never to talk about again and he certainly didn't want to sit around thinking about it either.

~~*~~

Vaughn sat at his desk quite a while before restlessness drove him to his feet. He paced the minimal square footage of his office and settled by the window overlooking the parking lot. Just beyond was Route 29, the traffic was moving steadily along the street as if just last night a little boy wasn't lying dead on that very pavement.

He'd left the Bentley house with a most horrible feeling in the pit of his stomach. Ellen and Robert had been hysterical once the phone call to the Lawrence house had confirmed their worst fears. Finally, at around six o'clock in the morning, Vaughn had stumbled back into his house. Dead tired, but still turning the details of the crime around in his mind. He'd tried to sleep but gave up at seven thirty. He'd taken a shower and driven to the station.

Mike Simms was still manning the front desk and Larry Fairfax was sleeping restfully on the cot in the holding cell. "'Morning, Chief."

"Good morning, Mike. How are things here?" Vaughn nodded his head toward the sleeping man.

"He's been screaming all night that he didn't do it. I'm sure 'doesn't remember doing it' would be a more appropriate term." Mike tapped a pen on the Formica surface.

Vaughn could only nod.

*Tap, tap, tap.*

"Has the coroner called anything in yet?"

"No, sir. The phone's been surprisingly quiet," Mike said, tapping relentlessly.

"Well, I'll be in my office. Let me know when Mr. Fairfax wakes up."

*Tap, tap, tap.* "Will do."

Vaughn now closed his eyes to the fast moving traffic before it made him nauseous.

A voice startled him.

"Couldn't sleep either, huh?"

Vaughn hadn't heard the door open until the sound of Perry Newlon's voice penetrated his thoughts. He shook his head at the Sergeant and took a deep breath in through his nose.

"No, but seeing how we're both here maybe we should just skip on over to the Lawrence house and get to the bottom of why that kid was out wandering the streets in the middle of the night."

~~*~~

The ride from the station to Elizabeth Lawrence's two-story home was done quickly and in silence. Both men pulled their hats down low to shield their eyes from the late spring sun. They were dressed very officially in their blue policeman's uniforms. Pants creased, shoes shined. The day was too pretty to be taking care of such ugly business. Vaughn had called ahead and learned that Jesse was still at Bear's although Nina was coming to get him later this afternoon.

"I'm going to need to talk to Jesse," Vaughn said to Bear when he answered the door.

"Yeah, I know. It's just that he's been through a lot too, you know. Go easy on him. He blames himself."

Bear moved aside and let the police officers enter the foyer. Perry reached a hand down to let Jesse's Golden Retriever lick it.

Vaughn could see through an open doorway to the left that Jesse sat beside his grandmother on a sofa, staring silently out the window. His pallor was evident even in the warm sunlight. The already dark circles under the boy's eyes were now coal black smudges.

"Chief. Perry. Please come in. We're just devastated about what's happened," Liz Lawrence rattled on, her complexion growing as red as her hair.

Vaughn regarded the woman with a nod before turning back to Bear. "Is it all right that we speak to Jesse alone?"

"Of course," Bear stepped into the room and took his mother's arm. "We'll be in the kitchen getting some coffee."

Perry heard Liz utter a small protest as she allowed her son to escort her from the salon. A room where she'd been told ten years ago that Jesse was on the way. Vaughn moved to the chair opposite from the couch and took a seat. Perry stood to one side, watching. The boy hadn't moved since either had entered the room. His eyes remained unfocused and staring towards the flower box in his grandmother's front yard.

"Jesse, is it okay if Perry and I ask you a couple of questions?" Vaughn tried to keep his voice soft and he glanced at Perry when the boy didn't answer.

Perry shrugged, stepped forward and knelt down in front of Jesse. "Jesse, I know you're upset about what happened to Ryan, but now you need to help us understand what happened to him."

Jesse turned his head slowly to meet Perry's gaze and Perry couldn't help but shudder at the coldness of the boy's eyes. "Everyone says Mr. Fairfax hit him. I guess that's what happened."

The statements were matter of fact. Said without emotion or sentiment.

"Okay, but what we really need to know is why he was in the road in the first place."

Perry's tone was even and non-judgmental. Vaughn watched the exchange between the two and was thrown back into his own childhood. He'd been about Jesse's age when his older sister, Leigh, was murdered. Even now, he could recall every detail of the police officer who'd questioned him.

~~*~~

The cop had been roughly fifty years old and getting rather soft in the middle. He held a toothpick balanced between his lips and Vaughn couldn't help but stare at it when the detective talked. His hair was artfully combed over the top of his head to hide his baldness, but the harsh overhead light of the dining room bounced off the shiny surface. Vaughn could tell he was tired although the hour wasn't late, as if he anticipated this case would keep him up all night.

"Didn't you hear anything? What were you doing up there in your room all alone?"

Vaughn had sat in one of the tall dining room chairs and cried as if his soul would never repair from the hurt.

"I didn't hear anything," he managed to say through the sobs. "Just the door slamming."

From somewhere in the living room a camera had flashed and Vaughn could hear his mother weeping in the kitchen.

~~*~~

"I already told my dad. Ask my dad," Jesse mumbled, bringing Vaughn back to the present.

"If it's okay, we'd really like to hear it from you, Jesse." Vaughn's voice cut into the conversation as he tried to make himself concentrate on the job at hand. He sympathized with Jesse but knew now there was no other way. As Chief of Police, he needed to get a handle on the death of Ryan Bentley and close the case as soon as possible. The loss was already starting to tear at the town and the rip was starting with Jesse Lawrence.

"I know you blame yourself for what happened to your friend but you have to know it wasn't your fault."

Vaughn knew in his heart that his sister's death hadn't been his fault but he felt guilty anyway. And no one would be able to convince him differently.

Thinking back to the coroner's words, Vaughn chose his own carefully. "No one could have known that Larry Fairfax was going to be driving drunk and that Ryan would be killed."

*No one knew but Margaret Yardley.* The sudden bubble-burst of that thought made Vaughn's head ache. He wished like hell the old woman had never come into the station that day.

"We had supper and then went to my room to watch a movie," Jesse volunteered.

Vaughn's mind flashed back and he shuddered despite himself.

*"Vaughn, listen to me. I need to talk to Shawn alone. I want you to play in your room then we'll make popcorn and watch a movie. Got it, kiddo?"*

"It was a scary movie and so we started telling ghost stories. I thought it would be fun to try and really scare Ryan so I told him my grandma's house was haunted. But he didn't think the game was so much fun. He freaked and said he wanted to go home. That he didn't want to stay in a haunted house," Jesse looked down at his hands and Vaughn watched a single tear snake a trail the length of the boy's cheek. "I told him he was being a baby but he wanted to go home anyway. I said, 'fine, go home then,' and I just got in bed and pulled the covers over my head."

Silent sobs wracked the boy's small frame but Vaughn needed to hear him say the rest. "Go on, Jesse."

"That's it. I heard him get his pack and leave the room. I thought he went to wake up my dad or grandma. I didn't know until my dad woke me up that Ryan was...that something had..."

Jesse broke down completely and covered his face. Perry put a reassuring hand on the boy's shoulder and stood from his stoop. Vaughn stood too.

"I'm sorry we had to put you through that, Jesse, but you really did help us. Thanks."

Vaughn and Perry met Bear in the foyer and after a couple of hushed words Bear went to his son. Just as he stepped through the front door into the sunshine, Vaughn saw Jesse cling to his father's arm and weep openly. He knew it would be a long time before the child would ever get over the death of his friend, if ever.

Vaughn hadn't gotten over his own loss.

~~*~~

Perry started down the front porch steps and made it halfway down the walk before he realized Vaughn wasn't following. "Need something, boss?"

"I'm just trying to get a visual on what Ryan would have seen when he left the Lawrence's," Vaughn said from under the porch roof.

"And?"

"And there are no street lights." Vaughn followed Perry's lead and met him on the sidewalk.

Perry was looking skyward. "Nope, no street lights."

"And the Bentleys live on Wildrose. That's nearly a mile and a half in the opposite direction from where Ryan was found."

Vaughn motioned for Perry to get into the police car. When they were settled with the doors closed, Vaughn spoke again. "Why would you suppose a little kid who was scared from telling ghost stories would decide to walk home in the middle of the night on a dark street?"

Perry shrugged and tried to make sense of the situation. "Maybe he thought Bear would be mad for being woken up."

"The kid's been scared by ghost stories, but still decides to walk along a dark street—and not walk directly home..."

The two men locked gazes. After a moment Vaughn turned over the engine and backed out of the Lawrence's driveway. "I've lived in this town for only six months but from personal experience I don't think that Bear's the type of person who'd get mad at a ten year old for waking him up. You've known Bear for years. What do you think?"

"Good point," Perry nodded as he spoke, "Bear's a good friend and a great father. But what about this street light stuff? Don't you believe Jesse?"

"His story just got me thinking is all. I just wish I could make sense of why. If the boy was really frightened, why he didn't go straight home?"

## Chapter 12

V aughn pulled into the station lot but didn't attempt to move the gear shift into park. Perry grabbed the door handle and regarded his superior. "You not coming in?"

"No. There's something else I need to take care of."

Perry swung his leg out onto the hot pavement and unfolded his body from the front seat. The sound of the car door shutting echoed off the municipal complex. He watched Vaughn Dexter leave the parking lot and head back into town.

Inside the station, Mary Randall, from the village office, pulled a fistful of pink message slips from the pocket of her polyester skirt. "You know I don't care for taking messages for the police."

"Yes, I know, but thank you," Perry replied automatically.

"Well anyway," Mary handed over the messages, "Some reporter from 'The State Journal Register' wants to talk to you or the chief. Margaret Yardley's called three times regarding Mr. Fairfax. Oh, and the Bentleys want to know when they can bury their son."

Perry pulled a deep breath in through his nose and let it out through his mouth. It was during these times he was almost glad he hadn't been appointed Chief. Vaughn was a standup guy, someone Perry held in high regard, but he wished like hell that he was privy to why Vaughn was questioning this open-'n-shut case.

~~*~~

Amy Agans felt Tim Rothwell's hand creep slowly up her leg and then touch the bottom of her shirt. She was glad that she'd reconsidered and put on the lightweight sweater— something she didn't have to tuck in. The thought made Amy feel naughty and she raised her arm slightly so the hem of the sweater inched above the waist of her jeans, inviting him to go further. Without hesitation, Tim's hand brushed along the smooth skin of her belly and up over her left breast. They were tucked back into the corner of a study desk deep in the library's stacks. The scent of musty books was overwhelming in the air and Amy took a deep breath of it.

"I love you, Amy," Tim whispered into her ear.

"Oh Tim, I…"

"Excuse me."

Amy pulled her mouth away from Tim's neck and gasped. She made a hasty attempt to pull her sweater down although Tim's clumsy hand was still underneath making it absolutely impossible.

"Mr. Cody, I'm so sorry. We were just studying and…" Amy stopped, unable to think of a good explanation as to how translating German had turned into a horny make-out session between the teenagers.

"Maybe there's been enough studying for today. Besides, I think it's a bit early in the morning for studying, wouldn't you say?" Cameron said tightly, his arms full of books he'd been returning to the shelves.

"Yes, of course."

Amy jumped from the chair and started gathering her things. Tim had been embarrassed into silence and chose only to hang his red-faced head in shame as he grabbed his backpack and started for the stairs leading to the library's main floor. Although for obvious reasons, he kept his backpack waist-level in front of him.

Amy took a half a dozen steps away from Cameron before suddenly turning back. "Please don't tell my mom, Mr. Cody. I swear I don't know what got into me. I don't usually act like that."

The palms of Cameron's hands became damp and clammy as they held the stack of books and, although Amy didn't notice, his breathing had become rapid. He forced himself to calm down before answering the girl. "Of course, Amy. We all make mistakes. Don't forget that I was young once too."

Her smile was broad and full of relief. She straightened her pink summer sweater again around her waist and turned to go. Cameron waited until she was completely out of sight before falling back against the shelf of books. He squeezed his eyes shut and took deep breaths through his nose, flaring his nostrils. At that moment he hated himself. For all he tried, Cameron couldn't erase the scene he'd just witnessed and what was more, the whole situation had left him aroused. It had been so long since he had allowed himself to love anyone physically. The two teenagers who had just left had been part of the group Cameron had seen the other night in the parking lot. The same beautiful face, the same body verging on adulthood.

Margaret Yardley had been right. Cameron was angry. *Damn* angry.

~~*~~

"Did you know?"

"Well, Chief Dexter, I won't say I'm surprised to see you," Margaret Yardley said ignoring his question, from the framework of her front door.

"You came to me the other day and said that something deadly was going to befall Larry Fairfax. Did you know that Ryan Bentley was going to die?"

"So you actually did listen to me," Margaret said, avoiding the obvious.

"Margaret, a little boy is dead and you seemed to know that something was going to happen. If you don't start talking, I'm going to have to arrest you. Now I'm going to ask you one more time. Did you—"

"I didn't know," she said flatly. The old woman stepped forward and pulled the door shut behind her. Vaughn involuntarily took a step back as she made a wide path the length of the porch.

"But you said..."

"I *know* what I said," Margaret retorted, interrupting the chief for a second time. "I could see that something bad would happen but I didn't know what or even when. It doesn't work that way."

"Well maybe you should tell me how it *does* work," Vaughn said, leaning against one of the porch's support posts; his arms were crossed casually but his insides were tense.

*I can't believe I'm standing here. Why am I relying so much on the rantings of a psychic?*

From his position, on the Yardley porch, Vaughn realized he was staring straight at the intersection of the highway where Ryan had been killed. Until then he hadn't recognized how very close Margaret had been to the entire situation.

"I told you at the station that I see things," Margaret began. "My grandmother saw them, my mother saw them and now I have the gift."

"I know you said he was wearing a dirty halo, isn't that what you called it? But what exactly is it that you see?" Vaughn continued before Margaret had a chance to answer the first question.

"Everyone has an aura, Chief. You've probably heard that from Dionne Warwick and her psychic friends. That much is true. Some people have a stronger aura than others. The colors of an aura can tell a great deal about a person if you really want to know the truth."

Margaret stepped away from the porch steps and removed one of the many necklaces she always wore around her neck.

"This was passed down through the generations of Yardley's."

She held it out for Vaughn to see. On the thin strand of fishing line was a row of multi-colored beads. Every bead, about the size of a pea, was a different color. "Each color represents a different emotion of the aura. I don't see it like what's represented around the Virgin Mary. I see it as a swirling cloud above the head."

Margaret moved her hand in a circular motion around her head of wiry hair for effect. "That is why I call it a halo."

Vaughn had quietly examined the necklace and then looked up to meet Margaret's eyes. He realized for the first time how very tired and old she appeared to be. As if the knowledge of another person's intended fate was just too much for her to bear. She'd known something was going to happen that concerned Larry Fairfax and had worried ceaselessly until the deadly event involving Ryan Bentley. But there was *something*. Something just below the surface, and it had Vaughn on edge. Something he couldn't quite make sense of. That was why he was at Margaret's house.

As if reading his thoughts, Margaret commented, "That's why I asked you if I could see Larry. I need to know that the halo's gone. That killing Ryan Bentley was the deadly event I saw in his aura. I said before that it was a gift, but in instances such as these it's more of a curse really."

Vaughn knew the answer before he spoke. "So everything you've told me is just based on a feeling.

What you're saying is that you don't have any concrete proof that Larry killed Ryan."

Margaret took a step forward, her eyes narrowed. "It almost sounds as if *you* don't have any proof, Chief."

Without a word, Vaughn pulled his muscular frame away from the porch post and started down the sidewalk. He didn't want Margaret Yardley to see the look on his face. If she could see auras, she might be able to read into his apprehensive expression. From her shadowed spot under the porch roof, Margaret called out. "Don't you want to know if I can see *your* aura?"

Vaughn stopped and somehow found amusement in her words. He smiled coyly to himself, turned and called back, "Unless there's a color on that necklace for workaholic, I doubt there's anything interesting to report."

Margaret smiled back a weary smile. A small breeze lifted the hem of her skirt and Vaughn watched it dance around her thick ankles. "No. There's no color for a workaholic, but there *is* a color for guilt."

The smile vanished from his face as soon as the words had passed her lips. "Good day, Margaret."

Margaret called out after him, raising her voice as Vaughn got farther and farther from her house.

"You carry a guilt, Chief Dexter, that's eating you from the inside out!"

By the time he'd settled in behind the wheel of his car, his breathing was fast and shallow. The whole time she'd spoken of her gift and the auras, he hadn't given himself completely over to believing in her abilities. After all, Larry Fairfax was a drunk. The whole town knew it. Wasn't it only a matter of time before he killed someone from behind the wheel of his Taurus?

But why did Margaret have to go and see through his tough, rigid policeman's exterior? She'd touched on a part of his life he'd spent the last twenty-five years burying deep inside. Whatever it was Margaret thought she saw, it was clear she didn't know the details surrounding the guilt Vaughn carried, and if it were up to him, it would stay that way.

His knuckles were white on the steering wheel, but just before he lost all control the police radio crackled to life. "Home base to Chief."

Vaughn snatched up the walkie-talkie and answered the call. "Chief Dexter here."

"Chief, its Perry. Susan just called. They are ready for Ryan Bentley's autopsy."

## Chapter 13

"Nina, I don't think it's necessary for Jesse to go home. He's perfectly safe here and besides, it's the weekend. That's the only time I get to have him."

Bear's voice was as tight as his grip on the telephone handset and he tried to keep himself in check less Jesse heard the conversation from where he sat across the hall.

Bear heard Nina take a few quick breaths and she finally relented. "Fine. In fact, I suppose it would be easier for you to keep him Sunday night too. I heard they're going to cancel school on Monday and I won't be able to take off of work to stay home with him. Can you take him to the shop with you, or to the funeral if they have it?"

It was the first time since the separation that Nina had asked anything of him. Anything except for him to get his stuff and get out of her house, that was. Bear was astonished into silence before pulling himself together. "Of course he can stay here. And if he doesn't feel like going into the shop or the funeral, I'll just stay home."

"You always were the hero, Bear," Nina stated, her voice dripping with sarcasm.

Bear opened his mouth to retort, but his mother stepped into the kitchen. He refused to show her how petty things had gotten between him and his estranged wife. "We'll see you Monday night then."

Without another word, Nina hung up.

"Is everything all right?" Liz asked her son.

"Yeah, mom, everything's fine. Where's Jesse?"

"Still in the salon. I'm going to get him a sandwich."

She opened the fridge door and began surveying its contents. Without a word, Bear slipped across the hall and sat gently beside his boy. With an arm around Jesse's shoulders, Bear could feel his bony shoulder blades protruding through the thin cotton of his t-shirt. It had gotten bad and now he feared that with Ryan's death it would only get worse.

"Hey, bud."

Jesse's voice was quiet in reply. "Hey, Dad."

"Listen I just talked to your mom and we think it's a good idea if you just stay here tonight and tomorrow night." Bear watched as Jesse's head snapped around to meet his gaze.

"I don't have to go back tomorrow night?" The anticipation of the question's answer was evident in Jesse's eyes.

"No. And if you want me to stay home from work—" Bear began.

"But tomorrow's Sunday. I always go home on Sundays." The outside light from the window was fading and made the whites of Jesse's eyes give off an eerie glow.

"Oh," Bear said, confused, "well if you want to go home, I can take you."

"No, Dad, no. I hate Sundays. Sometimes I feel like every day's Sunday. I hate them because I have to go back to Mom's. I want to stay here. I want to stay here forever." Jesse reached his arms as far around his father as he could and held on.

Just then, Liz Lawrence entered the room holding a plate and a glass of milk.

"Did you hear that, Grandma? I don't have to go home on Sunday." Bear watched as a broad smile spread across the young boy's face. It was the happiest he had seen him in quite a long time. He knew then that it would be possible for Jesse to overcome the recent tragedy in his life.

Liz set the plate in front of her grandson and happily watched him devour the food. It was the most she'd seen him eat in months. Now that some of the unpleasantness that had been in the house had passed, Liz remembered something she wanted to say.

"I've been thinking, Walter, maybe it's time to clean out your father's old office."

~~*~~

Vaughn moved through the quiet halls of the hospital with purpose. His shiny shoes made the only noise and soon his footsteps matched the rapid beating of his heart. The closer he got to the morgue the more he knew that the answer to his nagging questions surrounding Ryan Bentley's death lay behind those cold steel doors. Reaching a hand out to open the door, Vaughn hesitated. If the findings weren't consistent with the accidental death, he'd be unsure of his future in Rochester. He'd come to the small town with the intention of living a low profile life. No violence, no murder.

Before thoughts of his sister could enter his mind, Susan Barnes pushed through the heavy doors, clad in blue scrubs and a gown. She'd threaded her hair through a ponytail holder and clipped her long bangs back with a bobby pin. As always she looked lovely, despite the countenance of despair she wore on her face. "Vaughn, thank God you made it. The pathologist just made the first incision. I came out to look for you. I don't think you're going to want to miss this."

Without further explanation, Susan quickly ushered him into the hallway outside the autopsy room and fitted him with a gown, gloves and booties to protect his shoes. As they entered, Vaughn expected the mood inside the room to be somber. On the contrary, both of the forensic pathologists were laughing at something said before Susan had opened the door. They carried on their conversation as if no one else was around and they weren't hacking into the body of a ten-year-old boy.

Just as it had at the scene of the accident, the site of Ryan Bentley's body seized up everything inside his stomach. He was fixated on the pale skin. The harsh overhead light bounced off of the waxy surface of the body and glinted from the cold steel table it lay on. He glanced at Susan and wondered how she could appear so undaunted by the situation. She turned in time to see him staring at her and gave a weary smile. He blew a breath out through his mouth and nodded in return.

"I wanted to show you this at the scene but I never got a chance," Susan said, motioning for him to join her at the table. Vaughn took a step forward and wedged in between the coroner and the forensic pathologist. Again they laughed at something Vaughn didn't hear, choosing to ignore the chief. "I had a lot of questions about the condition of the body and since there was no obvious sign of death I brought him in for an autopsy."

Vaughn grunted in agreement and nodded his head. "What did you find?"

The boy appeared to be sleeping peacefully on the table except for the gaping hole in his chest where the pathologists were working. Ignoring his question, Susan threw a thumb over her shoulder and asked, "Did you get to see him before he was removed from the scene?"

"Yes, briefly. While the paramedics were loading

him up."

"Did you notice anything odd about the way he was laying?"

The nagging feeling Vaughn had been trying to identify all day began to take form in his mind. He recalled the paramedics loading the tiny body. The sheet had pulled back revealing the boy's upper torso. "Yes, now that you mention it. He was laying perpendicular to the road...but that wasn't it." Vaughn squinted his eyes in thought, then the answer came to him. "It was his arms. His arms were stretched over his head. Like he was reaching for something."

"Right. And as far as I know, no one had touched the body."

The coroner snapped a pair of latex gloves into place. "Also there appeared to be no external damage to the body," she continued. "I've seen a lot of victims that were hit by a car. Typically there are extensive injuries to the lower half of the body. Especially the ankles." She waved a hand over the boy's legs, which were perfectly intact.

"Even if he was laying in the road there would be tire marks on the body from being run over," Vaughn volunteered.

"Exactly. Hang on a second."

They stood silent while the pathologists closed up the chest cavity.

"Take a look at this." Susan motioned for the forensic pathologists to roll Ryan Bentley's body onto his side. Scrapes and cuts marked up the flesh of the boy's lower back and hips. "We've bagged his clothes for the crime lab. On the shirt tail and soles of his shoes we found mud and grass."

"He was dragged." It was a statement not a question.

"Exactly," Susan replied again. She helped lower

the body back to the supine position and the pathologists began preparing the head for an exam.

"Could he have been dragged by the car?" Vaughn hoped against hope that her answer would be 'yes'.

"Did you see any mud or grass on the road?"

"Good point," Vaughn said. He took a step back and took a deep breath in through his nose. "Damn." He didn't need to hear anymore.

Vaughn left the autopsy room and ripped the gown from his clothes. Suddenly his temperature was rising and he couldn't breath properly.

"I can't be for certain, Vaughn," Susan said, following him into the hallway, "not till the autopsy's complete. I mean there was no set lividity and the body temp was consistent so it *is* possible..." Susan's voice trailed off as she leaned against the green tiled wall. Vaughn could see she was making excuses.

"The boy didn't drag himself into the street, Sue." Vaughn placed his hands on his hips. He didn't want to hear her say it but he would ask anyway. "What is your professional opinion?"

Susan pulled the bobby pin from her hair and tossed her long, brown bangs out of her eyes with a flip of her head. "Larry Fairfax didn't kill this boy. Ryan Bentley was already dead in the road."

And just like that, the small, quiet town of Rochester lost all innocence.

~~*~~

Shannon slowly wiped down the windshield of Roger Thompson's old Plymouth and then grabbed for more Windex. He'd heard Bear and Jesse enter the shop that morning but so far neither had come out of the office to greet him. That wasn't like Jesse, but he'd heard people talking about Jesse's friend getting killed. Shannon felt bad. It seemed like lately he was always feeling bad about something. He knew that all things died eventually.

Only Sunshine had made her way into the garage. She sniffed in every corner to make sure everything was as she left it. Shannon liked Jesse's dog. Her coat was so shiny and smooth. Not like the animals lying in Shannon's back yard. The only dog buried there had mangled fur, matted together with blood and tissue. The thought of it made Shannon sick to his stomach and he turned away from Sunshine.

For a split second in his mind, Shannon saw the golden hair of the dog red with blood and tangled in clumps. He willed himself to stop. Counted to ten and began wiping down the windshield again. The glass was clean. No streaks anywhere, but the repetitive motion made Shannon feel better. Half a bottle of Windex and a roll of paper towels later, it would appear there was no glass in the car's frame at all.

Inside the office, Bear watched Jesse sit behind his desk, hands folded in his lap, legs not quite reaching the floor. Just yesterday, his son would have given anything to climb up in the creaky, leather office chair and spin it wildly around. Bear wondered if he'd ever get him back again. Maybe Katrina was right. They did need to get out of Rochester. Taking Jesse to New York City might just be the answer to let him get over the death of his friend.

Thinking of his sister, Bear glanced to the back wall of his office to see the picture of Katrina holding his young son. But in its place there was only blank wall. A frown creased Bear's forehead and his eyes moved to the floor to see if the picture had fallen. It was nowhere to be found.

~~*~~

Cameron Cody rinsed the plate and fork he'd used to eat a piece of the apple pie his mother had made for him. He stacked the lone dish in the rubber drainer next to the sink and watched the water silently drip onto the tray below. It was one of the saddest things he had ever seen.

He had closed the library early, nearly two hours ago and returned home when it was evident the townspeople wouldn't be venturing out. Word of Ryan Bentley's death had swept through the town like wildfire and now no one wanted to be seen carrying on the normal nuances of everyday existence. And that included visiting the library. He had closed up reluctantly. The library was his life. He knew that upon returning home, he would be faced with the vast emptiness of the two-bedroom house where he lived.

He longed for someone to share his life with. He wanted to see more than one dish in the drainer, to see a second pair of house slippers on the bathroom floor. But that just wasn't to be. Cameron Cody had condemned himself to a life alone. That was the only way he knew to avoid the evil that lay inside of him. If his parents only knew, it would kill them. There'd be no freshly baked apple pie or visits on Sunday afternoons. Several years ago, Cameron's parents had moved to a retirement village in Springfield, partly to give up the rambling old house where Cameron and his sister had grown up. And partly to be close to their grandchildren and great-grandchildren.

When Cameron looked at old pictures of himself as a child, he often wondered what the turning point was in his life that had made him this way. Was it the fact that his parents were much older than usual when he was born?

Cameron was a so-called medical miracle born to Ross and Elsa Cody when they were forty-five and forty-two years respectively. After the difficult birth of his sister, Debra, the Cody's were told they'd never be able to have another child. And perfectly content they were with Debra until, nearly twenty years later, Cameron was born. Ross and Elsa were thrilled with having a son but always in the back of his mind Cameron wondered how they would feel if they knew the truth. He would be ostracized from his family, from society. It was criminal— his wishes, his desires.

If only they had been content with Debra. She was perfect. The perfect child, the perfect teenager, and adult. She had married her high school sweetheart and gone on to have three beautiful daughters. Her interest in education had blossomed from her being a junior high Science teacher to principal of Meadowcrest Elementary in Riverton. He resented her happy life.

In his kitchen, Cameron slammed a fist onto the counter. How had it all ended up this way? How could he have let the situation get so far out of control? The anger swelled up inside him. It had affected his life and cost him his teaching job. But no one would find out. No one could find out. He could never let that happen.

As if from a trance, Cameron snapped to attention in his kitchen. He was breathing heavy and shallow. Somehow the dish and fork he'd placed in the drainer had ended up several feet in front of him on the floor. Droplets of water glistened around it, and at first he thought they were drips from the dishes, but he soon realized they were his tears.

~~*~~

Vaughn's drive back to the police station was quiet. Even the walkie-talkie remained mute. For a long while after arriving, the chief sat in his car staring out over the highway into the endless cornfields leading to the neighboring towns. For so long now, Rochester had remained in a bubble, untouchable from the outside world. Vaughn's guilt welled up inside and he was nearly unable to keep it contained. The mayor, Jim

Wagner, had hired him on the assumption that Vaughn could keep the town safe and running smoothly as it had for the last decade. He needn't be reminded that Jim never wanted a replay of the murders that had plagued the town in the past.

At last, Vaughn extracted himself from the vehicle and entered the short hallway leading to the squad room. To his surprise, Margaret Yardley swished through the open doorway holding a white cardigan sweater draped over her arms. The look on her face was one of pure dread and her simple statement shook Vaughn to the core. "He didn't do it."

"What are you doing here, Margaret?" The fight had left the Chief. He no longer desired a confrontation with this woman.

"I had to see him. I'm sorry." It seemed that Margaret had also called a truce. "Officer Loveland let me peek into the holding cell. But don't punish him, please. I can be very persuasive." A long moment passed between them before she spoke again. "He's still wearing the halo, Chief Dexter. Larry Fairfax didn't kill that boy."

Just as the last words passed the old woman's lips, Brendon Loveland stepped around the corner and paled when he saw the Chief. He knew he shouldn't have let Margaret Yardley see Larry Fairfax without permission.

"Margaret, I'd like to see you in my office," Vaughn said and turned to unlock his office door. Once the old woman had settled into a chair, Vaughn regarded Brendon. If he wasn't mistaken, the young man looked as if he might vomit at Vaughn's first word. For the time being, Vaughn needed to focus on the situation at hand and decided to let the boy off the hook. "Tell Mr. Fairfax he's free to go."

"Chief?"

"Just do it, Brendon," Vaughn replied. And the minute before he disappeared behind the closed door of his office he said, "Oh, and call the Mayor. He's going to need to hear this from me."

~~*~~

"Chief Dexter, what the hell is going on?" Jim Wagner's voice boomed through the phone. Vaughn had been dreading the call. Only moments ago, he'd escorted Margaret Yardley to the door and told her to go home. She'd insisted that Larry continue to be detained since his dirty halo was still present, but Vaughn had no authority to violate the man's constitutional rights. Even if he wanted to keep Fairfax under lock and key, he just couldn't.

Of course, he was kicking himself for not listening to Margaret in the first place. He'd dismissed her information and turned away when he should have let her see Larry Fairfax at the crime scene. Now he'd be working with nothing and had a cold trail not even forty-eight hours after the boy's death. If he'd paid attention, he could have had his men collecting more evidence and roping off the crime scene for further investigation.

But instead he'd instructed his officer to release their prime suspect and now he had the mayor yelling in his ear. "It isn't good news, Jim."

"It can't be. Brendon Loveland just told me you released Larry Fairfax. Are you not going to charge him?" Jim's voice had taken on the squeaky quality of a cornered mouse. Vaughn could sense his stress level but it in no way matched his own.

"We can't charge an innocent man, Jim."

"*Innocent man?* Vaughn, you need to tell me what's going on. Better yet, I'll just come down to the station and you can tell me in person." The line was disconnected before Vaughn could utter another word. Great, all he needed was the mayor hanging around questioning every move he made. Now his actions would be scrutinized. And if the mayor didn't feel he was competent to find Ryan Bentley's murderer, Vaughn would have to put up with the Springfield Police Department. Macho Cop would come back out with his crew cut and sunglasses, giving orders and taking over. He couldn't let that happen.

He needed a break.

He had a killer to find.

## Chapter 14

*Monday, May 23rd*

Katrina Lawrence stood outside the Woman's Choice Clinic and stared up at the sign. The sun over New York City was hot but that wasn't what was making Katrina sweat under her green short-sleeved t-shirt. This morning she had carefully chosen the outfit, pairing the t-shirt with her favorite linen pants, but in hindsight she had no idea why the decision had been so important. Of course, it isn't everyday you get to pick out the outfit you're going to wear to your abortion. Without breaking her gaze, Katrina felt her shoulders slump. She just wanted someone to tell her what she should do.

A sign.

But not the sign she was staring at. It was unnaturally pleasant, given the type of work that went on inside. It was sunny yellow with a melon-colored writing. The words 'Woman's Choice Clinic' were scrawled in fancy lettering followed by the silhouette of a woman with her arm around the shoulder of a child. Katrina wasn't sure if the image was supposed to evoke feelings of relief, or regret.

Maybe if there had been a throng of protesters waving their signs and spitting at her, she would have found it very easy to just walk on by. Skip her appointment. Pretend it never even existed. But no one blocked the door or cursed her. In fact, the people passing on the street went about their own business as if the clinic were nothing but a fast food joint or maybe a newspaper stand. Without anyone or anything to change her mind, Katrina went inside.

The interior of the building matched the sign. But in addition to the sunny yellow and melon trim, the walls were painted a nauseating blue, the shade of a robin's egg. The door shut automatically behind her, thrusting her into the tiny waiting area. Only four chairs lined the wall to Katrina's right. There were no magazines or reading material to pass the time.

On her right a large woman sat behind a window of bulletproof glass with only a sliding metal drawer and a silver circle that housed the electronic transmission for communication. Directly across from the entrance was a melon-colored door undoubtedly leading to rooms one of which you'd leave carrying the eternal question of whether or not you had done the right thing.

"Can I help you?" The receptionist's voice was shot through the electronic box, sounding like Darth Vader addressing Luke Skywalker. It startled Katrina and she clutched her purse.

"Oh, yes, I'm sorry. I have an appointment." Katrina cautiously approached the window but the woman was already consulting a computer screen.

"Name?"

"Katrina Lawrence."

"Do you have your payment in full?"

Suddenly the far door opened and from it came a girl no older than sixteen, and a nurse dressed in all white. The young girl was pale and held an arm across her middle. When the nurse whispered something, the girl nodded and accepted a packet of papers the nurse had been holding. She walked by just as Katrina placed her money in the sliding metal drawer.

*Look at me. Just look at me*, Katrina willed to the girl. *Look into my eyes and I'll see your despair and I'll walk right out of here.*

But the girl didn't make eye contact. She approached the entrance, went slowly through, and a sliver of early morning sunshine stole in before the automatic retractor slammed the door closed once more.

"Katrina?" The white-clad nurse was still standing in the open doorway. Her smile was the warmest thing Katrina had seen all morning, and for a just moment she thought that maybe this was the best decision.

"I wouldn't be a good mother," Katrina muttered to herself as she slowly walked towards the nurse. The nurse nodded but didn't comment as she took Katrina's arm. Behind the door, Katrina expected dark walls and looming shadows with doctors who laughed behind masks as they squirted an unidentifiable liquid from a medieval syringe.

But of course, there was none of that. Just more walls the color of a clear October sky. She was shuffled through the closest open doorway into a room where she placed her purse on the lone visitor's chair. Averting her eyes from the table in the center of the room, Katrina focused on the nurse as she thumbed through a chart. A couple of flips and she met Katrina's gaze.

"Just change into the gown and wait on the table." That warm smile again, and the woman left. Katrina was certain the nurse had smiled it hundreds of times. It was supposed to provide comfort and reassurance but she wasn't convinced. Maybe in a couple of years when all of this was behind her, she'd write a piece on abortion clinics for her magazine. Give the reality side.

Katrina's movements were slow and deliberate. She took great care in folding her t-shirt and linen pants. She tucked her undergarments in between the two and placed everything on top of her purse. Then slipped her sandals off and scooted them under the chair with her bare foot. A good estimate would indicate that the whole process had taken her only five or six minutes, yet no one had knocked on the door to gain entrance, or even checked on her. With nothing else to delay her, Katrina moved to the table and positioned herself on the edge between the extended stirrups. The contraption seemed foreign to her even though she'd been visiting doctors since her first period began at fourteen.

No sound came from beyond the closed door of her room and the minutes crept by. Katrina pulled the gown tighter around her body and crossed her dangling legs at the ankle. Unable to stop herself, she glanced down at her stomach and apologized. "I just don't think I can do it alone. You understand, right?" A tear fell from one of her eyes and made a wet spot on the gown. She wiped at the fabric and cringed at the roughness against her skin. No doubt they were washed in some industrial machine with harsh soap, worn by women before her who shared her inability to be a parent.

In a hasty attempt to erase the disturbing images from her thoughts, Katrina almost didn't hear her cell phone ringing. When finally the sound penetrated through her conflicting emotions, it startled her.

*Has someone seen me come in here? Do they know what I'm doing?*

Katrina slid off the table, bare feet thudding on the cold tile floor. She was starting away from the table when one of the stirrups seemed to reach out and grab her flimsy gown. Katrina tugged to release the hold of the metal arm and finally pulled away, with the tiniest of tears serving as a scar from the battle.

Unearthing her purse from the impediment of clothes, Katrina was frantic and practically spilled the entire contents in order to get to the ringing cell phone. One quick flip and the phone was at Katrina's ear.

"Hello? Hello?" Katrina glanced at the display screen and saw the words missed call. "Damn." She punched another button to bring up the phone number of the missed call and gasped out loud. The number had been committed to heart; Katrina could recite it in her sleep. There was no mistaking who had called.

*Jackson Graham.*

Katrina quickly hit the send button to reverse the call in Jackson's direction. It rang endlessly. Then, "You've reached Jackson Graham, attorney at law, please leave a message…"

"Dammit," Katrina exclaimed and slammed the phone shut.

*Why is he calling? What does he want?*

"Oh God," she uttered aloud.

Katrina looked around her.

What if Jackson was calling to tell her he'd changed his mind? What if he wanted her and the baby? And here she was getting ready to terminate her pregnancy. Maybe this was the sign she'd been waiting for.

Katrina clawed at the clothes she'd dropped on the floor and hastily threw off the abrasive gown. Just as she was sliding the beloved green t-shirt down over her waist, a soft knock sounded at the door. The nurse with the warm smile poked her head in between the door and the frame. When she saw that Katrina was dressed in her regular clothes a peculiar expression softened her face and she cocked her head to the side.

"Are we not ready yet, Katrina?" the nurse asked.

"Oh, no. I'm sorry. I can't do this. I'm sorry," Katrina repeated.

"That's okay." The warm smile returned and the nurse opened the door wide. "Well, if you change your mind, just call us."

On the verge of tears, Katrina stumbled through the door clutching her purse and cell phone against her chest. She burst into the empty waiting area and crossed the tiny space in record time, spilling out into the sunshine of the day. Everything was as it had been before she entered the clinic. People passed by on the street, oblivious of her presence.

Quickly, she redialed Jackson's number and listened to the ringing until the message picked up again. Katrina clamped the phone together and choked off a sob. She was surrounded by hoards of people in one of the most populated cities in the United States—and yet she'd never felt more alone.

~~*~~

Larry Fairfax crawled out of the police car and shut the door behind him. He turned just in time to see the officer pull back onto his street and drive away. Larry wanted to say something. He even went so far as to open his mouth, but no sound came out. There was nothing but a sour taste on his tongue. The police were quick to dismiss him. The young officer who'd released him from the holding cell had averted his eyes when he told him he was free to go.

There was no explanation and he didn't ask for one. He just wanted to go home. It had been nearly twelve hours since his last drink and the bottle sounded good. Looking up and down the sidewalk in front of his home, Larry saw no one. The town was eerily quiet for this beautiful sunny spring day. Any trace of last night's rain was gone with the clouds. Larry let himself into the front door, which he never locked, and closed it firmly behind him. The shades were perpetually drawn which blocked out the harsh light of the sun.

Just like the outdoors, the interior of his house was a virtual vacuum of sound. He could hear nothing. The battery in the clock on the wall in the living room where he stood had died long ago. The hands sat still at twenty-two after five. Morning or evening, Larry didn't know.

With every intention of passing through the room and entering the kitchen, Larry found himself moving towards and standing at the foot of the stairs leading to the second floor. He'd never even set foot on the bottom step since the night he had buried his sweet wife. Life had dealt Larry Fairfax a rotten hand. Everything he had cherished had been taken from him. Now everyone thought he was a murderer. It didn't matter that the police had freed him; that he hadn't been charged with a crime.

The town would be quick to assign his guilt; tried and convicted in the public eye. He envisioned that women would turn their children away from him when they passed him on the street. They would say that maybe he hadn't hit the Bentley boy with his car but sooner or later he would kill *someone*.

Before he knew it, Larry was at the top of the stairs. He'd ascended the wooden steps as if in a trance. Along the hallway in front of him were three closed doors. Larry shuffled along the floor in measured steps. He reached an arm out in front of him, his hand peeking through the sleeve like a turtle's head coming out of its shell. The doorknob was cool under his touch.

Over two decades had passed since the door had been opened and it squeaked in protest as he turned the knob and gave it a determined shove. The sight choked a sob in his throat. Everywhere in the room, he could feel the presence of his daughter, Marie. She had been such a beautiful girl, never caused trouble and had loved him and his wife unconditionally. Memories haunted Larry. He remembered playing catch with her in the backyard when she was nine and helping her learn to drive his wife's old five-speed.

Standing in Marie's room now, he smiled. His face was slick with tears and his nose had begun to run, but oddly he felt a sense of peace take over his body. Larry moved back into the hallway, leaving the door to his daughter's room wide open. Sunlight spilled in through the uncurtained window and brightened up the dark upper story of the house.

Across the hall from Marie's room was the bedroom he'd shared with his wife. She too had left a void in his heart when she left this earth. The bed was still unmade, just as it had been that last day of Betty's life when he had found her dead on the bathroom floor. Quick as his feet could take him, Larry went to the bed and lay down. The sheets and pillow were cool to the touch and he breathed in the scent of must and neglect. He reached for Betty's pillow and swore he could smell her flowery perfume just as strong as if she'd just been there beside him.

"It's time for me to join you, my love," Larry said aloud to the empty room. His eyes were clamped tightly shut and he could picture his wife and daughter standing side by side in the afterlife. Without a hesitating thought, Larry picked himself off the bed and started back into the hallway, dragging the white bed sheet with him.

His old joints and fingers were no match for his determination. Within minutes Larry Fairfax had tied one end of the bed sheet around several of the stair railing's spindles and the other end around his neck. He tugged at the tightened knots to ensure they would hold and then swung a leg over the banister.

Perhaps he hadn't meant for it to happen so fast but the jerky movements of the old man's limbs hindered by the bed sheet didn't give him time to get his footing. His other leg slid easily over the smooth wooden rail, wiping away the layer of dust. Larry sailed out over the empty space between the first and second floors of his house like a fallen angel. The flooring beneath him was fast approaching but he would never reach it. The bed sheet held tight, snapping Larry back up towards the stair railing for just an instant before settling him into a swinging pendulum.

If Margaret Yardley had been there, she would have seen Larry's dirty halo fade to grey, and then disappear altogether.

~~*~~

Bear put his shoulder to the wooden frame of the door and gave a shove. It gave with a loud groan from the old hinges, the sudden force of air into the darkened space upsetting the layer of dust that had formed, swirling it around Bear Lawrence's head. He swatted a hand in front of him and held his breath to keep from sneezing. But it didn't stop Sunshine. From behind him, Bear heard the dog sneeze several times and Jesse laughed at the sound. It was all music to Bear's ears. It was Sunday morning and Bear knew Jesse needed to get out of the house. It held too many reminders of what had happened in the last couple of days.

"Jeez," Jesse marveled as father, son and dog entered the office of the late Walter Sr., "when was the last time anyone was in this place?"

"I'd say not since you were born, buddy." Bear stepped around Sunshine's wagging tail and flipped the light switch on. Now visible, the dust hung like a cloud in the air. Doc's old office was nostalgic to say the least. It was tiled in alternating green and white squares reaching from paneled wall to paneled wall. Around the perimeter of the room several black vinyl chairs, now grey with filth, were positioned for waiting patients. Connecting the chairs at the corner was a squat table offering magazines from nearly fifteen years ago. Jesse picked one up, revealing a shiny, white Formica top outlined in grime. He gingerly replaced it in the same spot and wiped his hands on his shirt.

Bear moved behind the receptionist desk where his had mother worked most Saturday mornings. The top was as neat and tidy as her home. Pencils and pens in a cup sat next to several pads of message paper. All were arranged in close proximity to the phone. His parents hadn't used a computer but there was a typewriter reserved for preparing prescriptions. All patient records were hand-written and stored in numerous gray metal filing cabinets in a back room. Bear assumed most of the records were gone now, having been transferred to new doctors when his father had died.

Directly across from the entrance was the door to Doc's examination room. Bear opened it. The room was set up like every other doctor's office in the world. A secondhand examining table came out from the far left corner of the room. A visitor's chair sat patiently at the far right. Bear glanced around. To his right was a countertop serving as a makeshift desk, with a swivel stool shoved underneath. The countertop held glass containers of cotton balls, tongue suppressors, and alcohol swabs. On the left, two other doors were closed tightly. One led to the tiny half bathroom and the other housed patient medical records.

Curious, Bear approached the door and pulled on the knob. Time and humidity had warped the jamb and the old door groaned as if in pain. Another tug didn't produce the results Bear wanted and he conceded defeat. Just then Jesse and Sunshine came through the door to the examination room.

"This place is so cool. Why does Grandma want to get rid of it?"

"I guess she thinks she's held onto this stuff long enough." Bear shrugged. "Why don't you run out and get those boxes from the truck?"

"Okay, Dad." Jesse ducked back into the lobby. When Bear heard the outer door close behind his son, he moved once again in front of the jammed access to the file room. This time a quick jerk of the knob produced the results he wanted and the old doorway swung open wide. The inside was dark.

A sudden flash and sizzle came out of the darkness when Bear flipped the light switch and the bare old bulb in the ceiling burned out. One step into the space and Bear was swallowed whole by the gloom. He could make out the outlines of the metal filing cabinets and reached a hand out to touch their cool surface. The light from the examination room illuminated very little but Bear could see a shelf set two feet from the ceiling, home for five or six leather-bound books. He stretched up to pull them down and something with many legs clambered across his fingers.

"Here you go, Dad." Bear hadn't heard Jesse return and with haste pulled his hand back away from the shelf.

"Well, we should get packing if we're going to make any progress today. You start with Grandma's old desk." Bear backed out of the records room and lodged the door back into place. He could look at the books later. He had a feeling they weren't going anywhere. After all, they'd been on the same shelf for eleven years.

"Hey, Jess. What do you think about going to New York to visit your Aunt Kat for a few days?"

## Chapter 15

"Susan, what are you doing here?" Vaughn asked, surprised to see the coroner making her way towards him in the police station's parking lot. He hadn't heard another car pull in as he gathered his things from the passenger seat and assumed she'd been waiting for him to arrive. It wasn't early in the day but Vaughn hadn't expected to hear from the coroner's office until at least Tuesday. The revelation of her look was determined. Her mouth was set in a grim line, which made any hopes he had vanish instantly.

"I think you're going to want to take a look at this, Vaughn." She raised an arm and waved the piece of paper she held firmly in her grasp. A stiff breeze blew a lock of brunette hair across her lips and she brushed at it absently. Vaughn knew it had to be the autopsy report and was just as anxious to hear the results, so he could put this whole thing behind them.

"Yeah. Why don't you come on in?"

Vaughn led the way up the small sidewalk and entered the pass code to unlock the door to the police station. He hoped beyond all hope that he could usher Susan Barnes into his office without any of the officers in the squad room noticing. He needed a few moments alone with her to find out the facts of the autopsy report before he started answering any questions. Of course, he knew he could never be that lucky.

"Hey Chief," Phillip Downing Rothwell III stepped from the office marked Corporal and pulled the door shut behind him. Phillip's roots in Rochester ran as deep as the founding fathers. His great-grandfather, grandfather and father had passed down real estate that was purchased cheap and sold high from generation to generation. All were businessmen of the truest nature. The Rothwell name was synonymous with commercial property, mortgage lending and deals made with handshakes.

When Phillip the third was born, the family rejoiced that another legion of Rothwell's could march into the future of Rochester's landscape. They were devastated when shortly after Phillip Downing Rothwell IV was born, Phil moved towards a career in law enforcement. Although the family would never utter this aloud, all thought that Phil was making the biggest mistake of his life and would have to learn the hard way. Coming from money, they just knew that Phil's career of choice would not provide the adequate lifestyle for a wife and child. He would soon be back in the family business. Of this they had no doubt.

Now eighteen years later, Phil was still an officer of the law. Having been promoted to Corporal for the last nine of those eighteen years, Phil provided nicely not only for his wife and Phillip IV but also Jason, Timothy and his youngest, Kristen. Now the joke was on the Rothwell family, although the Rochester police officers did get a kick out of telling Phil that his name was far too fancy to put on a brass name tag.

Other than that, no one messed with Phillip Downing Rothwell III. At nearly seven foot tall, Phillip towered over everyone else including Vaughn. He finished locking his office and turned towards his boss. "Oh, Ms. Barnes, I didn't see you there."

"Hi, Corporal Rothwell. Nice to see you."

The awkward silence that followed was disrupted only by a phone ringing in the background and papers being shuffled in the squad room. Phil wasn't sure if the meeting between Vaughn and Susan was personal or professional but in any event knew he'd interrupted *something*. "Well, I was just on my way out. Is there anything you need before I go, Chief?"

"No, Phil, thanks. Brendon's in the squad room. He should be able to handle things. Oh, have you seen Perry?" Vaughn asked, having to angle his neck upward to address his Corporal.

"Perry left a while ago. Said he'd be back for his shift." Phil tossed his keys from hand to hand.

Vaughn nodded and held his office door open for Susan Barnes to enter. She gave Phil a slight wave before disappearing inside.

As he walked out, their lack of eye contact and tone of voice made Phil think that the Chief had finally found a good woman.

~~*~~

"Well?" Vaughn asked as soon as the door to his office was closed. Susan handed over the pathology report and took a deep breath.

"The autopsy confirmed it. Ryan Bentley wasn't killed by Larry Fairfax's car. In fact, there was no evidence that the car even touched him."

Vaughn nodded and scanned over the report. Most of it was gibberish to him. Medical jargon. And even if he could read it, he wasn't sure he could make his eyes focus. What had appeared to be a simple accident had officially just become a murder investigation.

"The temperature was relatively mild last night because of the rain so the body temp made it difficult to determine the exact time of death. But as the paramedics were loading the body, it started to show signs of rigor mortis. I'd been on the scene about two hours then. So I would say, Ryan had been dead at least three hours before Larry came along." Susan stopped a moment to gather her thoughts.

"I wish there had been maggots. Maggots are so much easier to work with."

"Maggots?" Vaughn questioned, not even sure if Susan was speaking to him.

"Maggots on a body can give you an exact time of death depending on how old they are. If they are in the larvae stage, just hatched under—"

"Susan," Vaughn stated, holding up his hand for her to stop her graphic explanation.

"Oh… sorry. Anyway, the official cause of death is blunt force trauma to the head. As you saw there was no exterior damage to the body but once we opened up the head, we could tell by the pooled blood."

"So someone hit the boy over the head?" Vaughn moved around behind his desk and sat down, indicating Susan should do the same. She brushed off his offer with a shake of her head and paced instead.

"Well, I can't be exactly sure of that. Most of the damage was done to the base of the skull. And remember the mud and grass in the boy's hair and on his clothes? I called the State Police Crime Lab before I came. They were able to give me some preliminary test results."

Vaughn straightened in his chair. This is how crimes were solved. Even the smallest, most insignificant piece of evidence could lead right to a murderer. "And?"

"Mixed in with the soil was motor oil with a weight of 15w40. The type used primarily in diesel vehicles. The grass clippings had torn edges as if they'd been ripped from the ground instead of cut with, say, a lawn mower." Susan tucked the strands of her long brown hair behind her ears, finally sat in the chair, and crossed her arms over her chest. "And there was one other thing. Deeply embedded in his scalp were tiny flecks of something yellow."

"Paint," Vaughn volunteered. He was tense with anticipation that her next statement would lead him towards Ryan Bentley's murderer, or at least to the scene of the crime.

Susan nodded vigorously. "Yes, paint."

"The kind of paint used for automobiles?"

"Possibly." Susan shrugged.

Vaughn slammed a hand down on his desk and picked up his walkie-talkie. He called out to Perry Newlon. From some unknown location came Perry's voice. "Go ahead, Chief."

"Perry, I need you to meet me at Bear's Auto Body now. I'll explain when I get there."

Vaughn bolted to his office door, stopped and regarded the coroner. "You might as well ride along. I think you're going to want to see this too."

~~*~~

"What's going on?" Gordon Newlon demanded of his son.

"I'm not sure, Dad, and even if I was I can't discuss it with you. Official police business, remember?"

Perry was still dressed in his uniform. He'd come home from the station to grab some sleep and a late lunch. He hoped that eating at home would encourage his father to eat as well—the man just didn't look good.

Perry was due in for duty in less than an hour but Vaughn's call meant his shift would be starting early. The police force was understaffed and lately he felt like he never got to come home. Not that there was anything at home for him. Not since Joyce had left. Maybe he should call her just to see how she was...

For a moment he was lost in whimsy until Amy Agans' voice interrupted his thoughts.

"See ya, Gordon," the young girl gave Perry's father a peck on the cheek and slung her book bag onto her shoulder.

"Off so soon?" Gordon pulled a ragged breath in from his oxygen tank.

"Yeah, I've got to grab a book from the library before it closes," she explained.

Jackie Agans moved through the dining room area with a glass of iced tea and sat it on the table beside Gordon. "I thought you went to the library on Saturday, honey?"

"Yes, but I forgot to check out one of the books I need." Amy downcast her big brown eyes and pretended to inspect her shoe-laces. She knew her face would be bright red. She and Tim had fled the library after getting caught by the librarian, but she wasn't about to tell her mother that was the reason why she'd forgotten the book.

Perry joined the trio in the dining room and fastened his holster-belt around his waist. "I have to make a stop at Bear's Auto Body, but then I'm heading to the station. You want a ride?"

"Sure," Amy was elated she wouldn't have to walk. She was just sorry Perry hadn't brought home one of the police cruisers.

The two said good-bye to their respective parents and made their way towards Perry's car. He opened the passenger door to let the teenager slide in.

"You still seeing Phil's boy?"

"Um, sort of."

Amy settled onto the blue cloth seat and placed her backpack on her lap. For a moment the conversation was halted as Perry shut her door and made his way around to the driver's side.

"'Sort of', huh? Well that doesn't sound too promising for ol' Tim, now does it?"

Perry backed carefully out of the driveway and couldn't help but glance at the young beauty in his car. She was young, he knew it, but her body was well-developed. The weather wasn't quite warm enough for shorts but Perry wished it was.

Amy was slightly taller than her mother with the same blond hair and chocolate eyes. She had the slender, taut body of a teenage cheerleader and he knew she'd be a heartbreaker. She'd fastened the shoulder strap of her seat belt and it pulled the red shirt she wore tightly against her breasts.

As quickly as he'd peeked, Perry looked away, ashamed of himself.

*She's a teenager for Christ's sake. 'Jailbait', they call it— and I'm an officer of the law.*

~~*~~

Margaret Yardley watched the police cruiser roll to a halt at the stoplight and then turn right onto her street. Her eyes stayed transfixed as the vehicle continued past her house until the dip in the road hid the car from view. The lights weren't lit and the siren was silent, but Margaret couldn't help but feel an ominous presence. She finished sweeping the front steps and sidewalk before ambling back up to the house. Shannon was coming over. She needed to prepare for his visit.

Once inside her museum of a home, Margaret carried a plain cardboard box to the back bedroom and opened the door. The sight always took her breath but she quickly composed herself and began tearing away at the packing tape to expose the fragile contents.

She wondered what the Chief would think of Shannon's hobby. Was she the only one willing to accept Shannon as he was? She doubted very much that Vaughn Dexter would be interested in anything else but how all those dead animals ended up in Shannon's backyard, and in her spare bedroom.

The doorbell sang out and Margaret stopped fiddling with the lid of the cardboard box. Maybe it would be best for her and Shannon to open it together.

## Chapter 16

Vaughn and Susan stood in the parking lot of the closed auto body shop and waited for Perry. The Chief continually checked his watch and then glanced towards the sky. The nights were getting longer as summer approached but Vaughn knew that once the sun dipped behind the row of trees along the road, the search would be difficult. Especially if they were looking for trace evidence that a boy had been murdered.

They were also waiting for Bear Lawrence to bring the keys to open the garage.

"At least Bear Lawrence didn't decide to open the shop today," Susan said, to break up the silence of the afternoon. It seemed that as a result of Ryan Bentley's death, the entire town of Rochester had decided to stay indoors.

"Yeah, that's true. The shop's been closed since Saturday at three. That should mean nothing's been disturbed since the murder." They lapsed back into an awkward silence and Vaughn again glanced at his watch.

Susan took the opportunity to take him in. It was no secret that she found him extremely attractive. His blond hair and deep blue eyes made him perfectly suited for the dark color of the Rochester police uniform. But she couldn't figure him out. Why would a man who could have any woman choose to be alone? Susan knew she wasn't unattractive but whatever she had to offer, it certainly wasn't what the chief was looking for. If only she knew something about his childhood, his hometown, anything. But Vaughn never opened up. If Susan didn't know better, she would think he was secretive for a reason.

Vaughn could feel the weight of Susan's burning stare but he made a point not to make eye contact. She was a beautiful woman. Someone who might make him betray his own vow to himself not to care about anyone. He didn't need a distraction right now, especially since he was in charge of solving a murder. Vaughn raised his head only when he heard the sound of a car approaching the garage. Perry Newlon drove up in his father's dark blue Buick Skylark and parked along the curb. Vaughn could see that someone was in the passenger seat.

"Got a ride along?" Vaughn asked as Perry walked over.

"Amy Agans. Said I could give her a ride to the library when I was done here." Perry glanced back over his shoulder at the car.

"You'd better send her walking. You're going to be here a while. Oh and call in some back-up," Vaughn advised, and motioned for Susan to follow him around the back of the building.

"Why? What's going on, Chief?" Perry called after the shrinking figure of his boss.

"Crime scene."

~~*~~

Bear Lawrence shook his head, hands firmly planted on his hips. "Can't say as I've ever bought any yellow paint, Chief. Not exactly a popular color for the type of cars I work on." He stood outside the auto shop of which he was so proud. He'd worked so hard to make the shop a success and now there were police crawling all over it. Combing through his papers and scouring the grounds.

"I gotta ask, Bear. Where were you on Saturday night?" the chief asked.

"At home. You know that. I picked up Ryan around six and took him back to our house to spend the night with Jesse. Around nine, they watched a movie. I never saw the boys again." Bear didn't seem offended by the chief's question. He answered frankly and quickly.

Vaughn flipped a couple of pages in the small notebook he was carrying and glanced around the side of the garage. They had found an old oil hold; a barrel where Bear kept his used motor oil after changes, before it was picked up and disposed of properly. It was an ideal place where Ryan Bentley could have gotten the oil on his clothes.

But so far, no yellow paint.

"So you're saying you haven't purchased or used any type of yellow paint in the last six months?"

"No, nothing like that." Bear was distracted, watching some of the cops as they pulled bottles of oil off the shelf and place them in a cardboard box. They were confiscating them. Looking for evidence.

Vaughn flipped the notebook shut and pulled a deep breath in through his nose. He could see Susan Barnes combing through the tall weeds surrounding the barrel of oil. The light had long ago faded and the beam of her little flashlight bounced off the rusted metal of the barrel. Perhaps the paint had spilled long ago, back when John Tavish ran the place. Maybe that's why Bear never recalled any yellow paint. Maybe it was already here. Vaughn took a hard look at Bear. He didn't think he was looking at Ryan's murderer. Typically someone with something to hide didn't let you have free rein on a suspected crime scene.

"And what about the boy you have working here for you? There's nothing you can think of that would cause you any concern about Shannon Marshall? And your son, Jesse, he hangs out with Shannon from time to time. He ever say anything about Shannon that might make you worry?"

Again Bear was shaking his head. He was clearly perplexed. First, Ryan Bentley should have been sleeping peacefully in Jesse's room when he was actually out on the streets of Rochester getting killed. And now Vaughn Dexter was standing in front of him questioning him about someone he'd left alone with his son. It was enough to push you over the edge.

"No. I can't believe that Shannon would have anything to do with this. I mean, Shannon?"

Bear Lawrence's tone was incredulous. Bear had given Shannon Marshall a chance when no one else would give him the time of day. He refused to believe it.

Suddenly a change in Bear's expression made Vaughn stand a little taller. Something tightened inside the chief's stomach and he thought this might be what he'd been waiting for.

Bear turned to the chief. "You know, come to think of it, Jesse did say something strange the other day."

"Strange, how?" Vaughn asked when Bear didn't elaborate.

Bear squinted his eyes in thought as he tried hard to recall the conversation he'd had with Jesse right before he dropped him off at Nina's last week.

"Something about animals. 'Shannon's animals', Jesse said."

"Animals?"

"Yeah." A slight dawning landed on Bear's face. "Jesse asked me if I'd apologize to Shannon for telling Ryan about his animals. He said he made Shannon angry 'cause he told Ryan some secret."

Now Vaughn was confused. "What would be so upsetting about that? Shannon has some secret pet?"

"No, that's just it. Jesse specifically said they were Shannon's *'animals'*. They weren't pets."

Vaughn reached up to the radio on his shoulder. "Base, this is Chief Dexter. I want a pickup on a suspect—one Shannon Marshall. Keep him detained at the station until I get back. Do you copy?"

"We copy Chief. We're sending a car now to pick him up."

Vaughn turned his attention back to Bear. "Thanks, Bear. I think Jesse may have just been a big help."

## Chapter 17

*Tuesday, May 24<sup>th</sup>*

Ryan Bentley's funeral was a solemn affair. The boy's parents stood at the front of the Catholic church in their best clothes, shaking hands and touching their eyes with wadded tissue. Vaughn stood at the back dressed in his policeman's uniform. He felt like it had become a permanent part of his skin.

The casket was light blue and full-sized. Vaughn wasn't sure he'd be able to handle his emotions if it had been one of those child-sized coffins. He hadn't been to a burial service since his sister, Leigh, was killed and he didn't want to be at this one. Throngs of people moved past him down the sanctuary aisle, most of them small children who'd gone to school with Ryan. Vaughn recognized very few people. He did see Jesse Lawrence sitting in between his father and grandmother with his head down and hands clasped in his lap.

Cameron Cody, the librarian, was sitting several rows behind them. Vaughn could tell he was nervous; he kept touching his small wire-rimmed glasses as if they were continually sliding down his nose. Across the aisle of the church was most of the Rochester police staff.

Phil Rothwell sat a head above his wife. His meaty arm was slung across the back of the pew and it reached nearly all the way to encompass his daughter as well. Perry had come in late, escorting his father. The going was slow as the old man was dragging a life-sustaining oxygen bottle. Vaughn had never before seen the old man—the man he had succeeded in office.

Without dwelling on it too long, Vaughn quickly scanned the rest of the church. Much to his surprise, the one person he'd been looking for was not in attendance. At the front of the church, he watched Pastor Sampson approach Ryan Bentley's parents and place a gentle hand on each of their arms. Whatever words the pastor uttered caused Ellen Bentley to drop her face into her hands and sob uncontrollably. On the front pew closest to Bob Bentley a fair-haired little girl of about four also began wailing in sympathy. Vaughn recognized the little girl as the Bentley's youngest daughter. Everyone took their cue to find a seat in the packed church.

Everyone except him—*he* watched the crowd.

He stepped back towards the entry hall of the church and waited for anyone to turn around and catch a glimpse of him. When no one did, he made his exit, letting in only the briefest slit of daylight. Another storm was brewing somewhere to the west of them. It would only be a matter of time before the sky clouded up and let loose a shower. His mother used to say that rain was God's tears. Today He'd be crying for Ryan Bentley. Vaughn folded himself into the driver's seat of his truck and tried to shake the image of the boy's casket from his head. He vowed to find the boy's killer. And with Shannon Marshall safely tucked in jail and the rest of the town attending a funeral, he knew this was the perfect opportunity to visit someone he had never met. Another woman that could tell him about Shannon's childhood, his life before Margaret Yardley intervened.

As he drove away, the crackle of the police radio brought more news of death. The very threads holding

Rochester together were unraveling as he watched and there was nothing he could do about it.

~~*~~

Margaret Yardley answered the door in her usual swirl of colored beads and pleated skirt. Answered it before Vaughn even had the chance to knock or ring the bell. "Well what can I say, Chief Dexter? You look like hell."

Vaughn regarded Margaret with his usual look of skepticism. "You would too if you hadn't been to sleep since Saturday morning."

"Come on in then. Coffee's brewing." Margaret stepped aside and Vaughn entered a time warp. The inside of Margaret's home was old wood and antiques. Every available space on the end tables and in the china cabinet was filled with miniature tea sets of every design and color.

There was no television that Vaughn could see, just an old brocade-covered couch perched on four intricately-carved legs. The arms were worn nearly thread-bare. Two wingback chairs completed the circle around a brick fireplace. To Vaughn, the space wasn't comfortable; he fidgeted in effort to avoid sitting on the ancient furniture. "Coffee brewing, you say?" he asked as he glanced around. "Were you expecting someone?"

Margaret moved past him and gestured towards her museum of a living room. "Yes, I was expecting someone. *You.*"

The chief nodded.

"You're here about Larry Fairfax," the old woman continued.

"Well it doesn't take a psychic to know that," Vaughn cracked.

"Why Chief," Margaret exclaimed, smiling back, "I do believe that was a joke." She made her exit into what he presumed to be the kitchen and he chose one of the chairs as the lesser of two evils. Only moments later, Margaret Yardley swished back into the room with a sterling silver tray and matching coffee carafe. When Vaughn peered over her shoulder as she poured, he was relieved to see normal sized cups and saucers. For a fleeting moment he was afraid he would have to be a guest at the Mad Hatter's tea party, drinking out of a thimble-sized cup shaped like a blooming tulip.

Margaret finished the chore and placed the warm cup in the Chief's hands. Vaughn noticed a slight tremble in her grip that sent ripples across the surface of the coffee. She settled onto the couch with a mighty groan of protest and took a sip from her own cup. "Well?"

"He's dead," Vaughn stated his reason for the visit matter-of-factly.

To his surprise, Margaret didn't appear to be affected by what he'd just said. She nodded her head twice and sipped again at the black liquid in her cup. "How did it happen?"

"Hung himself," he said again without emotion. "A reporter stopped by his house for an interview and discovered the body. Looks like he's been there all night."

Margaret knew that Vaughn was trying to keep the feeling from showing in his face but she could see his once guilt-colored halo flare from gold to nearly brown.

"Committed suicide," her tone was breathy as if she had been running, "so that was the cause of the dirty halo. Not killing the boy."

"Evidently."

"And you feel guilty about it."

Vaughn could tell it was a statement not a question. Figuring the psychic woman would be able to tell if he lied, Vaughn agreed. "I should have listened to you and kept him locked up. I'm sure I could have come up with some sort of excuse to keep him inside. At least until a psychologist came to talk to him."

Margaret shook her head and spoke softly. "It wouldn't have made any difference. You follow the law, Chief Dexter. You need more than excuses to keep people locked up. Besides, Larry was determined. And the law doesn't protect us from ourselves."

Vaughn narrowed his eyes. He wasn't sure the last statement was still referring to Larry Fairfax. He wanted to break eye contact but couldn't until Margaret reached across the coffee table towards the silver serving tray.

"Anyway, I came here for another reason. We've uncovered some evidence that has us looking at Shannon Marshall."

She was so startled by the comment, her hand lurched forward and spilled the delicate container of cream. The white liquid spread across the inside of the lipped tray.

"He didn't kill that boy if that's what you're thinking," Margaret exclaimed and busied herself with mopping at the spillage.

"Well I was going to ask what you thought of the boy, but I guess it's pretty obvious."

"He's a good kid, Chief Dexter. Just grossly misunderstood."

"I thought you might say that." Vaughn placed his cup of coffee onto the table in front of him and laced his fingers together. "I dropped by Shannon's house this morning while we have him detained for questioning and had a little chat with his grandma. Nice lady."

Margaret defensively tightened her eyes to slits. "Just what are you getting at, Chief?"

"The old lady mentioned you. You of all people, Margaret. Wanted me to know how sweet you are to Shannon. Told me you've helped him on more than one occasion." Vaughn locked stares with Margaret and he could almost feel her squirm under his intense gaze. "You see after my talk with grandma, she had no issue with me taking a look around. She told me to go right ahead. Alone. I don't think she gets out of her chair much anymore."

Margaret's face went pale and chalky. Her mouth must have suddenly dried out because Vaughn watched her lick her cracked lips. "You'll never believe what I found in the backyard."

"You don't understand..."

"Well then you'd better help me understand, Margaret." Vaughn's voice boomed off the walls in the old woman's living room. "You claim to be a psychic, to have all of these powers. You've been pushing me for weeks to finger Larry Fairfax as Ryan Bentley's killer. You've endlessly distracted me with showing up at the station and the crime scene. Am I supposed to believe you aren't trying to cover for Shannon? Did you help him kill all those animals, Margaret?"

"No, Chief, listen..."

"It's classic behavior. Profilers have proven it over and over. The murderer starts small and then works his way up."

Vaughn was so distracted by the heightened conversation he didn't realize that now both he and Margaret were standing, separated only by the coffee table.

Instead of the hysterical comeback Vaughn had expected, Margaret's response was calm. "I think it's time I show you something."

Caught off guard, Vaughn blinked several times. "What?"

Margaret motioned for him to follow her into the kitchen. The décor was outdated and slimy green and it matched his mood. He wasn't sure what he expected Margaret to show him but it wasn't what he saw out her back window. The porthole overlooked an attached screened-in porch that had several cages sitting on the sagging wooden floor. Two of the cages were empty. In the enclosure closest to where he stood, a rabbit was nibbling on a piece of lettuce. One of its ears was distinctly shorter than the other and ragged at the tip. Along the back of its neck, the rabbit's fur was shaved and Vaughn could make out a neat row of stitches that had just recently sealed a wound. The other cage was holding an injured bird whose right wing was bound with a popsicle stick and white tape.

"He doesn't kill or torture them, Chief. He *saves* them." Margaret's voice was barely above a whisper. The look on her face was all pride as she looked out into the porch. "Shannon has amazing abilities. Could have been a doctor; a veterinarian, given his love of animals and all."

"You mean to tell me that I'm supposed to believe Shannon Marshall sewed stitches into that rabbit?" Vaughn's tone was incredulous.

"Yes, that's exactly what I'm telling you. Shannon walks everywhere he goes. He doesn't have a car, or a driver's license even if he did. If he comes across an animal that's hurt or sick, Shannon will give his best effort to save the poor creature. Regardless of what he shows on the outside, Chief Dexter, Shannon is a highly sensitive boy. And that isn't a crime. He couldn't have killed Ryan Bentley. That isn't his nature."

"But what about all those graves in the back yard of his grandmother's house?"

"He isn't God," Margaret scoffed, "Some of the animals can't be saved. If they're mangled or torn up, Shannon gives them a proper burial in his back yard."

Something in the way she said the last sentence made him ask. "And if they aren't mangled or torn up?"

Margaret ambled back through the kitchen door and led Vaughn down a darkened hallway with two closed doors. Margaret stopped at the first door and opened it wide. Inside were dozens of animals. Birds caught in flight. Rabbits and raccoons sitting on all fours. Even a snake coiled up on a rock. But none of the animals moved. "I have a friend in Harvel whose husband is a taxidermist. He does the work for practically nothing. Seeing the animals restored to their natural state of beauty is soothing to Shannon. In his life, there *is* nothing else."

Vaughn stepped into the room and skimmed the contents with his dark blue eyes. Could the old woman be telling the truth? Was Shannon Marshall some saint to all animals great and small?

"You believe me, don't you? After seeing all this, you know in your heart that Shannon couldn't have killed that boy." She leaned against the doorjamb and bunched one side of her skirt in a firm fist.

"Just because he's good to animals doesn't mean he isn't capable of killing a human. You can't know. I'm following hard evidence."

Even to Vaughn, his voice was weak and unconvincing. "Thank you, Margaret, for the information."

Instead of acknowledging the Chief's comment, Margaret's countenance took on a look of whimsy. "Shannon's aura is the most beautiful shade of pink you could ever see. It not only swirls above his head but also envelops his entire body. It never leaves him. You see, a person's aura is affected by their mood and immediate actions. But there are people in this town that never lose their halos. Anger, happiness, purity, guilt. They never go away."

Vaughn had stopped listening. He made his way back through the maze of ancient living room furniture and let himself out.

For a long while after the door had shut behind him, Margaret stood gazing in at the beautifully-stuffed animals. She didn't admit it to the Chief, but the sight of them comforted her too.

~~*~~

"I thought I saw the chief in the back of the church," Perry Newlon said, leading his father over the wet cemetery grass back to their car.

"Yeah, he must have gotten called away about the Fairfax thing. Damn sad situation there," Phil Rothwell replied, walking a couple of steps behind his wife and daughter. "Do you really think Shannon Marshall killed that little boy?"

Perry sucked a sharp breath in through his teeth and shook his head slowly. "I don't know. That Marshall kid has a lot of problems. His family's messed up. He was constantly picked on in high school till he finally dropped out. Maybe he just looked at Ryan Bentley and was jealous of his perfect life."

"Yeah, you've got to admit the evidence does point in his direction." Phil agreed.

"What evidence?" Gordon Newlon stopped in his turtle-paced tracks and stared up at the tall police officer.

"I don't think…I mean…Perry?" Phil stuttered.

"Dad, we can't divulge that type of information. You know that."

"Listen here. I'm an old man, dying—but not dead yet. I was a police officer for thirty-two years. And a damn good one at that. Consider me a consultant for the investigation." Gordon's words rattled and wheezed from his chest. He was worked up and it was beginning to show in his pallor.

Perry looked around to see if anyone had witnessed his father's outburst before encouraging him to start walking again with a slight shove on his elbow. Perry didn't want to mention that even though his father was a good policeman and a great chief, the murderer of Marie Fairfax had never been caught. Nor had the disappearance of Mandy Getz ever been solved. Of course, back then forensic evidence wasn't a household term. Murders from Perry's childhood were usually solved based on luck and the murderer's ego. He debated over whether to share the information and looked to Phil for the answer—but Phil had looked away.

By sheer good fortune, they had reached Phil's parked car and he hurriedly tucked his wife and daughter inside before squeezing behind the wheel.

"Come on, Dad. Let's get in the car."

Once inside, Perry told the old man everything he knew about the autopsy, the grass clippings, the mud and the paint. Through it all, Gordon tapped his index finger on the knee of his good pants. He nodded every once in a while but didn't speak until Perry had finished. And even then he simply said, "Get me a cigarette and Vaughn Dexter on the phone."

## Chapter 18

"I think its best we just pull him out of school the rest of the week. He's a mess, Nina and there are only a couple of days left in the year."

Bear stood on the porch of his old house again, not invited in, like some unwanted salesman. Jesse hadn't said much since the funeral. The ride from the cemetery to Nina's house was all but silent despite Liz's efforts to engage him in conversation. They both knew Jesse didn't want to go home. When they pulled up to the dark house, Jesse had mumbled good-bye and disappeared inside. Now Nina stood before him wearing the rust-colored smock she donned everyday for work.

Nina nodded. She had agreed with him for once without a ten-minute argument. Maybe she could see from the tired look in Bear's eyes that he couldn't stand one more second of her hostility. She too was tired. Her aqua eyes were vacant.

"And I've been meaning to say this. I talked to Kat the other day after Ryan was killed and she thinks it might be a good idea if I take Jesse to New York for a couple of days to get away from here."

Much to Bear's surprise, Nina nodded again. "I think that might be a good idea too. I think Jesse needs to get out of here too."

"I can just take him back home with me if you want," Bear said.

"No. That's not necessary. I can stay home with him tomorrow. I'll think of something. And you can get things lined up with the shop. Will you close it down or will Shannon be running the place while you're gone?"

Bear could hardly speak. His brown eyes unfocused and for a fraction of a second he could see the girl he'd fallen in love with all those years ago. She hadn't asked about his work at the shop in years. He almost hated to ruin the mood with his next statement. "Shannon's been arrested for Ryan Bentley's murder."

"My God," Nina gasped and stepped out of the door onto the tiny concrete porch cap. "Are they sure? Oh Bear, do you think Jesse was ever in danger?"

Bear felt a surge of emotion well up inside of him. Nina hadn't blamed him. Her words weren't accusatory like he'd expected. Normally, the statement would have been something like, 'How could you, Bear? How could you have allowed Jesse around that murderer all this time?'

"No, Nina, I don't think Jesse was ever in any danger. I'm not entirely convinced that Shannon did anything wrong."

Nina's eyes were moist in the gloom of the day. Any sun from the day had long gone behind a cloud and stayed there. So far, there was no rain. "Would you like to come in for some coffee, Bear?"

*Yes,* Bear thought, *I would.*

But instead he took a step back from his wife and motioned towards the car. "Mother's waiting. If I had known I would've—"

But the moment was gone. Nina stepped curtly back up the step into the house and held the screen door open only an inch. "That's okay. Never mind. Will you be arranging to leave for New York on Friday when you pick Jesse up for the weekend?"

"I'll call Kat and finalize the details." Bear started walking away, then turned back. Nina still stood framed by the door, staring out over the yard. Her eyes were hooded in shadows and Bear wasn't exactly sure if she was looking at him or not. "He'll be okay, Nina. Jesse's a tough kid. We'll do whatever it takes to get through this."

He started walking away again and this time he kept going.

Nina closed her eyes and fought the tears. When she heard the sound of Bear's car door slamming shut, she winced.

*Will Jesse be okay? First the divorce, then Ryan's death—and I know Jesse hates me.*

She didn't know what to do. She was afraid her little boy was lost to her but still she couldn't help herself from locking up the house and going down the hall to his room.

~~*~~

Katrina lay on her overstuffed sofa in her beloved linen pants again. It was the third time she'd worn them this week. She wanted to get as much use out of them before her belly grew too large to enjoy their worn comfort. She twiddled the drawstring tie through her fingers and listen to the sound of her brother's voice. When Bear finished, Katrina furrowed her brow. "I'm sorry about everything that's going on there, Bear. I know how much you liked Shannon but some people just can't be saved. Sometimes they're born bad and I have to tell you he's always given me a creepy vibe. But anyway, I can't wait for you and Jesse to come to New York. It's going to be great."

"So we should fly out on Monday morning then?"

"Yeah, let's both get things squared away with work and then you'll have the weekend to pack and get stuff together. When you fly in, I can meet you guys at JFK."

"Kat, thank you. You've no idea how much it'll mean to Jesse to get to see you. He's grown so much, I'm afraid you won't recognize him."

Katrina could hear the smile in Bear's voice when he talked about his son. She hoped she could someday feel that way about the baby she was carrying. Right now there was no bond. There was nothing. Without movement or even a hint of a growing stomach, the pregnancy was still unreal to her. She was glad Bear and Jesse were coming now when there wouldn't be any questions to answer. In a few more months, she figured it would be Bear and Jesse that wouldn't recognize her.

Bear finished the conversation and disconnected the call. The inside of her apartment was quiet. Soon it would be filled with the sound of Jesse's boyish laughter and soon after that a baby would be there full time. Katrina tried to imagine what it would be like.

That day after Jackson's call at the Woman's Choice Clinic, Katrina had torn up their card. Even though nothing ever came of the mysterious call, Katrina was certain it was too early to make such a rash decision. She was only nine weeks pregnant which gave her plenty of time to come to an informed, intelligent choice about her future.

Katrina realized she'd stopped fiddling with the string on her pants and had placed the palm of her hand on her abdomen.

*A baby. What am I going to do with a baby?*

~~*~~

The hour was late and finally the sky, slashed open by a single bolt of white-hot lightening, released the rain. It came down in sheets outside Vaughn's office window and he couldn't concentrate as he narrowed in on the liquid sound. If he didn't get some sleep soon he was going to turn into a zombie. He ran a hand through his hair and then back down over his face. His mustache was getting long from neglect and he absently thought about shaving it off for the summer.

Tomorrow he was taking the day off but he still planned to go up to Springfield and see Shannon at the Sangamon County Jail. They'd transported him there early this morning while most of the town was occupied with Ryan Bentley's funeral. It was all they needed, to have a scene outside of the police station, especially when Shannon hadn't even been given the opportunity to tell his side of the story.

A single long hissing sound made Vaughn snap his head towards the door of his office. To his surprise, the old man he'd seen with Perry Newlon earlier at the funeral was standing in the doorway.

"You guys really should think about changing the pass code on that door."

"Chief Newlon." Vaughn stood from behind his desk. "For someone carrying an oxygen tank you're really quite stealthy."

Gordon Newlon cracked a smile and his laugh came out in a wet crackle. "Just call me Gordon. You can have the Chief title all to your self."

Perry Newlon's voice floated in from the darkened hallway, accompanied by a boom of thunder. "Dammit, Dad. I told you to wait on the sidewalk while I parked the car."

"It's all right, Perry," Vaughn called out and then returned his attention to the elder Newlon. "Please come in."

Gordon pulled in a drag of oxygen through the tubes in his nose and started across the floor of Vaughn's office. Not sure if the old guy would make it,

Vaughn came from behind his desk and moved the visitor's chair closer to the door, making Gordon's trek a little shorter. As the old man settled into his seat, Perry joined them. "I'm sorry to barge in on you like this, Chief, but my father insisted on meeting you."

"Oh? After all this time? What would make you come out on a night like this?"

Even as Vaughn asked the questions, he wasn't sure if he wanted to know the answers.

"It's about the boy, Chief Dexter. Ryan Bentley. I thought I could lend a hand with the investigation."

Vaughn sized up the shriveled shell of the former chief.

*What could he possibly think he could contribute at this point?*

"Lend a hand how, sir?"

"Well, I overheard Perry and some of your other officers talking about the case. I know you've arrested that Marshall kid and I know you've got some evidence that you haven't released to the public yet."

"I'm sorry, Vaughn." Perry began to say before Vaughn held up a hand to stop him.

"We'll discuss that later. Right now I'd like to hear what your father has to say on the topic." Vaughn wasn't preoccupied with what Gordon had overheard, but he was curious as to what the old man was about to say regarding the case. Right now there were no more leads than there had been the night they found Ryan Bentley's body.

Nothing at Bear's Auto Body suggested there'd been foul play and despite the mini-graveyard in Shannon Marshall's backyard, his home held no clues about a murder.

"The paint. The yellow paint." Gordon wheezed out the words.

"Yes?" Vaughn urged.

"Have them test it again. There's something that they're missing."

*That's it?*

Another round of thunder and lightening put a pause in the conversation.

"Why the paint?" Vaughn leaned forward, putting an elbow to his knee.

"Because it's one piece that doesn't fit. It was imbedded in his head, but where did it come from?" The breath was depleted from Gordon's lungs and he inhaled raggedly to make up for it.

"Well, they *are* running some more tests on several things we seized from Bear's Auto Body. I suppose I could have them take another look at the paint chips."

Gordon's next question caught Vaughn vulnerable. "Are you convinced it was Shannon Marshall?"

Vaughn leaned back and settled onto the edge of his desk. With legs splayed in front of him, the chief studied his feet for a moment. After another crackle from Mother Nature, Vaughn replied, "I'd like to see more evidence. We haven't really secured a crime scene yet and the motive is threadbare."

Gordon Newlon leaned forward and placed his hands on his knees. Deep coughs racked his body and tore themselves from his lungs with a noise that rivaled the outside thunder. Perry went to his father but the old man held up a hand to stop him. With his other hand, he pulled a handkerchief from his hip pocket and wiped the spittle from his lips. To Vaughn, the old man looked just a breath away from death. The entire conversation had taken out of him what days worth of breathing in the oxygen had provided.

Perry knew it too. "Dad, I think that's enough for tonight."

Without the usual argument, Gordon struggled out of the chair and let Perry lead him into the hallway.

Vaughn followed idly, keeping his distance from the pair. Perry opened the outside door and the wind picked it out of his hands instantly. It swung wide open, letting in the slashing rain and blinding flashes of lightening. Despite the inclement weather, Gordon Newlon stopped in his tracks and regarded Vaughn again. "Have them test the paint, Chief."

Vaughn didn't reply. Something in the old man's tone said it wasn't necessary. Even though Vaughn had meticulously combed through the evidence they'd collected and gone over every report from the crime lab, he knew he wouldn't deny the old man's request. He was only human, albeit a good police officer—the death of a child in his town had him distracted. His sister Leigh had been on his mind more than ever lately. It was something he knew he needed to put aside so he could focus on Ryan's murder. He mentally added the paint testing to his list of things to do tomorrow before he visited Shannon Marshall.

Then as quietly as they had entered, Perry and Gordon Newlon made their exit.

The door to the police station sealed shut leaving Vaughn in a deafening quiet surrounded by concrete walls and pictures of long-dead officers that paid the ultimate price to be a policeman.

Later, Vaughn would wonder just how long he had stood there staring at the door but seeing the past.

## Chapter 19

*Wednesday, May 25<sup>th</sup>*

Detective Donnie Parsons, the man Vaughn Dexter referred to as 'Macho Cop', and his partner Detective Alvin Lair stood in front of the interview room's mirror window and smirked at Shannon Marshall. The Rochester police department had brought the suspect in late Tuesday morning and since then the boy hadn't gotten a lot of sleep. Donnie had made quite sure that Shannon's rest had been disrupted several times during the night for mundane details such as height and weight, whether he was left or right handed. The strain of the last couple of days together with the interrupted slumber was taking its toll on the teenager.

Donnie had requested that Shannon be brought to the interview room nearly an hour ago. Although they could have unlocked the handcuffs enclosing the boy's wrists, Donnie told the officer to leave them. Shannon was dressed in the same dirty sleeveless black shirt and jeans he'd worn to bed Saturday night and Donnie was sure they'd served as his uniform the whole week prior. The kid's arms were lean and wiry from working at the auto shop, verging on adulthood. Donnie smoothed the top of this crew cut and watched as Shannon's head dipped once, twice before jerking back to its wobbly position on the boy's bony shoulders.

Donnie nodded to himself. *Almost there.*

Shannon's eyes closed briefly and finally he leaned forward in the uncomfortable, metal chair and placed his cheek on the table.

"That's my cue," Donnie said aloud and snapped his finger in the air. The two detectives left the tiny observation room and entered the interview room as loudly as they could. "Mr. Marshall."

Shannon wrenched his head off the table and regarded the detective with bloodshot eyes that appeared puffy and sour. "Yes?"

"I thought we could have a little chat about Ryan Bentley."

Donnie moved next to Shannon and remained standing so Shannon would have to look directly up at him. The angle was sure to hurt his neck and the harsh fluorescent light from above caused his already-irritated eyes to squint more. Alvin retreated to the far corner of the room, unspeaking.

"I didn't hurt him. He was Jesse's friend." Shannon's voice came out in a croak.

*He could probably use a drink of water, but he ain't smart enough to ask.*

"Yep, that's right," Donnie said, flipping through a folder he'd brought with him. He quickly scanned the entire statement they had gotten from Jesse Lawrence regarding the conversation between Ryan and Shannon at Bear's Auto Body. "Says right here that you got angry at Jesse's friend just the other day. Right before he was found dead in the road."

"I didn't do it. I wouldn't kill anybody." Shannon was already near tears.

"Oh no? What about that tidy little collection that we found in your back yard?" Donnie slammed the folder down on the table in front of him and Shannon jerked in response. His pallor was ghostly pale against his pink swollen eyes. The lack of sleep and intense interrogation were chipping away at him. The detective knew the boy was right on the edge. And if Donnie could just get the kid to confess before he suddenly grew wise and asked for a lawyer, then he'd be a hero for cracking the case wide open.

For a second, Donnie was silent and he perched on the edge of the table, absently picking at some nonexistent spot on his pants. Out of the corner of his eye he watched Alvin cross his arms and lean back against the stark white wall. Knowing the reaction he would get, Donnie didn't even look up as he said, "I've got a cousin named Shannon—But she's a girl."

"Don't," Shannon whispered and then raised his cuffed hands. He tried in vain to cover his ears but when he realized that the steel bracelets wouldn't allow it Shannon put his hands back in his lap.

"Yep," Donnie stood again, "one of those real girly girls, you know? All make-up and dresses." Shannon began rocking back and forth in the chair and was muttering something Donnie couldn't understand. The detective leaned in real close and raised his voice. "Is that what happened, Shannon? Did Ryan Bentley call you a girly girl? Tell you, you have a girl's name? And you got mad— You got real mad, right?"

Shannon rocked faster and muttered louder. Now both detectives could hear the words 'stop it', repeated over and over again. But Donnie didn't stop, he pressed on, pushing his mouth closer to Shannon's ear and talking louder to be heard over the boy's ranting. "That's what happened, right? That little boy was teasing you. Teasing you like they used to in school. Gathered all around you on the playground and made fun of you because you had a girl's name."

"Stop it!" Shannon lurched from his chair knocking it backwards onto the concrete floor. He stood wild-eyed in front of the detective, but Donnie knew it wasn't him that Shannon was seeing. There was nothing more in the boy's vision than schoolyard bullies. "Stop making fun of me. I'm not a sissy. I'm not a girl."

"You killed him didn't you, Shannon? Ryan Bentley said you had a girl's name and so you killed him. You couldn't hurt those kids back in school because you weren't big enough—but you *wanted* to. And now you're bigger. Bigger than Ryan Bentley. He had no right to tease you. And he knew your secrets. Your animals were a secret. Jesse should have never told Ryan about your animals, but he did. And you had to stop him. You had to stop Ryan from telling your secret and teasing you. And you killed him."

"Yes. I mean I don't know. He was teasing me. Jesse told him but I don't know why. Told him about the graves. And he said I had a girl's name and I wanted to hurt them. I did." Shannon was sobbing uncontrollably now. He melted at the knees onto the hard floor and put his face in his hands, hiding him behind a curtain of long, stringy hair.

Donnie turned to Alvin Lair and they exchanged a knowing smile. It said everything. You just had to know which buttons to push. Shannon Marshall was vulnerable. It only took one tiny detail to bring the man to a blubbering baby. He would have confessed to killing the Lindbergh baby just to get Donnie out of his face.

Alvin opened the door to the interview room for his partner and pointed a finger towards the hallway. "Shall we go type up a statement?"

"Yes, we shall," Donnie replied, dramatically.

~~*~~

Vaughn stood in the kitchen of his house and looked out over his back yard through the window above his sink.

*Why*, he wondered, *do they always put the window above the sink?*

Vaughn lived in one of the older houses in a neighborhood called Camelot. It wasn't a glamorous part of town but definitely livable. He had seen and bought the house in the same day and now, six months later, boxes still lined three of the four walls in the dining room area. He didn't plan on entertaining. He didn't even own a dining room table.

The hour wasn't terribly early. For once he'd been able to sleep without being plagued by the dream of his long-dead sister. He couldn't remember the last time he'd been able to shut his eyes and not see her as he last had. She'd been such a beautiful girl. Then a crime of passion had choked the life from her body.

*Dammit. I've got to stop doing this.*

Vaughn moved through the galley kitchen and picked up the phone. He consulted a list of numbers in an address book lying open on the calendar and then punched in the number to the State Police. Two rings, then a voice mumbled, "Crime Lab. This is Jake."

"Jake, this is Chief Vaughn Dexter of the Rochester PD."

"Hey, Chief, what's up? You guys seem to be having quite the busy week."

Jake, whom Vaughn had never met in his life, seemed to be talking through a mouth full of his breakfast.

"Yeah, it's been busy," he replied. "Say Jake, I couldn't get you to run some additional tests on some evidence we had at the Bentley crime scene could I?"

Jake took a moment to finish chewing and swallowed. When he spoke again his voice was clear and intelligible. "Sure thing. What type of tests?"

Vaughn tapped a finger on top of the open address book and the pages made a hollow fluttering sound as they slapped together. "I was hoping you could tell me. Something a little more in depth. Really narrow down where this paint came from."

The lab tech drew in a sharp breath through his teeth and Vaughn knew the answer wouldn't be good. "Problem is we just don't have that sophisticated of equipment. You're better off to have it sent to the FBI for testing."

"Is that something you could do for me?" Vaughn was in a hurry. He was anxious to get to the jail to see Shannon and he was sure Jake wanted to get back to his food.

"Sure thing, Chief. Just give me a couple of days, okay?"

Vaughn agreed, gave the man his cell phone number and disconnected the call. He quickly showered, shaved and dressed in jeans and a rust-colored polo shirt. Without socks he slipped on a pair of boat shoes and headed out of the house. His truck was a couple of years old but he loved it. It turned over smoothly and for a moment he felt like this was just a normal day off for him. He hadn't been able to dress this casually, or even relax, in nearly a week now. The feeling was long overdue.

Vaughn pulled to the stop sign at Route 29 and looked both ways. Straight across the road from his intersection, through the unevenly spaced-wall of trees, Vaughn could see the movement of equipment on the bike trail. The snort and groan of the machines had been quiet all weekend and yesterday's rain had halted the work. Now they were in full swing, moving dirt and clearing the path for the trail that would run all the way into Springfield. It would be a welcome addition to the community. Even he was looking forward to pounding the freshly paved surface when it was completed. It might even bring back a sense of normalcy following the craziness of the past few days. In his mind's eye, he could see mothers pushing strollers and elderly couples walking in matching sweat suits.

Vaughn flipped on the turn signal, looked again down the busy highway and then pulled out into traffic. Unfortunately, there was still some unfinished business at the Sangamon County Jail. Shannon Marshall had been arrested and it was still his job to get to the truth.

~~*~~

Bear loaded the last of the boxes into the trunk of his mother's car and dusted off his hands. "That's it for the lobby and exam room."

Liz stood back from the squat, brick building and admired the exterior. It was not architecturally appealing, or even particularly interesting, but everyone in town knew that behind the walls a great man had worked. The office was set off on a side street not far from Bear's Auto Body. It was located between two other buildings that were larger and open for business. One of which had been constructed after the doors to Doc Lawrence's office had been permanently closed.

The owners of the new building had offered Liz a great deal of money for the property but at the time she hadn't the heart to sell it. It was all her husband Walter loved to do and it was all she had left of him. Besides her children, of course.

Not one to show emotion, Liz patted a bony hand on her son's back and forced a smile. "Thank you, dear. I suppose you'll have the rest of it taken care of before you leave for New York?"

Bear knew that subject was a sore one. His mother wouldn't admit she was upset she hadn't been invited to New York to visit her only daughter. In fact, when Bear mentioned that maybe she should go along, Liz scoffed and claimed she was in no health to be traveling. He wasn't sure what he wanted his mother to say so he made a hasty attempt to steer the subject away from his pending vacation.

"Yeah—the Chief hasn't released the shop as a potential crime scene so I won't be going to work for a couple of days. And really all that's left is the room where dad kept the medical records."

Liz nodded her head, but Bear could feel the strain of their conversation. "Mom, can I ask you why you're getting rid of this place now?"

For a moment, Bear didn't think she'd heard his question, or if she had, she was choosing not to answer. Then at the last moment before Bear spoke again, Liz said, "I guess I felt like I owed it to your father to keep this place as homage to him. He was a great man. We were lucky to have him. Rochester was lucky to have him. I realize now that keeping this office won't keep your father's memory fresh in my mind. He'll be there, no matter what. Besides, I thought with everything going on between you and Nina, you needed to be close to your father. Here you can be."

Bear watched his mother smooth her long red hair back away from her face and get in behind the wheel of her car. He'd never heard his mother say a cross word against his father. And she was right—Bear needed to be close to his father. Needed something constant he could hold onto.

She drove slowly away. The day was beginning to heat up and Bear wiped his brow. He watched his mother's car make it all the way down the street and turn back towards the main part of town.

Back inside his father's old office, the heat was steadily rising and Bear was anxious to finish up the last of the packing. He loaded a couple of miscellaneous items into his arms and was just about to lock up when he remembered the leather-bound books on the shelf in the records room. He backtracked through the tiny lobby and set down the load.

Recalling what a challenge the door was a couple of days ago, Bear wiped any sweat from his palms and grasped the knob with both hands. He gave a mighty yank and to his surprise the door came flying open as if it had been well greased and in working order. Caught off-guard by the sudden laxity of the doorjamb, Bear went stumbling backwards across the room. He barely kept his feet underneath, nearly fell on his butt. Alone in the office, Bear laughed out loud at the spectacle he must have been.

He grabbed the books from the high shelf—there were six in all. He fluttered the pages open on one and saw his father's neat penmanship. Some sort of journal, he figured. It was then that he noticed a tiny wet droplet on one of the outside covers. Sweat was dripping from his chin. The heat in the office was unbearable. He gathered up the books and other items he intended to keep and headed for home. He'd much rather enjoy his father's thoughts and anecdotes in the comfort of his own air conditioning.

## Chapter 20

Cameron Cody finished stapling the summer bulletin board up at the library and stood back to admire his work. Sandpaper for the beach, cellophane for the water.

*Not too bad for this crappy town*, Cameron thought.

So lost in arranging the realistic beach scene, Cameron didn't hear the woman approach him. "Hey, Cameron, how are you?"

Startled by the voice, Cameron jerked and dropped his stapler. It clattered to the floor, the noise reverberating off the walls.

"Jackie. I didn't hear you come in."

Jackie Agans laughed and bent over to pick up the fallen stapler. "Jeez, the way you jumped you'd have thought I was mugging you." Jackie held the stapler out in front of her like a gun and said, "Give me all your money, librarian."

Cameron strained a laugh and took the stapler out of Jackie's hand with a flick of his wrist. "So what brings you to the library today?"

Jackie was short but Cameron didn't stand much taller than her. She made him nervous. If she'd been paying any amount of attention to him, Jackie would have noticed. At the moment she was glancing around. "I brought Amy by. I swear she's practically going to live here this summer."

"Amy's here?" Cameron jolted and spoke perhaps a bit too abruptly. Again, Jackie didn't notice. In Cameron's mind he could see Amy in her pink sweater, Tim Rothwell's hand traveling up under the hem. "And you? You in the market for a good summer read?"

"No. Not me. Never have been much of a reader. I guess Amy got that from her dad. Besides, I'm taking care of Gordon Newlon now, and he doesn't exactly give me any time to sit and read." Jackie fiddled with the strap on her purse.

The underlying look on her face made Cameron begin to sweat. He knew what was coming and he had no idea how to escape the situation.

"Listen, I'm cooking a big dinner tomorrow night. Amy's inviting her boyfriend over to celebrate the last day of school. I thought it might be nice if I had some adult company. What do you say?"

Cameron reached up a hand to push his glasses back up his nose and glanced back to his bulletin board. In the instant before he stooped to gather the cut-up pieces of construction paper and sandpaper, Cameron caught a glimpse of his reflection in the crinkled, metallic cellophane. His image was distorted and twisted. One eye distinctly set above the other, his mouth a smeared slash of red.

He looked like a monster. Like the monster he knew that lived inside of him.

"So Amy and her boyfriend are going to be there?" Cameron asked casually, as he bent to retrieve a scrap of ribbon that had fallen.

"Yeah, but I can only take so much teenager gab before I want to pitch myself into traffic. I thought a nice, grown-up conversation would be, well, nice."

Jackie moved on from her purse strap and shoved her hands into the pockets of her jean shorts. The more Cameron looked at Jackie, the more he could see a more mature version of her daughter. Jackie was lean and toned from lifting her home health patients. Her skin was starting to take on the brown hue of a central Illinois summer and she didn't cover up her face with a lot of unnatural make-up.

Cameron caught his breath.

*I can do this.*

Nervously, he wiped the corner of his mouth, and straightened his glasses. He could tame the monster inside. The other dinner guests would cause a distraction, he speculated. But then again, he'd never been so close to anyone for such a long period of time as the dinner would take. And then, what would happen after the last bite had been consumed; the last piece of dialogue had been spoken? Then what? He wiped a sweaty palm down his shirt.

"I'd love to, Jackie. Thanks. What time should I come by?"

~~*~~

Vaughn entered the county building through the Ninth Street entrance like a normal citizen. He emptied his pockets into a plastic basket held by a bored-looking cop with a large belly, and then walked through the metal detector. Nothing beeped or otherwise set off an alarm to put him under suspicion, so he collected his change and wallet. The hefty cop looked annoyed and trundled back to his post with the empty basket. Vaughn figured that if anyone really dangerous came barreling into the courthouse, the big guy wouldn't be able to chase him down.

Vaughn started down the hallway to the section of the building housing the criminals. He was just passing a bank of elevators when he heard his name. The doors to one of the elevators slowly opened back up and Susan Barnes stepped into the hallway. She was looking exceptionally tall and attractive in a brown pencil skirt and heels. Her white, sleeveless blouse was flowing and clingy all at the same time. She'd wound her long brown hair into a makeshift bun and secured it with a pencil. In her arms she carried a dozen or so files.

"Hey, I *thought* that was you. I was just heading up to my office."

Susan's smile was bright in the dreary building. Around them a multitude of people scampered in and out of the elevators taking care of business. Most were here for court appearances, or family visiting detainees. One woman sobbed into a handkerchief until the doors closed, choking off her breakdown, but Susan never broke eye contact with him. "You shaved off your mustache."

Vaughn rubbed his naked faced and smiled back. "Yep. My summer look."

"What are you doing here today?" Susan adjusted the awkward files in her arms and settled them onto her hip.

"Came to see Shannon Marshall. I thought maybe I could get some answers out of the boy. Make sure he has a lawyer, you know—cop stuff."

"Oh well, I'll walk with you." Susan fell into step beside him and they walked a moment where only their shoes had a conversation with the freshly waxed floor.

"Is it unusual for the arresting officer to take such an interest in the suspect?"

Vaughn shrugged. "I feel for this kid. He has nobody. He was raised by a grandmother that probably hasn't left the house in twenty years. I think it's amazing the boy's even survived this far."

"Do you think he killed Ryan Bentley?"

"I honestly don't know." Vaughn shrugged again. "All our evidence is circumstantial. Unless we can pick up some fingerprints somewhere, this case may not even get off the ground."

"Yeah," Susan agreed, "I wish we could have found that paint at the auto shop. Sure would have made things easier."

"Funny you should mention the paint. I got the strangest visit from our former chief last night. He insisted I have the crime lab test that paint further." Vaughn stuffed his hands in the front pockets of his jeans.

"Did he say why?" Susan asked, perplexed. A piece of brown hair broke free of the pencil and she slipped it behind her ear.

"Just said we were missing something. He's an interesting guy though. Did you ever work with him?"

"No, actually. All of the murders and missing person cases came way before I was coroner. And since I've been in office there hasn't been much going on in that town. Until now." Susan cringed and regarded him apologetically. "Sorry."

Vaughn waved a hand to dismiss her comments. No matter how guilty he felt, Vaughn knew the malevolent occurrences weren't his fault so he attempted to change the subject.

"I imagine you had Larry Fairfax in here."

"Yes. He came in on Monday." Susan shook her head and again had to place the piece of loose hair behind her ear. "Sad, really. He had no one left. No family, no real friends. The state's going to bury him pretty cheaply. I'm not even calling for an autopsy."

They walked again in silence until Vaughn, surprising even himself, turned to Susan. "If you are free, maybe we could grab some lunch after this." Susan's smile widened until he thought it might split her beautiful face in half.

"Yes, of course. That would be great."

Suddenly uncomfortable, Vaughn was relieved when a female police officer rounded the corner and began making her way down the hall towards them. He reached out a hand to stop her and asked where they could find the holding cell for Shannon Marshall.

"Parsons has got him in interrogation."

*Macho Cop.*

"What?" Vaughn didn't wait for an answer but moved quickly down the hall towards the interview rooms. Before he reached them, the sound of laughter quickly changed his direction and he followed it into a messy room of desks.

Detective Parsons held up a Styrofoam cup of coffee in a mock salute. "Chief Dexter, good to see you again."

"What's going on here, Parsons? I heard you had my suspect in interrogation," Vaughn said, loudly.

"Yeah, that's right. And it looks like you are a little late. Your boy confessed just about an hour ago."

The statement caught him off guard and he was sure the expression on his face betrayed him. His tone was incredulous when he finally found his voice to ask, "What? *Confessed?*"

"Yep. Show him the statement, Alvin."

Donnie regarded his partner, who waggled a piece of paper out for Vaughn to see. He snatched the flimsy sheet from between the thumb and finger of the cop and it irritated Vaughn that the other cops in the room found this hilariously funny. They were so full of themselves from cracking the boy, nothing could kill their jovial mood.

Vaughn scanned the document twice. Shannon Marshall's sloppy, childish signature was scrawled at the bottom.

"Where was his lawyer? Did you tell him he could have a lawyer?"

Donnie dropped his head and looked at Vaughn up through his eyelashes. "Don't you mean 'didn't *you* tell him he could have a lawyer?' Your boys arrested him. I believe they are called 'Miranda rights'."

"I want to see him, Parsons. You shouldn't have questioned him without me present or without a lawyer." Vaughn's blood pressure was rising. He couldn't believe the words in black and white on the paper.

*Did Shannon Marshall* really *confess to killing Ryan Bentley?*

"Well, I'm sorry you feel like we stepped on your toes, Chief but really you should be thanking us. We did all the dirty work for you. Don't you want to see that little boy's killer caught?" Again, Donnie regarded him with scrutiny. Vaughn knew if he wasn't careful he was going to give away the fact that he didn't truly believe Shannon killed Ryan.

"I'm just saying without a lawyer this stuff is hard to prove in court. They cry police intimidation or coercion or brutality." He handed the paper back to Alvin Lair. "I still want to see him."

"You got it, Chief." Donnie Parsons set his coffee cup on the only portion of the desk void of paperwork. "Follow me."

The detective's tone was less than respectful. Vaughn didn't like him and sure as hell didn't trust him. He watched the back of Parson's crew-cut hair as they stepped back into the hallway. Waiting outside, Susan Barnes stood with eyebrows raised as if asking, 'what's going on?'

He'd almost forgotten she'd been with him. Vaughn shook his head and apologized to Susan with his eyes. "I've got to take care of this."

Susan tried to keep herself from appearing crushed.

*There'll be no lunch with Vaughn Dexter today.*
"No, I completely understand. Go ahead."

Vaughn left Detective Parsons behind and entered the interview room where Shannon Marshall sat staring at the wall.

"Jesus Christ," the Chief muttered under his breath. *How long have they left him in here?*

Above the table, the boy looked devoid of any life. He sat unblinking as if the cops had taken the very life out of his body with the swoop of his signature. When Vaughn's eyes were drawn under the table, he could see Shannon's right leg jigging at an inconceivable speed.

"Shannon, I'm Chief Vaughn Dexter of the Rochester Police Department. I don't think we have had the pleasure of meeting before." Vaughn moved cautiously into the room. He didn't want to scare the boy whom he feared was on the brink of catatonia. When he received no acknowledgement from the scared young man, he stepped closer to the table. "I know you're scared and confused. I'm here to help you."

"No." The single word was spoken so softly and quickly that Vaughn almost missed it entirely.

"I'm sorry?"

"I don't want your help. I said I did it—now just leave me alone."

Vaughn could tell the boy was angry, but even his words couldn't convey the sentiment on his face. The teen's body was tired and Vaughn knew what little mental capacity Shannon had was fading quickly.

He sat in the chair opposite Shannon in attempt to get the boy to make eye contact with him. "If you don't want my help at least let me contact a lawyer. Someone who will work on your behalf. I saw the statement, Shannon. You do realize that you were confessing to a murder, right?"

Still no movement, save for the restless leg.

"I said I did it, now leave me alone."

"Shannon..."

"*Stop saying my name!*" Shannon screamed at the top of his lungs and leaped from the metal chair. "*Stop it. Get out. Just get out of here.*"

At the first movement of Shannon's body, Vaughn bolted from his chair and prepared for an attack, wishing like hell he hadn't worn his boat shoes. He'd been in fights with criminals before. When he worked the beat in Rockford, it wasn't unusual to have to wrestle with a violent husband on a domestic abuse call or even deal with the wild disregard of a crack-head in the streets. But Shannon didn't assault him. Instead he retreated to the far corner of the room and huddled inside his own skin as if trying to disappear altogether.

Vaughn breathed through his rush of adrenaline and relaxed his tense muscles. The boy was lost to him. Shannon would give him no answers today. To Vaughn, that meant the truth would never be known. He was still not convinced that Shannon Marshall had killed a ten-year-old boy, but he had no way to dispute it. For whatever reason, Shannon had signed the statement. It would hold up in court. The town of Rochester would get their conviction and everyone would nod their head and think 'I knew Shannon Marshall was trouble' or 'it was only a matter of time before that boy snapped'.

Thoughts of wanting to save the boy were met with angry questions about whom he actually *could* save. He hadn't saved his sister, Leigh, because he'd been just a boy himself. Now he was an adult who couldn't save a boy. Shannon would hang, or more accurately, get the death penalty. He'd live out his adulthood among the worst criminals in the state, and that was provided he survived the local jailhouse experience. With Shannon's fragile psyche, Vaughn figured he'd have another suicide on his hands.

The nightmare of the last couple of days was just culminating. There'd be more questions to answer and proof to provided—not only for the recent death, but to show that he could keep the town of Rochester safe. Although he wasn't so sure anymore that he could.

Before he could do anything to rectify the situation with Shannon, his tiny cell phone began ringing. Figuring it to be a waste of breath, Vaughn left the interview room without saying a word. Once in the hallway, he dug the phone out of his pocket and checked the caller id.

*Jim Wagner. The Mayor.*

"Damn you, Parsons," Vaughn muttered and flipped open the handset. "Hello."

"Hey, Vaughn, I just heard the good news," Jim Wagner's voice was cheerful as if he'd just won the lottery, and it disgusted the Chief.

"I wouldn't call it good news, sir. Ryan Bentley is still dead." Vaughn kept his tone even hoping it would bring the mayor back down to a level of seriousness.

"Yes, well, we can't change that but we can bring his killer to justice. And Detective Parsons just called me. A signed confession. Fantastic." Wagner ignored Vaughn's attempt at professionalism and continued his party of one. "I've decided to call a town meeting tonight to let the people know there's no longer a need to worry."

"Sir," Vaughn interrupted, "don't you think it's a bit premature for a town meeting? Maybe when I get back to the station—"

"No, I *don't* think it's premature, Chief Dexter."

The party was over. "I want this town back to normal and I want it done tonight. I'll expect you at the station within the hour."

Vaughn didn't bother to mention that it was his day off. He snapped the phone shut and squeezed it in his palm. He needed to think of something that would cancel the mayor's press conference. Then as suddenly as that thought passed through his mind, he paused. Maybe having the entire town—or the majority of it, anyway—in the same room would actually give him an opportunity he wouldn't get otherwise. Let the mayor bask in his ignorance of the situation. Vaughn had another motive for supporting the town meeting.

He flipped the phone back open and punched in the number for directory assistance. "Rochester, Illinois. Give me the listing for Margaret Yardley."

~~*~~

Susan Barnes moved through the silent corridors of the county building. She knew the hallways like her own home, which was ironic considering she practically lived at her office. The stack of files in her arms had grown heavy and awkward; she shifted them constantly from arm to arm to alleviate the strain on her back and shoulders. The smile she had given Vaughn Dexter had long ago faded from her face.

*What can I do to get that guy to notice me?*

For one brief moment, Susan had seen her opportunity to win Vaughn over. He'd asked her out to lunch without even her slightest hint. That was real progress over the last couple of months. Then that stupid, square-headed cop had gone and made a mess of everything.

*Poor Vaughn, on his day off, had to continually deal with the ignorance and incompetence of the area police.* Susan sighed, he was better than that and he was perfect.

*Perfect for me,* Susan thought. *When's he going to realize we'd be great together?*

She'd waited out in the hallway until the door to the interview room had opened and Vaughn had stepped out with his cell phone. At first she thought he was coming to find her. Coming to tell her he was finished and they'd be able to have lunch after all. Then she heard his side of the conversation.

*A town meeting?*

Perhaps she should make an appearance. She could be there to support him. Susan waited until Vaughn had stormed out of the county building before she made her way back to the bank of elevators. She pouted all the way up to her third floor office. She'd make him see. She just needed one night alone with him to prove it. She knew she wasn't getting any younger. She wanted a family.

And she wanted it with Vaughn Dexter.

## Chapter 21

The village meeting hall was stuffy and hot, and the buzz of conversation permeated the space like the sound of flies on rotten meat. The whole situation was making Vaughn's head spin and his stomach feel sick. Jim Wagner stood behind the podium at the front of the hall and fanned himself with a piece of paper. He was wearing his best suit, navy blue with a smart, powder-blue shirt.

He was grinning from ear-to-ear as if he'd just been awarded the prize pig at the county fair. Behind him, seated in folding metal chairs were Macho Cop, Donnie Parsons, and Donnie's commanding officer, Ronald Weirs. Vaughn had worn his police blues, but these two were not to be outdone. They had every award, pin, patch and crest spit-shined and gleaming proudly.

From the lack of clean breathing air it would seem that every citizen of Rochester had been packed into this tiny space. Vaughn felt a nauseating sense of *déjà vu*. Just yesterday morning he witnessed the same type of gathering at Ryan Bentley's funeral. Now everyone was here to listen as Jim Wagner patted himself on the back for leading his police force towards the direction of the little boy's killer. Jesse Lawrence sat between Bear and Liz except now Jesse's mother Nina was also with them.

Jackie Agans and her daughter Amy were sitting with the Rothwell family. He could see that Amy and the Rothwell's youngest boy, Tim, were discreetly holding hands between the chairs. Gordon Newlon sat in the back row as if that was the furthest his oxygen machine would let him come.

A few other people Vaughn had only met once or twice also piqued his interest. Roger Thompson, a friend of Gordon's, who still owned and operated the grocery store, appeared to be sitting alone. There was also John Tavish, who had sold Bear Lawrence the auto shop. Paula Atterberry delivered everyone's morning paper and two people from the post office were still dressed in their uniforms.

At the head of the room, the mayor motioned for everyone to take their seats and then hushed the assembly with a few taps on the podium's microphone.

"Good evening good people of Rochester…"

Vaughn immediately tuned him out.

Sneaking in the back door was exactly the person he'd been waiting to talk to. Knowing the mayor wouldn't be needing him for anything, he started towards the back of the room when movement caught the corner of his eye. Susan Barnes, dressed in black from head to toe, put up a hand and gave a little wave. Caught off guard, Vaughn almost stopped in mid-stride.

*What's she doing here?*

Vaughn tried to muster a casual wave back before continuing on his path until Cameron Cody stood directly in front of him. The librarian's face took on a panic-stricken expression and Vaughn saw him glance around several times. Cameron's skin turned a purplish-red color.

"Excuse me, Mr. Cody."

At first Cameron seemed confused to Vaughn, as if the words coming out of Vaughn's mouth had been spoken in a language other than English.

Cameron was seeing things differently. Vaughn wasn't here to talk to him. The cop hadn't said 'excuse me' as in 'I-need-to-talk-to-you'. He'd said 'excuse me' as in 'you-are-in-my-way'.

Cameron stumbled over his words and feet as he tried to get out of the police Chief's way, stuttering, "I'm...I'm sorry,"

Finally through the crowd, Vaughn slowly turned back and stared at Cameron. The man's reaction had been odd, hard to read.

*Is there some reason he doesn't want a cop approaching him?*

If Vaughn knew the mayor's speech would last awhile, he would've considered going back and approaching the timid man, but as of now, his time was limited and he needed to get to work. He had to get to Margaret. She might just hold the key to keeping an innocent life from being sacrificed.

He closed in and touched her arm.

"Am I late?" the older woman whispered so she wouldn't disturb the people standing around her.

Vaughn surveyed the crowd briefly, then replied in a hushed voice, "No you're just in time. The mayor just started talking and given that he's a pompous windbag, you have about twenty or thirty minutes. Now just look around. Tell me what you see."

After only a moment, Margaret replied, "There's a lot of fear in this room. The colors are mixing. It's hard to determine everyone's individual aura."

She shook her head and narrowed her eyes as if she could clear the air with the force of her mind.

It was a long shot—a crazy notion—but it was all Vaughn had.

"Just try. I just need to know if you see anyone with a dirty halo. A black one, right? Something that might lead me to the real killer." He looked around too, as if he had the same unusual gift as Margaret.

She stopped and looked up at Vaughn. "Since when did you become such a believer?"

Vaughn looked squarely at her.

"When you told me my aura was the color of guilt. You were right. I've felt guilty for a very long time. My sister was murdered and I wasn't able to save her. The guilt's old and deep and I've never told anyone about it. But you knew."

Vaughn felt a tiny weight lift from his shoulders as he shared the little bit of information about his sister. He watched as Margaret moved her gaze to a place just above his head.

"Perhaps you should talk about your sister more often. The color of guilt just dimmed a little."

"Will you help me?" he pleaded.

The psychic was his last trick in the bag. If Margaret wasn't able to see someone with a dirty halo then surely Shannon would go down for a crime he hadn't committed.

"I'm not helping *you*," Margaret jutted her chin defiantly. She couldn't admit that after all of her bad luck with the police officers of this town, this one seemed to be getting under her skin. "I'm here to help *Shannon*."

That distinction was of no consequence to Vaughn. "Whatever. Just hurry. When the mayor stops talking people are going to start filing out of here and I don't want you seen staring at people like a tiger sizing up a piece of meat."

Vaughn started to push on Margaret's elbow to move her in front of him, until he felt her resist. She pulled her arm from his grasp and faced him.

"I just want this to be clear to you, Chief. Your killer might very well be in this room but dirty halos don't stick around after the fact. Once the deed is done, the halo is gone."

"I know, but I'm hoping our guy's had these murderous thoughts on more than one occasion. If he's killed once, he might be planning to kill again. Then there'd be a halo."

As he spoke, Vaughn detected a note of empathy in Margaret's eyes. She could hear the insistence in his voice, or maybe she could see it in his aura.

Either way he was a made man, so he pushed on. "I need your help. You're Shannon's only hope."

"But what if *I'm* the killer?"

"Margaret—" Vaughn began, giving her a stern look.

"Okay, okay, I'll do it."

With that, Margaret began looking around too, intently surveying her way through the crowd. Each time Vaughn suggested someone, Margaret shook her head and give him a dismissive answer.

"Jackie Agans?" Vaughn asked.

"Lonely." Margaret replied.

"Jim Wagner?"

"Self-involved."

"Bear Lawrence?"

"Deeply saddened."

"Nina Lawrence?"

"Hmmm, she feels guilty like you do."

"Because of the divorce?" Vaughn asked absently.

"I don't know, Chief, there isn't a detailed explanation above everyone's head. Although that *would* make it easier." Margaret retorted smartly.

"Just keep looking. What about Cameron Cody?"

"That man is just angry, angry, angry. He hates the world." Margaret shuddered as if the librarian's cold disposition had a physical effect on her.

"Could he be our killer?" Vaughn asked, as much to himself as to Margaret.

Margaret, feeling compelled to answer, replied, "Could be. A lot of killers are angry."

With every intention of questioning Cameron Cody later, Vaughn couldn't help but satisfy his building curiosity. "What about the woman in black with the long brown hair."

Margaret scanned the crowd, "Ah, yes. *She's* in love."

An eruption of applause came as Jim Wagner concluded his speech with flare and flamboyance. He'd announced Shannon Marshall's confession. Spoon-fed it to the crowd, and they swallowed it down after clinking their glasses in cheers.

People started moving towards the exit and Vaughn and Margaret retreated to a more secluded corner of the hall.

"So there wasn't anyone in the room with a dirty halo?" Vaughn asked with just a shred of hope left.

"Oh, there was one person," Margaret said unflinchingly.

Vaughn stared at the woman as if she'd gone mad. "Well? Who is it?"

"Gordon Newlon."

Vaughn closed his eyes and let a sharp breath out through his nose. "I have a hard time believing that a man connected to an oxygen tank could have killed a ten-year-old boy and then dragged his body out onto the highway."

"Oh I highly doubt he's your killer either, Chief Dexter. The dirty halo Gordon wears is for his own impending death. It won't be long until the lung cancer takes him," Margaret said, sadly. Her face had taken on a drawn, worn look. "Would *you* want to know, Chief?"

"Know what?" Vaughn frowned.

"If you were going to die, would you want to know?"

It took a moment for him to realize what a burden Margaret's gift must be. To be able to see that someone's life was about to end would be an endless struggle between wanting to tell them and not ever wanting them to know.

Her eyes took on a glassy look as she said, "There might be something Gordon wants his son to know before he dies. Or maybe Perry would like to spend more time with his father. It could make all the difference in the way they live out the last couple days of Gordon's life."

"No, Vaughn replied firmly, "I wouldn't want to know."

~~*~~

Bear and Nina Lawrence stood in an awkward silence outside of the municipal complex while Jesse hugged his grandmother. Nina called out, "Let's go, Jesse."

Liz bent to the child. "I'll see you on Friday, okay kiddo? And then we'll get you all ready to go visit your Aunt Kat in New York. That'll be fun won't it?"

"Yeah, I guess," Jesse mumbled half-heartedly.

Liz stood to her full height and ruffled Jesse's auburn hair playfully, but the expression on her face was full of worry. The look matched that of her son, Bear. He grabbed Jesse in a tight hug and whispered into his ear. "This week'll fly by. I'll see you on Friday, okay?"

"I could just stay with you, Dad. Stay with you until we leave."

Bear glanced around to make sure Nina wasn't in hearing distance and was thankful to see his mother had commanded her attention for the moment. "Don't you want to spend some time with your mom before we leave on vacation?"

"No, Dad, I just want to stay with you. Or you could come home. Please come home, Dad."

Jesse was on the verge of tears and it was ripping the very heart from Bear's chest. If he didn't leave now he wasn't sure it would be physically possible to do so. He knew the divorce was hurting Jesse, but he knew in the long run it was the best move for everyone. He couldn't stay with Nina; it would kill them both.

Bear stood with Liz as Nina took Jesse's reluctant hand and led him to her car.

"I don't know how much more of this I can take."

Liz reached out a hand and placed it on her son's arm. "Maybe it's time we call a lawyer. Look into some sort of custody."

"Mom, you know I can't afford that. Nina either. That's why we're trying to figure things out on our own."

"Well I'm not worried about Nina—I'm worried about you and Jesse. If Jesse wants to live with you then we need to do something about it. I have some money stashed away and I think this is the perfect time to get it out and spend it."

Liz gave her son a bright smile in the dark of the parking lot.

"Mom, I couldn't."

"Oh yes you can—and you will. Now let's go home."

Bear felt something in his chest break loose and he fought his own urge to tear up. He gave his mother a hug. Things were starting to look up. Now that Ryan's funeral was over and his murder had been solved, Jesse could begin the healing process. He'd fight Nina for custody. He'd win, which would obviously make Jesse even happier. And they were about to go visit his sister, Katrina, whom he'd idolized his entire life. He was so proud of her. Kat had set her sights higher than this town and she'd been successful at achieving what she wanted. Bear couldn't wait to see her and he couldn't wait for Kat to see Jesse.

Yes, things were definitely looking up.

~~*~~

Cameron Cody slammed the door to his house behind him and tried to calm his rapid breathing. The Chief of Police had been coming right at him. Staring at him as if Vaughn could see right through him.

*And what if he can? What if Vaughn Dexter can see right into my soul? Will he know what I'm thinking? What's been festering in my heart all these years?*

He stumbled through the house, barely making it to the bathroom before vomiting in the toilet.

Cameron dry heaved until he thought his very insides would come out. Afterwards, he went to the sink and rinsed his mouth out with water. Then he removed his glasses to rub his eyes. When he finally felt the sick feeling in his stomach subside, Cameron looked up and stared into his reflection. It was fuzzy at the edges without his prescription glasses. He shouldn't have come back here to this town. Not after losing his job at PORTA High School. Everyone had speculated about him, started rumors about him and even avoided him. But no one knew the truth.

Maybe he should cancel his dinner plans for tomorrow night with Jackie Agans. He needed to keep a low profile. Especially if Vaughn Dexter was on to him. But then again, maybe he *should* go. He could act normal, as if nothing was wrong. Maybe that would take the Chief's suspicion off of him.

And Jackie Agans was a nice lady. Maybe if he just had a woman in his life, any woman, the monster would be satisfied. Cameron looked at himself in the mirror again and saw Vaughn Dexter bearing down on him.

*Then again maybe not.*

~~*~~

"Did you cancel the poker game?"

Gordon Newlon settled into his recliner with a glass of ice tea and a fresh bottle of oxygen. They'd been home from the town meeting now for a little over an hour. Gordon tried to find a comfortable spot in the chair and then took as deep a breath as the cancerous cells would allow. It was then that he realized comfort was no longer an option.

"Yeah," Perry replied tiredly, twisting the top off a bottle of beer and flopping down on the couch close to his dad, "Figured no one would feel like getting out this weekend. Maybe next Saturday. Although I heard Bear's taking his boy to New York to visit his sister Katrina. You remember her, Dad?"

"Oh yeah, pretty girl, real bright red hair. Your mother always said she'd wished you had red hair."

"But neither you or mom have red hair. Where did she expect me to get it?" Perry chuckled at the memory of his mother.

Gordon shrugged. "You know how your mother was. She was always pulling that kind of thing out of a hat."

The two Newlon's sipped their drinks in silence for a moment and Perry worried about how quiet the house would be when his father finally died. For now he needed noise. He took another drink before admitting, "I was thinking about calling Joyce."

Gordon barked a cough and Perry couldn't tell if it was necessary or if the old man was just stalling. Finally his father said, "Yeah, that's probably a good idea."

"I miss her, Dad. I was a fool to drive her away." Perry leaned up and hung his head in his hands between his knees.

"I know what you mean." Gordon's voice was practically a whisper. "I spent a lot of time on the job when you were little. I used to think your mother must have been a saint to put up with me."

Perry raised his head. He'd never heard his father sound so sentimental about his wife.

"I think the only thing that kept her sane was you, Perry. You were a lifesaver for both of us. I probably never told you this before but I was so proud the day you became a cop. I know I wasn't the best father but when you followed in my footsteps I could have burst with pride."

Gordon's eyes had taken on a misty, wistful look and Perry wasn't sure if maybe he'd become delirious from the fresh oxygen.

"Were you disappointed when they passed over me for chief?" Perry sniffed.

Gordon shook his head. "Hell no. I've no doubt you would have been better than me. You did a great job in those couple of months you was acting chief."

"Thanks," Perry had to stop and clear his throat, "thanks, Dad."

"So." And just like that the moment was over. Another agonizing drag from the oxygen tube.

Then, "Did Vaughn call about the paint?"

Perry blinked and cleared his throat again. "Not sure. I didn't get a chance to talk to him tonight. He was talking to Margaret Yardley at the press conference."

Gordon nodded his head to save his precious breath. He'd talked enough for one night. He knew the paint chips would open up new doors in the investigation of Ryan Bentley's murder. No matter what Jim Wagner wanted to believe. Even though the mayor had told the town Shannon Marshall was guilty, the former chief just couldn't quite accept it. Forensic science was a wonderful thing. And he was afraid if they'd had that same technology twenty years ago when Marie Fairfax had been killed, Rochester would be a different place today.

They'd never truly solved the girl's murder and finally, after months of no leads and no evidence to go on, Gordon had given the town what they wanted.

A random act of violence.

But times were different back then. *Simpler*.

Three years later when Mandy Getz had disappeared, Gordon prayed they'd never even find a body. Her parents were quick to assume she'd just run away. Although Gordon didn't want to admit it, his police force didn't exactly break the time clock looking for the missing girl. Nobody wanted there to be a killer in their town. It was just too unbearable. People moved to Rochester to be safe.

A couple of years later, Gordon had heard about a girl who'd been found dead about a year after Marie Fairfax was killed. She was from Mechanicsburg—just down the road from Rochester, but most decidedly out of Gordon's police jurisdiction.

And one from Edinburg who showed up dead about five years after Mandy Getz's disappearing act.

Gordon didn't know how many crimes he could sweep under the rug. He was thankful when the malicious behavior just suddenly stopped. He heard no more tales at the coffee shop of beautiful young teenagers being massacred, or that had vanished. And he stopped worrying about being such an inadequate Chief of Police. After a decade of speeding tickets and otherwise ordinary police business, he'd felt it was time to retire.

Gordon remembered thinking the new chief had been lucky. The first unnatural death in Rochester in nearly twenty-one years, not counting the missing Getz girl, had been a simple hit-'n-run. Then Shannon Marshall confessed to the boy's murder. The whole situation was spiraling out of control and he figured Vaughn Dexter was in the same situation he'd found himself in so many years ago. Vaughn was looking for a killer who seemed to be a phantom. But Gordon had a feeling Vaughn wouldn't give up as easily as he'd done.

Maybe that's why he'd gone to the new chief's office.

*Am I feeling guilty for not catching Marie's murderer? Is the lung cancer a nasty form of revenge?*

Now at the hour of his death, Gordon felt the need to make the situation right. He'd no doubt that his son, Perry, would have been a good chief. Perry had always been conscientious and caring. More like his mother, Esther, than himself.

Perry caught his dad staring at him out of the corner of his eye. "Want me to see if there's a ball game on?"

"No," Gordon breathed deeply through the tubes in his nose, "Go call Joyce."

## Chapter 22

"Bear, um, I need to ask you to come with me." The young police officer was nervous. He squirmed under the harsh illumination of the porch light as if he were not the one in the police officer's uniform. Bear pushed the screen door completely open and squinted at Brendon Loveland.

"It's nearly eleven o'clock. Can't this wait?"

Brendon had been a part of the Rochester Police Department for only two months and he wasn't here because there was a problem with Bear, himself, but all be damned if the man wasn't intimidating him. "No, sir, it can't."

"What's this all about, Brendon? Does the chief need to get into the shop again?"

Brendon stepped back as Bear passed across the threshold and let the screen door bang behind him. With downcast eyes, the officer turned his hat in a nervous circle in his hands and glanced repeatedly at the ground. He really didn't want to be the one to tell Bear what was happening across town but the Chief had sent him. Brendon was determined to prove his abilities. The call had come in about forty minutes ago. Since then a rush of Rochester Police and rescue personnel had been summoned from their beds to attend to the escalating situation.

"I'm not at liberty to divulge information at this time..." Brendon began the rehearsed speech he'd practiced in the car, before Bear interrupted him.

"Brendon, please, this is *me*. I stuffed you in a locker after the Homecoming game the year you were a Freshman and I was a Senior. Tell me what's going on."

Brendon took a deep breath. What would it hurt? Bear would find out soon enough about the situation developing at Nina's house. "There's a problem with Jesse."

Bear stood dumbfounded. The thought had never even occurred to him that something might be wrong with Jesse. He'd just assumed that Brendon was here for him. Of course, he had no idea why but nonetheless, Jesse had never entered his mind. Now panic began to rise in Bear's body and an uncontrollable shaking took over his usual robust frame. He'd watched Nina pull out of the municipal complex parking lot just hours ago and everything was fine. Now all he could think about was Ryan Bentley lying cold in the street. "Oh God, what's wrong? Is he all right?"

Brendon had no idea how to approach the question. Jesse wasn't hurt but things were definitely not all right. "Get in the car, Bear. The faster we get over to Nina's the sooner this can all be over."

For now that seemed to satisfy Bear and, without a backward glance, he started for the police officer's car. Brendon motioned for the distraught father to join him in the front seat and they began their drive. The distance between the two houses wasn't great but the roads seemed to stretch out in front of them. He was surprised that during the course of the trek, Bear never uttered a word. He could hear the man taking in great breaths and exhaling forcefully through his nose almost in effort to keep from vomiting. The officer squinted through the windshield and then realized that all of Bear's heavy breathing was causing the glass to go opaque. He reached down quickly and flipped on the defroster.

From the moment they turned onto the street where Bear had lived only six short months ago, they could see the buzz of something happening. Several police cars were lined up in front of the house and someone had strung that obnoxious yellow police barrier tape from the mailbox to a tiny tree, bending under the weight of the pull. With Bear ahead of Brendon, they shouldered their way through the gathering crowd and stepped onto the front lawn. Behind him, Bear heard someone say "First the Bentley boy and now this. *Our* town has never seen so much tragedy."

The very sound of that sentence threatened to make Bear physically ill but he refused to react until he'd discovered what was going on inside the house. Every light was ablaze, spilling out through the windows into the moonless night to meet up with the pulsing strobes of the police cars. The harshness was blinding and he nearly collided with the chief of police as he stumbled towards the small front stoop.

~~*~~

Vaughn Dexter reached out and grabbed Bear's arm as he slammed towards the house. From the look on his face, Vaughn could tell that Bear was confused and frightened at what he might find. Bear clutched at him like a drowning man and pleaded, "Chief, what's going on in there? Is it my boy? Is he all right?"

Vaughn nodded his head. "He's not hurt, Bear. Calm down. We called you over because Jesse was asking for you."

More confusion clouded Bear's expression. "What is it? Is it Nina?"

"Before you go in there's something I want you to know," Vaughn said, ignoring Bear's questions. "Jesse's in trouble. He's holding a gun on himself."

"*What?*" Bear nearly laughed out loud. What the chief was saying was ridiculous. Incredulous really. What in the world was a ten-year-old boy doing with a gun pointed at himself?

*And where the hell is Nina?*

"Do you have any idea where he could have gotten the gun?" Vaughn's voice rose above the confusion in Bear's head. At first he shook it, having no idea where the gun had come from, but Bear remembered Nina saying, 'You still have things here at the house that you should probably pick up someday. I've tried to clean everything out as best I could".

"Wait, no, it could be mine. I bought a gun a couple of years ago for protection. I never took it when I moved out."

Vaughn was nodding in understanding but the movement, coupled with the throbbing red and blue lights, was making Bear even more nauseous. Somewhere behind the house, Bear could hear Sunshine barking at the chaos.

"Okay, let's go get Jesse." Vaughn put a hand on Bear's shoulder and steered him into the house.

Bear saw that there were men dressed in black suits with large automatic weapons lining the interior of the living room and hallway. Surely they weren't here to harm Jesse, but why were they here? And how could this have been going on across town while Bear sat in his father's old recliner watching a rerun of Seinfeld?

Bear stepped to the threshold of Jesse's bedroom and the scene within nearly shattered his hold on sanity. Nina was sitting cross-legged on the bed wearing nothing but a t-shirt and white cotton panties. The bed covers had been torn completely from atop the bed and were lying in a heap on the floor. Her face was as white as paste and smeared with tears and snot, still running from her eyes and nose. She'd pushed her black hair away from her face but a strand had matted itself to her cheek. In her left hand, Nina clutched the handset of the cordless phone. An angry red light on the keypad was an indication that the phone was on. If Bear listened close enough, he could hear the steady beeping of a phone left off the hook for too long.

Although disturbing in appearance, Nina was no match for Jesse's anger. He stood to the right of the bed, in between Bear and Nina. He appeared smaller than his normal self, his shoulders hunched. He was so much different than just a few hours ago when Bear had seen him.

Jesse was dressed in his boxers and a t-shirt from one of his summer baseball leagues. On the front were the words 'Bear's Auto Body' and on the back across the shoulders their last name was spelled out over the number eleven. The name 'Lawrence' was long on such a small shirt and had to curve in a semi-circle from shoulder blade to shoulder blade. The little boy's hair was disheveled and stood up in a spot above his right ear. At the angle from where Bear stood, he couldn't see the boy's face and could almost believe that what the chief had said was a lie. But when Jesse shifted his stance, Bear got his first glimpse of the boy's outstretched arm. In Jesse's hand was the gun. It was steady and true, pointed right at his own chest.

Bear opened his mouth but was afraid nothing would come out when he tried to talk. He cleared his throat gently so as not to startle the boy, then softly said, "Jess? It's Dad. Did you need to see me?"

At first he didn't think his son had heard him, but slowly the boy took his eyes from Nina and turned it in Bear's direction. The gun never wavered.

"Dad?" Jesse asked, as if at first he didn't recognize the man he resembled so much. Until now, the boy's face had been stoic but when he saw Bear, tears welled up and spilled over his lower lids. Jesse made no effort to wipe them away. Nina sat frozen on the bed, crying silently—she hadn't looked up at the sound of Bear's voice. For the moment, Bear didn't acknowledge her. "I can't live here anymore, Dad. I want to live with you. Can we go to Grandma's now?"

"Well, I'm sure that can be arranged, Jesse, but first I think they're going to want you to hand me the gun."

"I can't," Jesse stated matter-of-factly and turned his attention back towards Nina.

Sweat dripped down Bear's temples. He was afraid he'd cut off his vital communication with his son. He fumbled over what to say next. "Just because you don't want to live here anymore doesn't mean you have to hurt yourself. I'm sure Mom would let you come stay with us for awhile. Isn't that right, Nina?"

"No, she won't," Jesse's voice raised several notches in volume and Bear could feel the SWAT team tensing up behind him. They'd be forced to act if he wasn't able to gain control of this situation.

Vaughn kept post just outside the bedroom door in the hallway. He was sure that letting Bear talk to Jesse would be more effective than having a hostage negotiator come in. So far things were not going as easily as he'd hoped.

"Okay, okay," Bear held out his hand in effort to calm Jesse, "let's not talk about mom. Let's talk about us. Okay? Remember when we went fishing last summer on Sangchris Lake? That was fun, huh? Just you and me, camping and fishing."

Bear watched Jesse slowly turn back towards him, small shoulders shaking under the sobs.

"We could plan another trip for this summer. Make it a tradition, you know?"

"I remember that trip," Jesse's whisper was barely audible, "You said that Ryan could come too, but at the last minute he got sick."

"That's right," Bear silently kicked himself for not remembering. He knew Jesse's wounds were still fresh from losing his best friend. They'd attended Ryan's funeral only a day ago. Bear clenched his fists and wasn't surprised to find them wet with sweat. He realized that sweat was trickling slowly down the sides of his body. It dripped off his jawbone onto the shoulder of his shirt. "Well, buddy, what do you say? Why don't you put the gun down and we can go start planning another fishing trip?"

Jesse screamed in Nina's direction. "Ryan won't be able to go this year either because he's dead! He's never going to get to go and it's all *your* fault!"

For a moment took the gun off of his tiny body and shook it in her face. She cowered lower into herself and whimpered.

"No, Jesse, don't," Bear shouted, involuntarily taking a step into the room, but Vaughn jerked him back by his belt. "It isn't your mom's fault that Ryan died, Jesse. That was a terrible accident. It was nobody's fault."

"Yes, it was, Dad, you just don't know. You don't know," Jesse said, loudly. He reached up his free hand and wiped the streaming tears from his eyes.

Behind Bear, Vaughn spoke up. "Jesse, its Chief Dexter. I did what you asked. I went and got your dad. Now I need you to help me, okay?"

No reply came from the boy but Vaughn pressed on. "Maybe there's something you need to tell us about the night Ryan died? Something that maybe you haven't told us yet?" Vaughn could feel the sideways stare from Bear Lawrence. He kept his gaze trained on the boy.

"No," Jesse shook his head violently, "I don't want to tell you anything."

"Jesse, if you know something that could help the policemen you need to tell them." Bear's anxiety level was creeping towards an all-time high. They knew Ryan hadn't been hit by Larry Fairfax's car. Even Bear had been called in for questioning after Ryan had been found dead. He should have been safe in bed at the Lawrence house. But he wasn't. Why? Now, in the public eye, Shannon Marshall had been tried and convicted. Could Jesse have seen who hurt Ryan? That could mean that Jesse had been in danger too. Bear stared hard at Nina. Did *she* know the real story?

"Jesse, do you hear me?" Bear was surprised that his voice had taken on an air of authority.

"I wanted to tell you, Dad. I've been trying to tell you. But I just can't. I don't want to say."

"Why not, Jesse? You can tell me. You can tell me anything. I'm sorry I haven't been listening much lately but I'm here now. Tell me."

"It's too late," Jesse replied, "I told Ryan and he died. I don't want you to die too, Dad."

"Nothing's going to happen to me, son. I promise."

The boy wept openly now. He wiped at his nose with the back of his hand and took a couple of deep breaths. He'd moved towards the bedside table so he could keep his mother and his father in view at the same time. Now Jesse Lawrence closed his eyes and removed his finger from the trigger.

Vaughn knew this would be the moment to take back control of the situation but they may never hear what Jesse was about to say. The chief feared that tapping this ten-year-old boy's knowledge might be the only chance they had to solve the murder of Ryan Bentley.

Jesse's voice was tiny and his face was pinched with pain. Not physical pain, but the kind buried deep inside every one of us. Pain that should never be felt by a ten-year-old.

"We snuck out that night," he started, "We went out the window and climbed down the TV tower. We just wanted to have an adventure. We just wanted to check out the new bike trail. Are you mad?"

Bear was caught off guard by the sudden question and actually huffed a laugh. "Mad that you snuck out? Yeah, a little."

A ghost of a smile passed over Jesse's lips and he continued, "There were some machines there. You know, left by the workers. We thought it would be cool to sit up on the cab and look at the stars."

After a moment of silence, Vaughn quietly asked, "Is that where you told him... your secret?"

Bear watched as a tear slide out from Jesse's closed left eye and glistened a wet trail down the boy's cheek. He had no idea what secret Vaughn could be referring to but obviously Jesse did. He nodded his head slowly and frowned. "I just couldn't keep it to myself and Ryan was my best friend. I thought he'd understand."

"What is it, Jesse?" Bear begged his son to reveal what dark tale he held secret. His insides felt as if they'd gone liquid with anticipation.

The silence that permeated the room for several moments felt tangible.

"I told him that someone touches me," Jesse blurted the words out and then popped open his eyes to gauge the reaction from Bear. When he saw none on his father's face, he continued. "They touch me in a bad way. In places that I don't want them to touch."

It seemed the air in the room was being sucked out. Bear's ears were ringing and he felt like he was hearing Jesse from underwater.

*Am I hearing the boy right? Is someone abusing my son?*

"Was it Shannon Marshall, Jesse?" Vaughn asked into the room.

"No," Jesse stared directly at the chief and then swung around to face his mother, "it was her."

Bear might have collapsed if he hadn't felt Vaughn take a strong hold on his belt. He shifted his gaze back and forth between his son and wife. He didn't want to believe what he was hearing. Everything had taken on the quality of slow motion. The chief of police was visibly stunned.

Bear's voice quivered with accusation. "What's he saying, Nina? What have you done to him?" He wanted to storm into the room and grab her around the neck and shake the answers out of her. During the course of Jesse's story, Nina had pulled her legs up to her chest and put her forehead onto her knees. Her damp black hair had fallen forward to cover what was left of her face and she sat still as a statue.

Jesse continued. "She used to come into my room on Sunday nights and lay with me. I don't know why. I didn't ask her too."

Jesse had been a distraught little boy sobbing uncontrollably. Now that he was able to speak the truth at last, he was in complete control of his emotions. Wise beyond his years and relieved to be free of the hideous secret he'd held inside. "Then she started touching me. Telling me that if I loved her I'd let her do it and that it was okay if I touched her. I didn't want to, Dad, she made me."

Bear couldn't speak but nodded his head to let the boy know he understood.

"Only on Sundays though. Every Sunday since you moved out."

Bear found his voice. "That's why you always asked to stay with me after our weekend was over. Because it was Sunday and you didn't want to come back here."

"She always said I couldn't stay with you because it was a school night but that wasn't the reason. And now school's over but..." Jesse's voice trailed off and he hung his head. His arm, tired of holding the gun, dropped to his side and the weapon slid slowly from his hand and thudded to the floor. Bear shook free of Vaughn's grip and went to his child. He gathered the boy's small frame in his mighty arms and held on tightly. With his foot he pushed the pistol toward the police chief. Bear felt Jesse return the hug and wondered if maybe the damage Nina had done to their son could somehow be undone.

Vaughn stooped and retrieved the handgun, passing it to one of his officers as the cops began swarming around the bed. Perry Newlon grabbed Nina's arm above the elbow and helped her off the bed while Brendon Loveland left to rifle through Nina's bedroom closet. He came back almost immediately with a pair of jeans for the woman to slip into. Vaughn moved to her side once she finished dressing and produced a pair of handcuffs. It wasn't until he began reading her the Miranda rights that Nina began crying again.

Perry and Brendon took her out of the house while Bear shouted behind them:

"How could you, Nina? Your own son, for Christ's sake! How could you?"

~~*~~

Bear sat on the couch holding his son tightly wrapped in a blanket one of the faceless medical technicians had produced. Several of them were crouched in front of the boy taking his vitals and asking him questions. After the ordeal, Jesse's entire body had seemed to deflate and he lay limp against his dad, not speaking.

Perry Newlon entered through the front door and took a spot on the opposite end of the couch from Bear. "Bear, man, I don't know what to say. I'm sorry all of this is happening."

Bear stroked the top of his son's head, he felt clammy and sweaty and he was in fear that Jesse was in shock. "How couldn't I've seen this?"

"Don't beat yourself up. You couldn't possibly have known," Perry said, supportively.

"Yeah, but all the signs were there. Jesse was losing weight and his grades were dropping. He even tried to talk to me several times over the past week. I just kept thinking that all of this was because of the separation." Bear shook his head and frowned.

"You couldn't have known," Perry repeated.

Behind him, the chief spoke. "I am going to have Jesse transported to the hospital. He needs to be checked out and he needs to get some rest."

When Bear started to protest, Vaughn held up his hand. "Don't forget Jesse was holding a gun on himself, Bear. He was desperate. He maybe never intended to pull the trigger but his mother was abusing him. If anything he's going to need to talk to a mental health professional."

"Yeah, you're right—but I'm going with him," Bear insisted as the ambulance driver brought in a stretcher.

Jesse was in near catatonia as Bear lifted his tiny body onto the stiff white sheets, then watched as a woman pulled a heavy blanket up to the boy's chin and strapped him in for safety. Bear waited until she'd wheeled Jesse towards the ambulance and was out of earshot. "What's going to happen to Nina?"

"We're going to take her to the station for questioning. Then transport her up to the Sangamon

County jail for an arraignment and to formally charge her." Vaughn explained as gently as he could. "If what Jesse says is true, Nina could be going away for a very long time."

Unable to control himself any longer, Bear exploded into sobs and fits of anger. "My God, she's his *mother!* What kind of mother does this to her child? Was it me? Was she trying to get back at me? I could kill her for what she did. How's Jesse ever going to be the same again? First Ryan and now this. Everything's been taken from him. He's got no childhood left!"

"We're going to get him some help, Bear. We're going to help him get through this. He has you and his grandmother. That's what he needs right now. Jesse needs you to be strong and to show him that he can have a normal life."

Vaughn watched as Bear nodded and pulled in a deep breath.

Bear was visibly distraught when he spoke. "You're right. Thanks Vaughn. It's just enough to make you crazy, you know?" Bear reached out to shake Vaughn's hand and then disappeared out the front door and into the back of the ambulance.

Vaughn stood in the open foyer as the medical vehicle drove back out onto the street and flipped on the lights. No siren.

Again, the Chief felt an overwhelming sense of *déjà vu*. Just a few days ago, they'd watched an ambulance take Ryan Bentley's lifeless body to the morgue. But tonight the little boy inside could be saved. They'd pull him back from the edge of an abyss that no child should ever have to look down into. No one should have to be saved from their own mother.

# Chapter 23

### Thursday, May 26<sup>th</sup>

$A$nother sleepless night of paperwork and loose ends had left Vaughn Dexter feeling like a tangled knot of pain and emotions. He reached up and rubbed the back of his neck and stretched through a cramp threatening to cripple him. He hadn't gotten home until well after two o'clock. Nina Lawrence had proved to be quite a piece of work. She had cried nonstop from the moment Brendon and Perry brought her back to the station until he ordered her to be taken up to the County jail.

Through her sobs, Nina had insisted that she hadn't hurt Jesse but he had to wonder if she really knew the reality of what she was being accused. Maybe she didn't think that what she was doing was hurting the boy. The entire situation had reaffirmed for him another reason not to get romantically involved with anyone. Just another explanation as to why he wouldn't knowingly bring a child into this world. There was too much suffering and pain as it was.

*Did I really ask Susan Barnes out yesterday?*

Vaughn groaned and threw an arm over his eyes.

After tossing and turning in his bed for a couple more minutes, restlessness drove him into the kitchen.

The clock on the microwave said ten till seven—he'd been home long enough. There'd be an endless list of follow-up things to do at the station and he was determined to make it up to the jail before Macho Cop had any more time to question yet another one of his suspects. Not that Nina wouldn't deserve the type of treatment that particular detective dished out.

Before he had the chance to think another thought, he heard his cell phone ringing from somewhere deep inside the otherwise silent house. Quickly Vaughn retraced his steps and found the pants he'd shed hours ago on the floor in the bathroom at the end of the hall. He dug into the front pocket and produced the still ringing phone. The number didn't look familiar to him but he flipped open the small silver handset. "Hello."

"Chief Dexter?"

The male voice didn't sound any more familiar than the unknown number. "Yes."

"It's Jake—from the crime lab."

It took a moment to put the name and the place together. But even after realizing who he was talking to, he was still confused. "Jake. I wasn't expecting to hear from you for a couple of days."

"Yeah, well you called pretty early yesterday and I have a certain, shall we say, 'lady friend' over at the FBI lab." Vaughn could tell Jake had a smile on his face even over the phone line.

"Well let me just grab a pen and let me know what you've got, okay?" Vaughn dug through a drawer on the end of his kitchen counter and then scribbled a circle of ink on an envelope to make sure the pen worked. Jake waited patiently, singing a tune by ACDC under his breath. "All right what have you got for me?"

"Seems the paint was pretty easy to isolate. It's manufactured for a specific company, used exclusively on their equipment," Jake said.

*Equipment?*

"What company?" Vaughn urged, not really needing or wanting the full technical explanation.

Jake continued as if he hadn't spoken. "It makes sense with the 15w40 oil you found too..."

"Jake," Vaughn said through clenched teeth.

"What? Oh right, you've probably seen it a million times. The color's actually *called* 'Cat Yellow'."

"Caterpillar," Vaughn said, answering his own question from moments ago, "The paint was from a piece of Caterpillar equipment."

A scene flashed before Vaughn's eyes. It was yesterday and he was about to turn onto Route 29. Across the street, through the trees he'd seen the heavy equipment contracted by the Illinois Department of Transportation to clear the trees from the land where the bike trail was being built. Two of the machines had been yellow.

Cat Yellow.

In his mind, Vaughn heard Jesse Lawrence say, *"There were some machines there. You know, left by the workers. We thought it would be cool to sit up on the cab and look at the stars."*

"Dammit," Vaughn swore and then realized he was still on the phone with the lab technician. "Thanks Jake. I really appreciate your, um, lady friend, getting to this so quickly."

~~*~~

Vaughn abandoned all ideas of a decent breakfast. He quickly showered and dressed in his uniform then jumped into his truck. He was torn between going to the county building and the hospital. If Jesse had been on the trail that night with Ryan, he might have seen more than he was telling. Maybe he was scared. Maybe he'd left before anything had happened to Ryan. Whatever the truth was, he wanted it and he wanted it *now*.

He drove recklessly towards the highway and dialed his phone with one eye on the road.

"Mike, I want you to call the mayor. Have him get a hold of someone at the Department of Transportation who's in charge of the trail and let them know we're securing it as a crime scene. Send Perry or Phil out to the trail and have the construction crew halt work on the bike path. Tell them to take possession of any and all machinery. I want them collecting and processing anything they think might be evidence."

"Should I let the mayor know where you are?" Mike Simms' voice was professional on the other end of the line.

"You can tell him I'm on my way to the hospital to question a possible witness. I should be back in a couple of hours. I want to be kept informed on the progress at the trail. Oh and Mike—call the county jail and have Shannon Marshall put into isolation. I think we might just have our killer by the end of the day."

~~*~~

The emergency room at Memorial Medical Center was quieter than Vaughn had expected. Upon passing through the automatic doors, he knew he'd commanded the attention of the triage nurse. She reached up to smooth the hours of exhaustive work out of her hair and tried in vain to push the Harlequin romance paperback she'd been reading under a pile of folders.

At this relatively early hour only three chairs in the waiting room were filled. In one a young man in his early twenties was holding a bloody rag under his swollen nose. To his left a man slightly older than Vaughn was pinning back the hair of a woman while she dry-heaved into a trashcan.

Vaughn removed his hat and continued toward the nurse.

"A boy was brought in last night by ambulance. Jesse Lawrence."

The edge in the policeman's tone froze the smile on the nurse's lips and she quickly turned to her computer. Vaughn noticed the same smile on her employee badge next to the name 'Sarah'.

After several taps on the keyboard, Nurse Sarah made eye contact with him. "He's still in room sixteen. They haven't been able to get him a room on the psych ward yet." Sarah stood from behind the desk. "I could show you."

Vaughn held up the hand that wasn't holding his hat and treated her to a heart-warming smile. "That won't be necessary. Thanks Sarah." He left her flustered and flushed as he moved towards the emergency room doors. The automated entrance opened with a hiss of released pressure and exposed the flurry of activity. Doctors and nurses moved about in a well-choreographed dance of white lab coats and blue scrubs. They carried charts and vials or were escorting patients to and from their rooms. No one paid attention to him. The presence of a police officer was an everyday occurrence in this environment.

The Chief walked the polished floor, shoes squeaking with every step. Room sixteen was on the far side of the center desk where the medical personnel gathered. The door was shut.

Vaughn rested his hand on the door handle and wished he didn't have to drag Jesse through this. He'd been through enough. But if the kid could lead him to Ryan's killer it would be worth it. He knocked quickly and stuck his head in the door.

Jesse Lawrence looked small on the gurney. He was sleeping soundly, as if he'd never been forced to hold a gun to his own head. Vaughn could see he was wearing a powder blue hospital gown and a plastic admittance bracelet was swimming around his thin, right wrist. Bear sat vigil in one of the uncomfortable visitor chairs. His head was laid back against the wall, eyes closed. The only sound in the room came from a harshly ticking clock above the door. Bear stirred and opened his eyes. "Chief?"

"Yeah, Bear, I was wondering if I could speak to Jesse for a minute."

Vaughn came all the way into the room and closed out the hallway noise with a click of the door.

Bear looked at his peacefully sleeping son. "Can't this wait? I really want him to get some sleep."

"I know and I'm sorry, but Jesse said something last night that I need to ask him about. I think he might know something more about Ryan's murder than what he's telling."

Bear nodded his okay and then stopped him again almost immediately.

"Before you wake him up, I was wondering about... Nina."

Vaughn blew a breath out threw his nose and wished he could keep Bear from any more pain. "I saw her right before she was sent up here to Springfield. She called her parents and they were headed over from Peoria. They've already got a lawyer. She wouldn't say a word to us."

"I just can't make myself believe it, you know?" Bear's anguish was scrawled across his face. The events of last night had aged him beyond twenty-eight years. "I don't know what this is going to mean for Jesse."

"It could be bad," Vaughn said, truthfully. "If Nina pleads not guilty and this thing goes to trial, Jesse could be forced to testify in court. It would mean reliving this whole nightmare again."

Bear clamped his eyes shut tight and Vaughn wasn't sure if this father was trying to suppress tears, or block out what he was saying. "God damn her."

"Dad?" Jesse's voice made the expressions on both of the men's faces change instantly. They turned to the young boy with smiles.

"Hey, sport. How ya feeling?"

"Okay," Jesse said and shrugged. He regarded Vaughn with a skeptical look. "What's he doing here?"

"He needs to ask you some questions. Are you up to it?" Bear's voice was gentle and soothing.

"Like what?" Jesse asked.

"Well," Vaughn said, stepping up, "you said something last night that kind of got me thinking."

The chief watched as Jesse's face paled to a ghostly white. No doubt he'd been trying hard to forget what had transpired the previous night and here Vaughn was dredging up the topic again.

"What?" Jesse's tiny whisper could barely be heard.

Vaughn pulled one of the visitor's chairs up and sat down at Jesse's level. He could see the boy's eyes were shifting back and forth nervously between him and his father. "You told your dad that you snuck out, right?"

Jesse looked at Bear and Bear nodded with a half smile as if to say, 'It's okay.' "Yeah, we snuck out. We just wanted to see the trail and see the machines."

"Jesse, you know that was the same night that Ryan was killed, right?"

Jesse didn't speak but quickly nodded his head twice.

"Last night you said that you told Ryan your secret. The secret about your mom coming into your room."

Jesse squeezed his eyes shut and balled the end of the sheet into his clenched fists. Vaughn could see he was going to be angry for a long time.

"Yeah, I told him."

"Then you said that it was your mom's fault that Ryan died. Why did you say that, Jesse? Did you see something while you were on the trail? Was someone else there besides you and Ryan?"

"No," Jesse replied quickly, "no one else was there."

Vaughn paused for a moment and took a deep breath. "Jesse, I need your help to find out who really killed Ryan. But that means you have to tell me the truth. Did your mom find out that you'd told Ryan?"

"No." The boy's answer was blunt.

"Jesse, no one's going to hurt you. If you saw someone else there, someone that hurt Ryan then you need to tell me who it is. I'll protect you. Your dad'll protect you."

"I'm telling the truth," Jesse exclaimed, his voice raising an octave. "There was no one else there. God, why don't you believe me?"

Vaughn held up his hand in surrender, afraid he was going to lose the valuable information that Jesse held inside. "Okay, okay. I do believe you, Jesse. If you say there was no one else there, then there was no one else there."

~~*~~

Behind Vaughn, Bear realized his breathing had become more rapid. He couldn't blame Jesse for being angry with the Chief of Police. He didn't want to be hearing what the chief had to say either.

*Did Nina find out that Jesse had told Ryan what was happening? Was she on the bike trail that night?*

Bear could hardly believe that the woman he'd married, who'd carried his child, could have killed a little boy to keep her secret safe. But then again, until last night he never would've believed she could have done anything as heinous as sexually abusing her own son.

He spoke in a surprisingly even tone. "Jesse, I think you need to tell us exactly what happened that night."

The reply was a long time coming. The hands of the clock slammed forward. "I'm afraid."

"You don't have to be scared," Bear said, stepping around Vaughn to get to his boy. "Just like the chief said, no matter what, I'll protect you."

~~*~~

Vaughn patiently watched the exchange between father and son. The same dialogue kept running through his head.

*Say it. Say who killed your friend.*

Jesse took a ragged breath. "I never told anybody what she did, you know? I just couldn't"

*Say it. Say who killed your friend.*

"We were just sitting up on top of the cab and talking about stuff and I had to tell somebody."

Jesse's voice was breaking under the weight of his emotions. Tears formed in his eyes and instantly started spilling over onto his cheeks. Bear pulled the boy into his arms but he'd become a rag doll. His stare was a million miles away.

"I knew that if I told Ryan he wouldn't say anything to anybody. He'd keep it a secret. But he didn't."

*Say it. Say who killed your friend.*

"He got real crazy when I told him," Jesse sobbed. "He said I should go tell my dad. I didn't know what to do. I told him 'no'. I didn't want to upset anybody. I said I just wanted him to keep it a secret. But he wouldn't listen."

Vaughn saw Bear pull the boy tighter against him. They wore matching expressions of grief.

Jesse continued, "He started to climb down the machine. He was going to tell my dad. I didn't know what to do. I tried to grab his shirt but..." The boy was near hysterics now. He shook his head violently back and forth trying to rid the image of his friend's body from behind his closed lids. "I tripped. I tripped and I pushed him. I pushed Ryan and he fell."

Something in Vaughn's chest tightened around his lungs like a vice. He tried to pull in a full breath but couldn't. He wet his lips with a tongue that felt like sandpaper and waited for Jesse to finish. The boy hadn't been lying. There had been no one else on the trail that night. Nina Lawrence hadn't heard her boy across the distance whispering her devilish secrets. Shannon Marshall hadn't used Ryan Bentley as a human sacrifice.

Tears continued to stream from Jesse's eyes but his sobs had settled down, to just the occasional hitch from his body.

"Oh Dad, It was a long way to the ground. Ryan hit the machine's bucket and he just laid there. I climbed down as fast as I could but..." Jesse wiped his nose with the back of his hand and looked up at Vaughn. "It was an accident."

Vaughn stood and placed a hand on the boy's shoulder. "Everything's going to be okay, Jesse. Thank you for telling me the truth. You did the right thing. Bear, can I see you outside?" Bear clung to Jesse and rocked him gently back and forth, ignoring Vaughn's request.

"Its okay, Dad. I'll be all right."

Bear studied his son. He'd survived so much. He seemed more of an adult, handling this situation better than himself.

Jesse had killed Ryan. It was an accident, but Jesse was the reason Ryan was dead. *No, it can't be true.*

"Why didn't you just tell me what happened? I could have helped you."

"Everything just started happening. I was trying to pull Ryan across the road and I saw a car coming so I ran and hid. Everyone kept saying that Mr. Fairfax had killed him. I was scared to say it was me."

"Why were you pulling Ryan into the road?" Vaughn asked.

"I was trying to get him to Ms. Yardley's house," Jesse explained. "Shannon told me she brings his animals back to life. I thought she could make Ryan come back to life too."

*Shannon Marshall. Why did he confess?*

Vaughn led Bear out into the hallway. "Jesse's going to have to make a statement for the district attorney's office. It's the only way I can get Shannon released."

"What's going to happen to him, Vaughn? Are they going to arrest him?" Bear was clinging by an emotional thread. "Why is this happening?"

"Bear, I need you to calm down," Vaughn urged and reached both of his hands out, grasping Bear just above the elbow. "While he's in the hospital for psychiatric care, there's nothing we can do. I can have the court reporter come here to get his statement. I want him to get through this as much as you."

"It was an accident. It was just an accident. You heard him." Bear couldn't be calmed.

"I know. I *did* hear him. I'll talk to the state's attorney, but it isn't up to me. Just get Jesse settled in a room and call your mother. You need to go home and get some sleep or you won't be any good to Jesse."

Bear nodded and did his best to straighten his appearance. He ran his hands through his hair and then down over his face. "Right. Okay."

Vaughn gave Bear's arm a squeeze and then started out the doorway he'd entered over an hour ago. "And call a lawyer, Bear," he called back over his shoulder.

This time the emergency room was buzzing with activity. Sickness and injury everywhere he looked. He tried to move quickly through the triage area but when he glanced out into the sea of chairs, he saw his sister,

Leigh, staring back at him. Seeing her froze the chief in mid-step and he choked off a cry.

Leigh continued to regard him with her unblinking eyes. Her long, blond hair was parted down the middle and had been gathered in a loose ponytail over her left shoulder. She was dressed in the same outfit he'd last seen her wearing, bell-bottom blue jeans and a white tunic top. The pale white skin was marred only by an angry red mark that stretched from ear to ear around her neck. Across the room, he could see a tiny smile play on the girl's lips.

"Officer?"

Vaughn knew the voice was talking to him but he reluctantly pulled his eyes away from the sight of his long-dead sister. "Yes," he croaked.

"Were you looking for someone?"

Turning now, Vaughn looked at the ever-helpful Nurse Sarah. She was still sitting behind the desk and this time hadn't even bothered to put down her romance novel. "No. No, I'm sorry." He shifted his gaze quickly back to the lobby but Leigh was gone. Her chair sat empty among the others, vacated for eternity. "No, everything's fine." He left as quickly as his feet would carry him out the door.

*What's the matter with me?*

He silently chastised himself. He needed some sleep. The strain of this past week including the events transpiring over the last twenty-four hours would be enough to kill any man. The truly unfortunate part was that everything was centered on a ten year-old boy. One who should be excited about going to summer camp, or outside playing fetch with his dog. Now his whole life was hanging in the balance.

Again, Vaughn's thoughts turned to Shannon Marshall. He just hoped he could get to the jail in time.

~~*~~

Susan Barnes held her gloved hand above her head and squinted through the sun. *Is that Vaughn leaving the emergency department?*

"You gonna need anything else today, Ms. Barnes?"

"What? Oh no, thanks."

Susan regarded the mortician as he shut the door of his hearse. She'd just released Larry Fairfax's body. There'd be no grand funeral, or twenty-car processional. He'd died alone and now he'd go to the grave alone. She hoped someone was waiting for him on the other side. She turned her attention back to the emergency room parking lot, located about a hundred yards from where she stood, but she could no longer see the handsome man she'd taken for the chief. Susan smiled to herself at the thought of him.

*Of course it wasn't Vaughn. What would he be doing at the hospital this early anyway?*

She snapped the latex gloves from her nimble fingers and waved a last good-bye to the driver of the hearse. She wished she could have talked to Vaughn last night at the town meeting. She was ready to tell him how she felt about him. She was ready to hear him say it back. Forgetting the nasty business of cutting up dead bodies, Susan dramatically flung open the heavy metal door and whistled all the way down the hallway to the morgue.

## Chapter 24

P erry moved quietly out of his father's bedroom and put a hand to his face.

"I tried to make him as comfortable as I could but I thought you'd want to know." Jackie Agans backed out of Gordon's room and closed the door behind her.

Perry nodded his head and placed his hands on his hips. "Thanks Jackie. I knew he was getting bad but coughing up blood? Damn." Perry tried to keep his voice low but each word grew in inflection and decibel.

"I didn't mean for you to have to leave work. I'm sorry, Perry. Any other night I would have stayed." Jackie wrung her hands together in anticipation and prayed that Perry wouldn't guilt her into canceling her plans.

"Oh no, Jackie, no way. You get out of here and go cook your dinner," Perry said and shooed Jackie down the hallway. "I'll take care of the old man. Vaughn has plenty of guys and besides he knows about Dad."

Although Perry was trying to put Jackie's mind at ease, he really didn't care if Vaughn needed him or not. He'd left the crime scene at the bike trail in the very capable hands of Phil Rothwell and had come home to his father. The talk they'd had the previous night had opened up doors closed for over twenty years. Suddenly Perry saw his dad in a different light. He was just a man.

Not the iconic, unbreakable Chief of Police that Perry had built him up to be.

Jackie collected her purse and dug through it to retrieve her keys. "Does it look like it could rain out there?"

"It sure has clouded up since lunch time."

Perry's voice took on a strained note. He was anxious to get Jackie out of the house and get back to his father. He really hadn't been able to fully look at her since that day in the car with Amy. His mind flashed back to the girl's red shirt being pulled tight against her breasts by the seatbelt.

"Well, call if you need something, Perry. Anything."

"Yeah, thanks," Perry placed a hand on the doorjamb. "Say hi to Amy for me."

~~*~~

At the courthouse, Vaughn grabbed Margaret Yardley by the elbow and hissed, "What the hell are you doing here?"

He led her into a hallway off the main corridor.

"I came to see Shannon. I need to see him." Margaret explained.

"Yeah, I've heard that before." Vaughn grumbled.

"Why? What are *you* doing here, anyway?"

Vaughn eyed Margaret but wasn't shocked by her audacity, inquiring about his business at the courthouse.

"I've been here all day trying to get a hearing for Shannon. Jesse Lawrence admitted this morning that he pushed Ryan Bentley, accidentally killing him."

"My God," Margaret gasped as her hand fluttered to her throat. "Does that mean that Shannon is free to go?"

"Not until the state drops all the charges, which is why I'm here. Conveniently, the state's attorney isn't answering his pages and no one can find a judge."

"Oh Chief, that's wonderful news. I mean, not about Jesse, but Shannon—"

"You never said what you were doing here, Margaret," Vaughn interrupted.

"What? Oh, I came to give Shannon my support, but the visiting hours are over. I need to get in there, Chief. I don't know how long he can hang on like this."

Vaughn furrowed his brow. Now he knew Shannon was innocent, he wanted to help the boy more than ever. Margaret had done what he'd asked her and now he would do what *she* asked.

"I have a plan that just might work. But you need to let me do all the talking."

Margaret grinned, "You got it." She hiked her large purse higher on her shoulder and fell into step behind him.

He couldn't believe he was about to go through with this, but he needed to see Shannon too. After yesterday's confrontation, he figured he'd need Margaret to get through to the boy.

They approached the visitor's sign-in desk. Vaughn was thankful he didn't recognize the officer behind the desk. The cop looked tired despite the fact that it was only early evening. "I need to see one of the detainees. Shannon Marshall." Vaughn pulled the clipboard towards him and started filling out the appropriate section on the visitor page before the officer had a chance to respond.

"And your friend?" The officer pointed towards Margaret, half hidden behind the chief's broad shoulders.

"Oh. Mr. Marshall's attorney—she'll be needing to speak with him as well."

The cop behind the desk narrowed his eyes instinctively as he took in Margaret's eccentric appearance. Vaughn was sure they were had. But either the officer didn't question his honesty, or else he just didn't care, because he shoved the clipboard toward Margaret.

"Sign in, please."

Margaret appeared to panic at the thought of writing her name but Vaughn gave a slight nod of his head to indicate that she should pick up the pen. And now. The old woman scrawled something on the piece of paper and he couldn't help but lean over to see what she had written.

'F. Lee Bailey'.

Vaughn fought to control a grimace. The odd pair moved towards the door that would lead them to Shannon's cell when the desk officer stopped them. "Wait just a second."

Vaughn with his back to the man closed his eyes and sighed. "Yes?"

"What are you taking in there, ma'am?" the officer pointed to Margaret's large purse.

Margaret stuttered, "What? Oh this? This is my, uh, my briefcase. Lots of legal papers in there. Yep, most stuffy lawyers carry a leather bag but I prefer to—"

"Come on, counselor," Vaughn said through clenched teeth. "We need to get into see your client."

The officer buzzed them through the door and led the way down a darkened hallway.

~~*~~

Shannon Marshall sat huddled in the far corner of his cell. The cot smelled of mildew and stale cigarette smoke. It made him want to vomit so he'd retreated to the corner and sank to the hard concrete floor. He wasn't sure what to do now. He had no idea what was going to happen to him now he'd confessed to killing Jesse's friend. He shook his head and tried not to think about it.

At first, he thought jail might not be so bad. They fed you and gave you someplace to sleep. But he knew he wouldn't be in a cell alone forever. Eventually he'd be transferred to Joliet or Marion and thrown in with the general population. Once there the other criminals would have a field day calling him a girl—and worse, treating him like one.

If he could have mustered the energy he would've cried. He'd cried so much over the last couple of days that he wasn't sure that his eyes would even produce tears. Maybe he should have talked to the chief. He'd said he wanted to help him but he just couldn't believe that was true. He'd trusted people before and now look where he was.

He'd seen Bear talking to the police outside of the body shop the day after they'd found the boy's body. Did Bear tell the police that he had killed Ryan?

*No, no, no...*

He shook his head and covered his ears to try to keep the voices from talking.

*"Yep, Bear thinks you're no good just like everyone else. He was only being nice to you so he could work you like a dog."*

"No, he was my friend," Shannon whimpered.

"Marshall." The voice was loud and bounced off his eardrums, leaving them ringing. "You've got a visitor."

Shannon peeked out from behind his nearly-closed eyelids and saw the guard coming toward the cell door. He obediently picked himself up and went to the bars as the door was unlocked and opened. He was trying to separate reality from his imagination. "Chief Dexter?"

"That's right, Shannon. I brought your lawyer." Vaughn said it loudly, hoping Shannon wouldn't tip off the officer. But Vaughn didn't think that Shannon even heard him speak, because when the boy saw Margaret, he nearly choked on his own breath.

"Maggie?"

Margaret waited until the officer had retreated back down the hallway to his post before she regarded Shannon.

"Oh dear, Shannon, what have they done to you?" She pulled the boy into her arms and held him like a baby while he cried buckets.

"Help me, Maggie. I don't know what to do. I said I did it. I told them I killed him," Shannon sobbed.

"Hush now, dear, we'll get this all figured out." Margaret led him to the cot and made him sit. "I came for a pleasant visit. Not this."

Shannon nodded his head and wiped his nose with the back of his hand like a small child. He didn't speak for fear that his voice would betray him and he'd start crying again.

"I came to show you this." Margaret produced the large purse from over her shoulder and quickly looked around before opening it. Vaughn had stepped down the hallway to give them some privacy.

When Shannon peered inside the purse he could see a white box about the size of a take-out container. Margaret carefully opened the lid and revealed a tangled mess of branches and straw that had been fashioned into a bird's nest.

"It's a nest," Shannon managed to say, although Margaret wasn't sure if it was a question or a statement.

She nodded in response. "That's right. A bird's nest I found just above my porch light two nights ago. The same day they arrested you."

"Was there something in it? Was there an egg?" Shannon's voice began to take on a light quality and Margaret watched the boy's aura turn from the muddy green of despair to the pink of tranquility he usually wore.

"Not an egg, my dear, but a tiny baby bird abandoned by his mother." Margaret stroked the twisted branches as if seeing the bird still snuggled deep inside.

"Did he... die?" Shannon swallowed a mouthful of emotion and his chin quivered at the thought, but Margaret was quick to reassure him.

"Oh no, quite the contrary. I watched the nest all day waiting for the mother bird to come back and feed her tiny baby. When she didn't return, I took the nest down from my porch light and moved it into the house. I made sure the baby bird was warm and had lots of yummy worms to eat."

Margaret paused as Shannon smiled and his pink aura grew brighter and more vibrant. "And you know that even through all of that, our little bird has managed to survive. He's growing stronger and stronger every day."

"You are such a good person, Maggie." Shannon peered into the white box for another look at the bird's nest.

"You're a good person too, Shannon," Margaret replied and brushed a strand of Shannon's hair from where it had plastered itself to his forehead. "They know you didn't kill that little boy."

"No. I didn't."

"You are like my little bird, Shannon Marshall. Your mother might have abandoned you but you're strong. Deep inside, I know you'll survive too."

"Will you help me?" Shannon pleaded.

"Yes, I will," Margaret responded immediately. "Just like that little bird, I'm going to take you in and help you once we get you out of this mess."

"But I'm in jail and I don't know how to get out." Shannon was near tears again.

"That's why Chief Dexter's here. He came to tell you that you're going to get to go home very soon. I don't have many years left, Shannon but whatever I do have is going to be spent making sure that you get what you need."

Margaret reached out and placed her hands about the boy's face. "Your parents have no idea what they missed out on."

Margaret felt Shannon's head fall against her hand and a single tear snake down his dirty cheek and onto her finger. Without realizing it, she'd also closed her eyes and was taking in the sense of Shannon's goodness. With a tiny smile playing on her lips, Margaret opened her eyes and saw the last thing she ever expected.

Vaughn Dexter, smiling too.

~~*~~

Patrick Monahan readjusted his tie and listened to the boy's taped statement for the fifth time. Now serving his third year as the Sangamon County State's attorney, he'd never heard anything quite like this and was certain he never would again. Pat knew that if he hadn't been present for the ten-year-old's statement, he would have been hard pressed to believe it was for real.

Pat called out for his assistant. "Angie? Have you got that motion to drop the charges against Shannon Marshall ready for me to sign yet?"

"Hot off the press." His assistant's voice made an entrance before she did. She bounced over the threshold and waved the motion just out of Pat's reach.

He wasn't paying attention. He'd bent over his worn leather blotter, making quick notes on a piece of paper. "Is that kiss-ass intern still here?"

"Pat!" his assistant admonished, "Yes, he's right outside."

"Good," Pat said and ripped the piece of paper from his notebook. He exchanged papers with his assistant. "Give this to him and tell him I want it drafted tonight before he leaves."

"Pat, have a heart. It's almost four-thirty now." The woman glanced down at the paper her boss had just given her and gasped. "You're filing charges against that little boy?"

Pat grabbed his suit jacket off the back of his chair and wrestled into it. "That 'little boy' is a pathological liar. He lied repeatedly to the police and was going to let not one but two different men take the fall for what he did."

"He was being abused by his mother. He was scared."

"Well, all that remains to be seen. Maybe he's lying about that too." Pat squeezed past the woman in his tiny office and grabbed the note out of her hand. "If you won't give it to him, then I'll do it myself."

Pat left his assistant alone and shocked and went in search of his kiss-ass intern.

~~*~~

"Let's pack it up guys. There's a storm moving in," Phil Rothwell shouted, towering over the other officers and crime scene technicians on the Lost Bridge Bike Trail.

The day had been a scorcher. Working on the partially-asphalted surface of the bike trail, combing the grass and dirt for clues, had been similar to working on the surface of the sun. The underarms of Phil's uniform were dark with sweat stains and the triangle that formed between his massive shoulder blades had turned his blue uniform black. The rain might be a welcome sight although it wouldn't help the already-destroyed crime scene. Phil grabbed the cell phone off of his hip and dialed up the chief. "I gotta tell ya, Chief, we ain't got much here."

"Phil, yeah, I'm glad you called. I'm sorry I didn't have a chance to call you guys off but I've had a strange twist of events."

Vaughn gave Phil a run-down on Jesse's confession. "I went straight to the court house to get Shannon Marshall released but it was too late to get all the paperwork in place and get him a hearing. I've been here all day."

Phil was flabbergasted. "My God, that poor family's been through hell this past week. Makes me want to go home and hug my kids, you know?"

Of course, Vaughn didn't respond.

He didn't know. But he didn't want to say to Phil that he was glad he didn't have any offspring. He knew that Phil and his wife didn't have a life outside of their four children.

He tuned back into Phil's voice. The man hadn't stopped speaking even in the wake of his silence. "...but they just grow up, you know? One day you blink and they don't want to kiss you goodnight or even have you drop'em off at school. Tim's going to be sixteen years old next month. Rarely even eats at home. As we speak he's at his girlfriend's house. Kids!"

## Chapter 25

Cameron arrived at Jackie's house at six o'clock sharp. He stood nervously on the cracked concrete porch cap for several tense moments before he worked up the nerve to ring the doorbell.

*What if this doesn't work? Oh God, what am I doing here?*

But God wouldn't answer his question. Over the years Cameron had asked many times why the Lord had made him the way He did. Cameron just wanted a sign—but of course nothing ever came.

"Hey you." Cameron was startled at the sound of Jackie Agans' voice. "Is there some reason you're just standing out there on the porch?"

"N-no," Cameron stammered, "no reason."

Jackie pushed open the screen door and then flinched as a bolt of lightening cut across the sky. "These storms are relentless. Well, come on in then."

Cameron shouldered past Jackie into the almost non-existent foyer and found himself peering into the living room. It was shabby and second-hand but he didn't notice. His attention was immediately drawn to the couch where Amy and her boyfriend Tim sat cuddled on practically the same cushion. Amy was leaned in close, whispering softly in Tim's ear. Cameron felt a familiar heat creep up the back of his neck as he watched the young boy knead his hand into Amy's taut thigh.

"What'cha got there?" Jackie's voice intruded into his lustful thoughts and he turned to her, making the effort to erase the annoyed look from his face.

"Oh this," Cameron regarded the bottle of wine he was holding. "It's a 'thank you', for inviting me."

"Oh, that's real nice, Cameron. Thanks." Jackie's voice dripped sugary-sweet and Cameron had to keep himself from physically gagging. He tried to appear nonchalant as he moved his attention back to the teenagers on the couch, and was startled to discover that Amy had crossed the room and now stood only a foot from him.

"Hi, Mr. Cody."

"Amy. How are you this evening?" Then glancing over Amy's shoulder. "Hello, Tim."

"Hey." The boy lifted a hand in a wave.

An awkward silence followed, since Cameron wasn't sure what he should do. He'd never been invited into a woman's home for a date, until now. The moments ticked by agonizingly slow. Everyone stood about with frozen smiles and shifting eyes until Jackie broke the silence. "Well, we should eat."

A collective sigh of relief, none louder than his, filled the room.

The four of them shuffled into the small dining room and took their seats. Cameron sat with Jackie to his right, Amy to his left and directly across from Tim Rothwell. He watched helplessly as Jackie filled his plate with heaps of meat and vegetables she scooped out of a crock-pot. "We are having pot roast. It's my Amy's favorite."

He smiled at Amy. "Good choice. It smells delicious."

Amy's nose crinkled. "Not to me."

"What?" Jackie stopped in mid-scoop. "You've been craving this all week."

"It's weird. I don't know—I just don't feel good all of a sudden." Amy shook her head and pushed back from the table.

Cameron watched Tim snake a hand across the table and reach out for his girlfriend. "You okay?"

As suddenly as the situation had started, it was over. Amy took a deep breath and smiled. "I'm fine. Just a little queasy for some reason." She lifted her plate high above the centerpiece on the table. "I want a lot of carrots, Mom."

Jackie's relief was obvious as she obligingly scooped the orange spears onto her daughter's plate. For a moment everyone munched in silence. Rain began to fall and quite suddenly gusts of wind rattled the windows. He glanced around, feeling stiff and uncomfortable. He choked down a chunk of the dry meat and took a sip of water.

Jackie broke the silence by clapping her hands together. "The wine. Can I get you a glass?"

"Yes, please," Cameron almost pleaded. Maybe that would help to calm him. He couldn't help but feel sorry for himself. How was it that he could have lived his entire life without ever really acquiring any close friends? Of course, he knew the answer to this question.

He would never allow anyone to get close to him. They might be able to see right through him. See the real Cameron.

*The one who lies awake at night fantasizing about what he would do if he were able to really live—he would release the beast inside him and let it feed on every desire that had ever flashed through his wicked mind.*

Cameron took the room in again with his dark eyes. He settled his gaze on Jackie. She smiled a closed-mouth smile as she swallowed a piece of masticated beef. He dipped his eyes to the bare expanse of flesh between her neck and the valley of her breasts. Her chest was heaving as if she was enjoying the fact that she had his attention. Her pale melon-colored top was low-cut and slung even further down when she leaned forward, which she did freely.

Across the table, Tim was hunched over his food as if it was the last meal he would ever eat. Cameron watched as the boy shoveled potatoes smothered in gravy into his awaiting mouth. He stopped every once in awhile to wipe his lips with a napkin he held tightly in his left hand. Tim parted his ample lips and forked in more of his dinner.

To his left, Amy was silent. He couldn't help but tear his gaze away from Tim to see what she was doing. Her fork was still balanced in her right hand, but both hands lay idle on the table. He noticed that full-figured breasts were also heaving, so much like her mother's. But on second glance, Cameron noticed the girl was wearing a pale, uncomfortable expression. She gulped in great breaths and her eyes looked watery in the overhead light.

Apparently Jackie had caught on to what her dinner guest was watching because Cameron heard her say. "Honey, are you all right?"

Amy shook her head and then stopped as the motion of her head was making her feel sicker. "I think I'm going to be…"

And then without warning, Amy opened her mouth and spewed the remnants of her recently-consumed dinner back onto her plate. Cameron heard Jackie gasp and jump from her chair. Although disgusted, he couldn't tear his eyes away as Amy sat helpless while wave after wave of vomit, rivaling the quantities produced by Linda Blair in 'The Exorcist', expelled from her body.

Jackie appeared in Cameron's peripheral vision holding a hand towel. She shoved the cloth up under her daughter's chin and with a firm hand escorted her from the table. Amy appeared to have emptied all of the contents from her stomach but was now crying uncontrollably. Cameron and Tim sat stunned at the table. They stared at each other unblinking. Neither knew exactly what to do.

Cameron mentally shrunk away from the mess on the table and tried to pretend like the smell wasn't going to cause a chain reaction. He could hear the two women in the bathroom somewhere behind him. Jackie was talking fast, asking her daughter a million questions. Amy continued to cry.

"Let's see if there's something to clean up this mess," Cameron heard himself say, something most surprising to him.

"You mean the puke?" Tim appeared absolutely horrified at the thought but got up and followed Cameron into the eat-in kitchen. They dug around in cabinets and drawers until they found a pair of rubber gloves and some trash bags. Cameron also grabbed a roll of paper towels.

The two men hunkered over the table. Tim scraped the uneaten food from the plates into a trash bag as Cameron gathered the silverware and glasses. At one point they stood close enough for Cameron to catch a whiff of the teenager's cologne. It was strong, spicy and he wore it well. The type of scent you'd expect from a football player and the boyfriend of a beautiful girl.

Jackie appeared in the doorway, disheveled and distraught. "I don't know what happened, she's just sick to her stomach." She stopped and looked back towards the bathroom, where everyone could hear Amy throwing up again, then realized what was happening with Cameron and Tim.

"Oh Cameron, you don't have to clean that up."

He felt sorry for her. She'd painstakingly planned this evening with him and now it had been ruined. And somehow he felt unnaturally relieved. The situation with Amy had provided him with an out. No awkward walk to the car where he would be expected to kiss or hug Jackie good night. "It's no problem, really," he said, indicating the mess on the table. "We'll just clean this up and get out of your way."

Jackie seemed more upset by Cameron's wanting to leave than her daughter being sick. "You don't have to go."

Amy's voice came from the bathroom. "Mom?"

Jackie glanced back over her shoulder and then faced Cameron once more. "I'm sorry, but thank you. Both of you."

She started back towards her daughter and then remembered. "Oh no—I was supposed to take Tim home. I certainly can't let him walk in this storm. Would you mind, Cameron?"

*And there it is*, Cameron thought, *the words I've been dreading. Does she really expect me to get into my car with Mr. All-American Football and make small talk?*

He didn't want to be alone with this boy, with anyone for that matter. He wouldn't be able to speak. He'd be too busy fighting his inner demons. Despite all of this running through his mind, Cameron heard himself say, "Sure, no problem."

Jackie was visibly relieved. She gave him a quick smile and exited the room.

Cameron and Tim finished their task and stacked the dishes in the kitchen sink. "I should get home," Tim said and threw a thumb over his shoulder towards the door.

"Oh, right. Come on then."

Cameron led the boy to the door and then watched as he dashed into the pouring rain. He was about to follow when Jackie's voice stopped him. When he turned around, he was surprised to see how very close she was. He hadn't heard her approach at all.

"I'm sorry the evening turned out this way," she apologized.

Momentarily stunned into silence, it took him a moment to respond. "That's okay. I hope Amy gets to feeling better."

Jackie reached out and touched his arm just below the elbow. "Will you come back some other time?"

"Sure." Cameron tried to sound convincing but was pretty sure Jackie could tell from the tone of his voice that he wouldn't be coming back. She nodded and he ventured out into the cold, wet night.

Tim had already settled himself into the front seat of the car. It seemed to take a long time for Cameron to fish the keys out of his pocket and find the ignition. He'd been holding in a stale breath of air and released it when the engine roared to life. Tim flipped down the sun visor above his head and fiddled with his wet, tousled hair as Cameron wiped the water droplets from his wire-rimmed glasses. The silence was thick and uncomfortable.

"You'll have to tell me where you live," Cameron spoke.

"Oh right," Tim chuckled and flashed a row of perfectly white teeth. "I live outside of town. You know where Oak Hill Road is?"

*In the country?*

Cameron didn't want to be here. In the car with this handsome boy who just reminded him of everything he wasn't. Tim flipped his hair back again with his long fingers and Cameron saw him kneading those fingers into Amy Agans' leg.

*They're having sex. No matter what Jackie wants to believe. They're so young. Too young.*

The voice inside his mind was loud and brash. He pulled the car onto the street and tried to concentrate only on the road in front of him. A song familiar to Tim was playing on the radio. Cameron heard him humming along and tapping out the rhythm on his blue-jeaned thigh.

Cameron gritted his teeth together and fought every urge not to just take his speeding car and drive headlong into the next telephone pole. Something was building inside him. He didn't know how to fight it—it was nothing like he'd every felt before. His grip tightened on the steering wheel and he took Oak Hill Road out past where the streetlights ended. Darkness enveloped the car, the rain only illuminated in the yellow glow of the headlights. He was breathing calmly through his nose but he could feel a sheen of sweat break out onto his upper lip. His glasses were slipping down his nose. Soon he couldn't control his emotional turmoil. It swelled like a massive wave and crashed through his body like a tsunami.

"So," Cameron started, "you like having sex with Amy Agans?"

## Chapter 26

Elizabeth Lawrence nodded numbly into the phone receiver as if the person on the other end of the line could hear her head moving. She glanced across the hospital room at her grandson Jesse. He was asleep in the adjustable bed and she turned her back so he wouldn't be woken by the sound of her voice. "I just don't understand, Chief. It was an accident."

"I know, Mrs. Lawrence. I'm sorry you had to hear about this tonight. I just thought it was better that you and Bear know."

"But how can they charge a ten-year old boy with involuntary manslaughter?" Tears crept into Liz's eyes and she fought the urge to sob out loud. Her son, Walter, had gone home only an hour ago at her urging. He'd barely had any sleep in twenty-four hours. Now, she'd have to call him and tell him the latest horrible news. She didn't even know anymore who the victim was.

~*~

On the other end of the line, Vaughn Dexter didn't have the answer to Liz Lawrence's question. He'd heard from the mayor only a half an hour before he called the hospital that the Sangamon County State's attorney was pressing charges. He'd exploded in anger.

"Are you telling me the state's attorney's office didn't have time to get Shannon Marshall out of jail but had time to file charges against Jesse Lawrence?" Vaughn had screamed at his superior.

The mayor had no answers for him. Vaughn hoped the mayor was as sick over the whole situation as he was, but there was absolutely nothing they could do about it.

Vaughn heard Liz whisper into the phone, "I have to call my son."

"Of course. Please tell Bear if he needs anything to let me know. I'll try to help in anyway that I can."

~~*~~

Liz disconnected the call with the chief and closed her eyes. How would she tell Walter Jr.? It would kill him. She dialed her home number reluctantly and listened to the ringing. Perhaps he'd gone to the auto shop to relieve some stress. Maybe he was just out driving around trying to make sense of the past couple of days. Liz heard Jesse turn over in his sleep. The sheets rustled softly around him.

Just when she was about to give up, a groggy voice answered.

It was all she could manage, just to say, "Walter."

Bear was instantly awake. "What is it? Is Jesse okay?"

Liz glanced again at Jesse to confirm that he was fine. "Yes, Jesse is fine. But Walter, Chief Dexter just called. The state's attorney reviewed Jesse's statement and—"

At that point Liz heard her son whisper the word 'no', but she couldn't keep herself from telling him. "—they're going to charge him."

"*What?!* Oh God, why are they doing this?"

Something in Bear's chest ripped free and he sobbed into his hands. He couldn't even stand to talk to his mother anymore, and threw the phone against the wall, where it exploded into pieces.

~~*~~

Bear tore through his room destroying anything he came in contact with. Books and shelves crashed to the floor as lightning strobed the inside of the room turning his destructive behavior into a maniacal dance. The thunderous storm was feeding his rage as he grabbed his jeans from the floor. A loud clap echoed through the otherwise empty house and reverberated in his ears, leaving them ringing.

Bear couldn't breathe. He felt alone more than ever in his life. His wife, the woman he had pledged to love forever, the mother of his child was in jail. In jail for abusing their son.

For killing his innocence.

For putting him into this horrible situation in which there was no out.

Bear's sister Katrina, who had been his only confidant for so long, was far away in New York—inaccessible in his time of need. His mother was at the hospital, albeit emotionally distant. He'd always had a good relationship with her. And his dear father was dead in the ground. Now of all nights in his life since Walter Sr. had left this Earth, he needed to be close to his father. A quick flash of lucidity cleared his head.

*The journals.*

Since the problems with Jesse, Bear hadn't had a chance to open the books he'd taken from his father's office. He dropped to his knees and rummaged through the chaos he'd created on the floor.

Lightning slashed the sky and thunder boomed again. He couldn't hear over the pounding of the rain against his window. He searched like a madman, unable to remember where he'd left the journals in his hazy existence of no sleep and mental exhaustion. Not finding the journals in the pile, he moved like a madman on the hunt, first through his bedside table and then the standing chest of drawers. They were there inside the top drawer, resting on folded underwear and paired socks.

He clutched the six books to his chest as if they held the cure to his mental ailments. He would be healed by his father's words. Whatever lay inside, the hidden messages of the journals would stop the hurt he was feeling for his son and for himself.

Suddenly the room was all wrong. Bear felt too large for the space. He shouldn't have taken the journals from the office. His mother had never insisted on selling the place. He left the house in jerky, exaggerated movements. He raced into the rain, feeling it drench the thin white t-shirt he wore. With no shoes on his feet, Bear jumped into his truck and slammed the door. He drove with one hand on the wheel. The other clutched the journals to his chest. He drove too fast. His foot was heavy on the accelerator.

Running a red light, Bear turned onto Walnut and continued to John Street. He slammed the gear shifter into park and leapt from the truck, not even bothering to close the door behind him. The door to his father's old office was locked. Bear pulled and clawed at the doorknob in anger. He leaned his head back and screamed into the sky.

The pure animal scream tore from his throat. He crushed his full weight against the door. It held fast. Unable to control his emotions, Bear balled his hand into a fist and bust through one of the panes of glass in the door. The jagged edges ripped and tore at his flesh, but he couldn't feel the pain.

Rain came down in sheets. His clothes were soaked clear to his skin and were plastered against his body. He reached through and unlocked the door from the inside. He clutched at the doorjamb like a drowning man, afraid to fully let go lest he fall headlong into the sea of his emotions. At last he broke down and sobbed out loud although the storm covered his anguish. His tears mixed with the pouring rain and ran in an endless stream down his cheeks and dripped from the end of his nose. Finally, Bear released his grip and entered the long-abandoned office.

The interior was dark and quiet. Bear shivered with cold. He continued through the lobby and went to the tiny medical records room were he'd first discovered the books. He flipped a switch and the bare overhead light, now flaunting a new bulb, cast an ethereal glow in the diminutive space. Bear sank down to the floor against one of the filing cabinets and opened the first journal.

*'Elizabeth is pregnant. Can you believe it? I am going to be a father.'*

Bear read on, line after line, page after page until his eyes could no longer focus on the words. He fell into a fitful sleep and dreamed. Maybe he'd failed his father all those years ago, but now... now he'd make up for it.

~~*~~

Margaret pulled back the curtain when she heard the roar of the truck zoom past her house on Walnut. The lightning flashed just long enough for her to see the logo for Bear's Auto Body on the door. She shook her head, sad.

*Poor Bear Lawrence. His son's killed a little boy. Maybe not on purpose but in any event, Ryan Bentley's dead because of Jesse Lawrence. Oh, the pain they must be feeling.*

Margaret had been shocked when Vaughn Dexter had approached her at the Sangamon County Jail. It would explain why she couldn't see the murderer's dirty halo. Jesse Lawrence didn't have murderous thoughts. It wasn't his intention for the boy to die. And besides, a child's halo is nearly impossible to determine. Their emotions change rapidly, mudding the waters of the aura. The different colors would swirl together like a psychedelic rainbow. If Jesse was happy, sad, angry or elated, Margaret would never be able to distinguish which.

She let the curtain fall back into place and retreated through the empty house. She retrieved the empty bird's nest out of her purse and carried it to Shannon's trophy room of stuffed animals. There was a nice place for it beside a swallow perched on a tiny fake twig. Margaret had lied to Shannon. There had been no bird inside for her to save. The nest had probably been abandoned for weeks. But she wasn't lying about wanting to help Shannon.

Now that he was going to be released from that dirty jail cell, she had a lot of planning to do. She would teach him. She would educate him. She would make him a productive citizen of their great society. Life would be returning to normal in Rochester soon and she wanted Shannon to be returning right along with it.

~~*~~

Shannon Marshall lay on his back on the smelly cot and stared at the ceiling. Suddenly the scent wasn't as revolting as it had been previously in the day. This was the last night he would spend behind bars. The chief had told him the lawyers were dropping the charges against him because of Jesse Lawrence's confession. Shannon was to be a free man. He marveled at the fact that the chief had actually helped him. Helped him like he said he would. No one had ever done that for him before, except for Maggie. She was his friend.

*His friend.*

Shannon thought of Jesse Lawrence. He was sad for the boy.

*How could these things have happened to a great kid like Jesse? He's got a great family and lots of friends at school. Not like me.*

He'd never had the opportunities Jesse had. But it was Jesse who was going to jail. At that moment, Shannon almost wished he could have taken Jesse's place. If Jesse had just kept his mouth shut, everyone could have just gone on believing that he'd killed Ryan Bentley. He realized he owed a lot to the Lawrence's. First Bear had given him a job and trusted him at the shop and then Jesse had befriended him. He vowed to stand by him, or at least try to.

Shannon thought of the rest of Jesse's family. His mom. His grandma. And his aunt, Katrina. He could picture Katrina's red hair and smile. Just the way she looked in the pictures in Bear's office. He was in love with her. But she lived far away.

Tomorrow, when the police gave back his personal effects, they'd return his empty wallet, a pair of tennis shoes two sizes too small, a pocket comb and the picture from behind Bear's desk, of Katrina holding a two-year old Jesse smeared in peanut butter.

~~*~~

Vaughn took a long pull off of the Bud Light beer and looked out of his sliding glass door at the storm. It rivaled his mood, miserable and tumultuous. The rain was relentless. It had started before he got home from the station and he figured he'd be waking up to its wrath in the morning. He wanted to run outside and let the water pelt his body. Drown his thoughts and let him forget the events that had turned this beautiful, quiet small town in to a haven for pedophiles and tragedy.

Vaughn watched the wind violently whip the small oak tree in his backyard near to death. It was bent at an unnatural angle and surely it would be broken by morning. Already trees had been felled by the wind, and the news had reported the far edge of town was without electricity.

Another swig from the bottle and the beer was gone— Vaughn's third since he'd come home. He'd thought all of this was over for the Lawrence's but now Jesse would have to go through a trial. They'd all have to relive the last week of their lives, down to the very last hideous detail. Jesse would be dragged through discussion after discussion about his mother's sexual advances on him. He knew kids were strong, but just how close can one walk to the edge before finally just falling over?

*I've failed again.*

He pictured his sister's spirit once more, serenely sitting in the hospital waiting area, her long blonde hair like spun silk. He rather preferred this image to the one of her sprawled on the couch in their house where they'd grown up. Her eyes wide open and unblinking, the angry red mark under her chin darkening by the second. He'd never recovered from her death. Vaughn figured that Jesse would never live a day for the rest of his life without seeing his friend's body tumbling off the end loader and lying still against the ground.

He tossed the beer bottle into the trashcan under the sink and made his way down the dark hallway to his bedroom.

Vaughn brushed the beer taste out of his mouth, but couldn't bring himself to look at his reflection in the mirror. He hadn't managed to save anybody. After all of this was over, he'd hand in his resignation to Jim Wagner.

He settled in between the sheets and turned off the bedside lamp. The lightening flashed in and lit up the room as if he'd never turned out the light. He wouldn't sleep. How could he?

A cold chill ran the length of his spine and gooseflesh pimpled his bare chest. Vaughn looked over at the empty spot beside him and wished like hell that tonight, of all nights, he wasn't going to sleep alone.

~~*~~

Susan Barnes parked the car only a half a block away from Vaughn's house and watched until the last light had been extinguished. She was shivering from excitement or cold, she couldn't tell which. The engine was still running so she could keep the windshield wipers operating. His house was quaint, old in years and style. From what she could see in the bright moments of the lightening, the siding and roof were gray, the trim around the windows white. No ornamental foundation shrubs or bushes had ever been planted for landscaping. It was a plain rectangle with a door, three windows and an attached two-car garage. Vaughn's pickup truck sat on the concrete apron of the driveway being pelted by the fat droplets of water falling from the sky.

She imagined him.

*He's in there, lying between the sheets, his arms casually crossed behind his head…or lying loosely at his sides.*

Susan closed her eyes. Leaning her head back against the headrest, she imagined herself emerging from the tiny master bathroom and joining him in the bed. The sheets were crisp and cooled her freshly-washed skin. The white silk nightgown she wore was long, almost to her ankles and Vaughn loved to see her in it. He ran a hand along her thigh, up over her hip towards her breasts, bringing the soft fabric with him… leaving her body exposed and tingling.

Susan giggled. It shouldn't be too hard to convince Vaughn Dexter to invite her into his bed. As far as she could tell, he was interested in no one else, and she damn sure intended to keep it that way.

She sighed, put the car in gear and pulled away from the curb. It was nearing ten o'clock. It had been a wonderful fantasy, but she needed to get home and get some sleep. Tomorrow she had two autopsies to perform. One was an old woman who had been found dead in her home by her daughter, who only stopped by to check up on her mother twice a week. Who knew how long it was that her mom had sat dead in her own excrement. The other autopsy was a thirty-year-old mother of two. It was an obvious overdose, whether intentional or not. It was Susan's job to find out.

As Susan made her way back to Springfield, she decided she was spending entirely too much time with dead bodies. Now somehow she had to catch the attention of one very alive one, Vaughn Dexter's.

~~*~~

Perry opened his father's bedroom door for the eighth time since he'd arrived home. Gordon Newlon still lay there propped up with six or seven pillows, making it easier for him to breathe, if that was even now possible. An oxygen mask used at night was now attached to the slender green tank on the floor beside the bed.

Gordon gasped at breaths, sounding a little like Darth Vader. Perry was just relieved to hear the man breathing. Perhaps he could convince the old man to go to the hospital or at least to the doctor, tomorrow. Of course, he knew Gordon wouldn't do that. He'd be too afraid they'd lock him up in some hospital room while he wasted away, just as his mom, Esther, had done before she finally died. It had been a miserable end to an otherwise tolerable existence.

*Will this night ever end?*

The storm outside was raging at full strength. He heard the wind and rain pounding against the outside of the house. He wouldn't sleep tonight. He knew that his father didn't have long. He'd make the remaining few of Gordon's days as comfortable as possible.

When Jackie Agans had called him at the station and told him his father had started coughing up blood, he felt his heart jump into his throat. When his father was dead, he'd be alone. No mother, no siblings, no wife to help him with his deathwatch.

Perry had to admit that taking care of and putting up with his father these past couple of years had been trying. Now, faced with his father's impending death, it almost took his breath away. Gordon had told him to call Joyce. He should. He needed to. He needed her.

After making sure the old man was in fact still breathing, Perry left in search of the phone. It was getting late and it would be silly to call her now. And yet he found himself dialing the familiar number of his in-laws house in Salisbury.

She answered on the third ring. Her voice sounded fresh, as if it weren't ten o'clock at night.

"Hello?" Joyce said, for the second time.

Perry was struck mute. Just the sound of her voice brought tears to his eyes. Why had he called? It was a stupid thing to do. He disconnected the call, and sat pinching the bridge of his nose. Maybe he should have fought to get the job as Chief of Police. Maybe then he would have had something to look forward to every morning. Right now it was just the same misery every time the daylight crept into his room and forced his eyelids open.

The same job, a dying father... and no wife.

The despair and depression covered him like a cloak. Was this what they called a nervous breakdown?

Perry looked up and realized he'd been sitting there holding the phone for nearly a half an hour. Time again to go check on his Dad.

~~*~~

In New York, Katrina was oblivious to the events that had transpired for her family back in Rochester, Illinois. She finished writing the story for her column and closed the laptop computer. It was late. Probably after one o'clock, but she wasn't tired. She moved through her apartment and retrieved the last carton of ice cream she'd bought last weekend.

*Peanut butter. Yum.*

She was expecting her brother and nephew on Monday. There was plenty of time for her to ready the guest room and set out extra towels. She was excited she'd be seeing her family. Excited that they'd get to experience her life in New York. She'd lived in Illinois and there was no comparison.

Maybe the trip would spur Bear into realizing he had more potential than just running the small body shop he owned back home. If anything Jesse would get to encounter the opportunities existing outside of their small Illinois town.

Those thoughts made her smile. She decided maybe she *was* tired after all. She replaced the carton of ice cream into the freezer and rinsed the spoon. Going to her bedroom, she peered over her tiny view of the city and felt its life pulsing up from the busy streets. She stood hugging herself as she watched. Nothing could pull her away from New York. For some reason that last statement running through her mind made Katrina think about her baby. She glanced down at her belly. She still wasn't showing— no sign she was pregnant. She could raise a baby in the city. People did it all the time.

*But do I want to?*

Katrina crawled between the covers and pulled them up to her chin. It wasn't something she wanted to think about right now. Instead, she'd think about Jesse running towards her at the airport, his excited voice telling her all about his first plane ride. She would marvel at how tall he'd gotten, and she'd squeeze Bear in the tightest hug allowable before serious injury.

~~*~~

Later, Katrina would remember that last thought and wonder how things could have gone so tragically wrong for her family. She'd question how life could be so unfair and malicious. She'd wonder how a sister-in-law who'd been a high school beauty could turn into a mother who molested her own son. How a nephew so full of promise could be broken and scarred forever because of a simple push of his hand. How her brother, once the center of her universe, could become the unrecognizable shell of the man she once knew.

How going home again could be the redemption she sought—even if she didn't know it at the time.

THE END

**Preview excerpt for the continuing book...
Month of Sundays, Book Two: Grace of God
coming soon from Beacon Books Publishing**

Katrina clamored out of the cab of Bear's tow truck and shut the door. The parking lot of the municipality complex was quiet in the early afternoon hours. She couldn't tell if the library was open. Only one other car graced the asphalt where Katrina had parked. It looked abandoned. She made her way toward the police station and pressed the button to be allowed access into the locked facility.

"Can I help you?"

"Um, yes, I am here to see Chief Dexter," Katrina replied.

A faint buzz sounded from the electronic box and Katrina hurried to pull the door handle while she was still being granted access. A man dressed neatly in his policeman's uniform was coming out of what looked like a very busy room.

"Kat?"

*Dammit, I wish everyone would stop calling me that.*

"Perry, hi. An officer of the law now, huh?"

Perry stood dumbfounded for a moment. Katrina was as beautiful as he remembered when they were growing up. The eight years she had been absent from Rochester had done nothing to mark it's time on her. Still a slender woman with blazing red hair, her white-toothed smile stood out from her creamy complexion with intensity. "What? Oh yeah. The cop life is in my blood. But you, you look fantastic. How are you?"

*Pregnant,* Katrina thought but instead answered, "I'm great, thanks. Hey, listen is the Chief in. I really need to speak with him."

Perry nodded his head in understanding. "You bet. He's in his office right now. I sure hope Bear and Jesse get through this mess all right."

Katrina started walking towards the door that Perry had indicated was the Chief's. "Thank you, Perry." She waited until he had retreated back into the noisy squad room before knocking softly on the police chief's door.

"Yeah, come in." A voice grumbled from the other side.

Pushing the door open wide, Katrina wasn't sure what she had expected but it certainly wasn't this. In hindsight, Katrina had assumed that the new chief of police would be a stout overweight, elderly man on the verge of retirement. His policeman's uniform stretched to the limit across his mid-section with buttons ready to explode. Something a little similar to what Gordon Newlon had resembled when he held office.

But quite on the contrary, the man before her was more like a soap opera cop. One hired only because he had been born to wear the uniform. The only straining was around his stone hard biceps. His shaggy blond hair was stylish and his piercing blue eyes were staring at her. "Can I help you?"

Trying to recover from her initial shock, Katrina cleared her throat and averted her eyes to the tile floor in front of her. "Yes, Chief, I am Katrina Lawrence. Jesse's aunt. I am here to assist with his release."

She watched Vaughn stand up from behind his desk and had to crane her neck upwards now to look into his eyes. He was tall and lean. And Katrina was instantly reminded how long it had been since she'd been held by a man. This also reminded her that she was pregnant. The flush of heat gone, Katrina again tried to concentrate on why she was here.

"Please sit down," Vaughn said, indicating a chair in front of his desk.

Katrina went to one of the visitor's chairs and tried to make herself comfortable which wasn't easy to do under the intense gaze of this handsome stranger. "I am really sorry about this whole situation with Jesse. It was just one unfortunate event after another. I was just as shocked as Bear to learn that the state's attorney plans to file charges against Jesse."

"I need to know how to get him out of this, Chief Dexter—"

"Please," Vaughn interrupted, "call me Vaughn."

"Okay, Vaughn. Will there be a trial? What is going to happen?"

Vaughn took a moment to reflect on what he was about to say. For some reason he was finding it very difficult to hear anything inside his head, except this woman saying his name over and over again. It had rolled out of her mouth with a delicious dip of her lower lip. Who *was* she? She had said Jesse's aunt, but where had she come from? Close by, far away? She was dressed smartly in tan Bermuda shorts and a sleeveless black top and her red hair was vivid against her pale complexion.

Vaughn realized he wanted to know more. Maybe it was the events of this last week that made him more aware of his mortality, or maybe it was his dead sister showing up at the most inopportune times, or maybe it was this stranger before him. In any event, Vaughn was drawn to her as he had never been to another human being since losing his sister. He had to focus. "You need to get a lawyer."

Katrina nodded her head. "I'm working on that."

"Good," Vaughn replied and perched on the corner of his desk. "Until you get that lawyer, we won't be able to find out what Pat Monahan is up to."

Katrina was oddly comforted when Vaughn said the word *we*. As if he was in this with her. As if he was willing to help. Katrina felt herself lean forward in her chair.

"Then," Vaughn continued, "If the charges aren't dropped there will be a trial."

Katrina blew a breath out through her nose and let her eyelids fall shut as she placed a hand over her rolling stomach. *Please don't let me throw up*, she thought miserably.

"Are you all right?"

"Yes... it's just... I hate this," she muttered.

# ABOUT THE AUTHOR

Courtney E. Michel has previously, independently published a romantic suspense novel, *Idle Tuesday,* has contributed several articles to a local newspaper, is routinely published in *The Springfield Writer's Block*, a literary magazine and is currently being considered for publication in the popular *Chicken Soup for the Soul* series.

The continuation, *Month of Sundays, Book Two: Grace of God* is due out in 2007 along with the conclusion, *Month of Sundays, Book Three: Hour of Healing*. Her novella, *Phobophobia*, is coming in 2008 and she has a work in progress called *All On A Saturday Night.*

At present, Courtney lives in Illinois with her husband and two sons.

For more information on Courtney and her books, please visit her website at www.michelfiction.com.

*BEACON BOOKS PUBLISHING*

www.beaconbookspublishing.com